Trapped

Ruby Moone

jms books

TRAPPED

All Rights Reserved © 2017 by Ruby Moone

Cover design by Written Ink Designs | written-ink.com

The story within is a work of fiction. All events, institutions, themes, persons, characters, and plots are completely fictional inventions of the author. Any resemblance to people living or deceased, actual places, or events is purely coincidental and entirely unintentional.

No part of this book may be reproduced or transmitted in any form or by any means, graphic, electronic, or mechanical, including photocopying, recording, taping, or by any information storage retrieval system, without the permission in writing from the author and publisher.

JMS Books LLC
10286 Staples Mill Rd. #221
Glen Allen, VA 23060
www.jms-books.com

Printed in the United States of America

ISBN: 9781543043624

For Steve. Thank you for understanding.

Trapped 1
The Wrong Kind of Angel 237

Trapped

Chapter 1

THE LORDLING'S EYES were miserable again. Sam had been watching him for a while, quite unnoticed, and saw him pace the bedroom, run a hand around the back of his neck, and then pour two glasses of brandy. It was the good brandy, not the cheap shit they usually served in the club, which indicated just how important his client was. His client. Sam smiled a little. He was gorgeous. Young, probably only a year or two younger than his own four and twenty years, but smaller than he with a slight, elegant yet willowy build. After the first night that he had visited the club he had only ever wanted Sam and Sam had been more than happy to oblige. When the misery faded from those eyes there was something beautifully boyish about him. Charming, unspoiled, and quite, quite irresistible. He'd thought of him as The Boy for some time. He had no idea of his real name, and beneath those aristocratic clothes that probably cost more than he would earn in ten years, he was most certainly all man, but that elusive boyishness called to something lost within Sam. His heartbeat picked up and he swallowed before speaking and drawing attention to his presence. Today was important. Today was the day. He had spent the last couple of weeks planning his escape, his future, his new life. All he had to do was persuade his boy, his lordling with sadness in his eyes, that he was going to help him.

"Henri," the boy said with a smile. The misery lifted to be replaced with something warm for a moment. Henri was the name Sam used when working and the boy went by Maurice to protect his identity. He strode to where his boy stood, took his face in his hands, and kissed him. Hard. The boy moaned into his mouth and clung to his shoulders. Given the disparity in their sizes he sometimes worried about hurting him, but Maurice never complained. The kiss became bruising, and as usual, Sam was as hard as iron in moments. He could never really fathom the effect the boy had on him, but he liked it. He was the only client that made him so hard so fast. The only client he ached to be with. As he was visiting the brothel three times a week, he was with him a lot. Sam dragged his mouth away, but held the boy's face in his hands. "Maurice, my beautiful Maurice."

He was beautiful, too. Fair skin, light blue eyes, and fair hair that, in candlelight, sometimes had an auburn cast to it. He looked ethereal. Ethereal. Sam liked that word and since he had heard it, and learned what it meant, he decided it embodied Maurice. Ethereal. Those light blue eyes were burning now. Wide, unblinking, flicking back and forth as he looked into Sam's eyes.

"Clothes off." Sam used his commanding tone. The boy liked to be commanded, and tonight he needed him to be as compliant as usual, if not more compliant. "I think I will fuck you fully clothed today." He knew the boy liked the feel of his rough clothes against his skin to begin with, but afterwards he loved nothing more than to lie on Sam's naked chest and rub his face in the dark hair that grew there.

Sam stood back as the boy peeled off his clothing and folded it. He was always tidy. He was clean, too, and in Sam's profession that was definitely something to appreciate. His own size and weight usually meant that he was pulled for the men who liked to be mastered and rogered hard, but not many of them thought to present themselves clean, bathed, and fragrant like Maurice did. As the clothes came off, Sam could smell the soap from his skin. A waft of sandalwood and a hint of leather. He was slender, but surprisingly muscled when he took his clothes off. All lean and hard without a spare inch on him, and exactly how Sam liked his men. When Maurice finally stood naked before him, cock jutting and weeping, Sam wanted to kneel and take it into his mouth, but that wasn't part of the game. Instead, he stood tall, shoulders back, unbuttoned the fall of his breeches and pulled out his own rock hard cock. He always returned the favour, and made sure he was clean and bathed, so he thrust his hips a little and rubbed himself. The boy's mouth was open; his eyes riveted.

"On your knees."

He dropped to his knees before him and looked up.

Sam pushed out his cock towards him. "Suck me." His breath caught when the boy's cool, slim hands took hold of him, still shy even after all these weeks, caressed him gently, and then took him eagerly into his mouth. He was incredibly inexperienced. He still gagged if he got too much in, and tended to nibble and lick rather than giving a good hard suck, but it was wonderful and Sam loved it. Loved that tentative, shy touch that was somehow moving. After a moment he took the boy's head in one palm and started thrusting gently. Maurice had asked for this, paid for this, but Sam could never quite bring himself to do it hard. He thrust until the boy's eyes watered and then pulled off.

"Get up."

The boy stood, wiping his mouth with the back of his hand.

"On the bed."

The boy scrambled up and Sam's cock ached at the sight of him when he got onto all fours. His back curved and as Sam got up onto the bed behind him he ran his fingers down its length and enjoyed the shudder it elicited. He took the oil from the bedside and poured a little into his hands and rubbed them together. What he really wanted to do was kiss him again, lick him all over until he was a quivering mess, then suck him until he almost came but what the boy wanted was his cock, and the boy was paying. Sam teased his hole a little and watched him tense. He pushed and heard the boy gasp. He noted that his hands were bunched into fists, and his head hung a little low and wondered if there was anything amiss, but this was hardly the time to bring it up, so to speak. Instead he focused on pleasing him. He circled again and this time pushed harder until he got the entrance he sought. The boy moaned and pushed back so Sam plunged harder, swirling his finger around, opening him until he could add another finger and thrust deeper. The boy shouted aloud and Sam curled his fingers until he found his sweet spot and Maurice threw back his head and let out a long sobbing moan.

"Hard." He panted. "I need it hard tonight, Henri. Hard."

The boy was sweating and shaking. Sam got more of the oil and ran it all over his cock that still poked through his clothes, added more to the boy and then lined up. He hesitated; he was big and the boy was terribly tight.

"Now, for God's sake, now." He was panting and pushing back, so Sam took hold of his shoulder and pushed in. The moans he had been making had been of pleasure, but the sound he was making now sounded more like pain so Sam paused and rocked a little to ease the way, then pressed in slowly until he was fully seated. He brought his legs up so that the boy would feel the roughness of his breeches and he grasped his hips so he would feel the edge of his coat and shirt. With a growl he withdrew, pushed back in, and when the sounds were of genuine pleasure he set up a deep, slow, rhythmic thrust that made him push back with sobbing breaths; then he fucked him as hard as he dared.

He was so damned beautiful; tight and hot. Sam had to concentrate on not spending immediately. He thrust hard, but held him close. The high-pitched keening sound interspersed with harsh pants suggested he was hitting the right spot so he kept it up. Hips snapping in short, harder thrusts, and then long and deep. The boy moved to take his cock in his hand and Sam slapped his arse. "No touching until I say."

The hand moved immediately but the imbalance made his other arm buckle so Sam pushed him down so his face was in the pillow, arse still canted upward, and held him tight as he rode him. He didn't think he could last much longer, his boy was simply too much, so he pulled up his hips until he could get his own hand around and grabbed his cock. It was hard and wet so Sam used one hand to hold him and maintain his balance and one hand to pump him as hard as he could whilst he pounded into him relentlessly. The boy howled and bucked and writhed as he spent and Sam fucked him through every second of it, hammering out his own release which contorted his entire body.

He collapsed on top of the boy. As his senses returned he had to admit that was probably one of their best goes. Perfect. Absolutely perfect. He moved as the boy squirmed beneath him.

"Undress please," the boy said, not looking at him.

Sam rolled off the bed and his head swam. He hesitated before unbuttoning himself, hesitated for just a moment, but then took a breath and went ahead.

TRISTAN TURNED HIS head to one side to watch his lover undress. Lover. What a joke. His lover was the man that he paid to be attentive, loving, but hard. Henri was so beautiful it hurt to look at him. Over six feet in height and with broad, manly shoulders he was magnificent. Long, dark wavy hair curled about his head and looked as though it needed the attention of a barber. It made him look gloriously debauched. Added to that were his eyes of a clear, almost crystalline, greenish-grey hue that seemed to see everything. It made him nigh on irresistible.

The man stood now, carefully removing his clothes so that Tristan could crawl onto him and be held. The two things that brought Tristan back time after time was the man's powerful body that at once could overwhelm him, pin him to the bed, and bring unutterable pleasure, but then could hold him as though he were precious. Sometimes they just lay there in the flickering candlelight, sometimes they talked. It felt for that short time as though someone actually gave a damn about him. As though he were loved. Tristan hated that he needed both things, but not enough to stop him coming back for more. Not ever enough.

Tristan rolled to the side and took one of the cloths by the side of the bed to clean himself. When he had done, he looked up to find Henri naked. His stomach was taught and his thighs hard with well-defined muscle. His cock was still half hard even after the pounding he had given him. Tristan allowed his eyes to linger there. Henri walked to the bed and climbed on so Tristan moved to give him room to lie beside him, but then stopped.

"Wait." He sat up and grasped the man's shoulder.

"It's nothing, please."

Tristan was staring in horror at Henri's back. It was covered in bruises. Long red welts that looked as though they had been laid there by a cane.

"What happened? Who did this to you?" Tristan ran his hand gently over the marks, but he flinched so he stopped.

"I swear it's nothing." He laid back and opened up his arms, but as much as Tristan wanted nothing more than to lie on him, to rub his face in the soft hair that filled the gap between those dark nipples, he couldn't think of adding his bodyweight and pressing on the bruises. Instead, he lay beside him.

Henri looked puzzled. "Would you prefer not to..." He gestured vaguely.

"I want to, but tonight I will hold you."

At this, Henri looked downright baffled but Tristan held out his arms and awkwardly, the big man shuffled over so that he could lay his head tentatively on Tristan's shoulder. He relaxed after a moment, gathered Tristan up in his arms, and snuggled into him tightly.

"Would you like to tell me what happened to you?" Tristan said.

Henri drew up one leg and inserted it between Tristan's. "I...I don't know where to begin."

"Henri..." Tristan hesitated and sifted his fingers gently through Henri's dark curls, his eyes following the movement. He didn't know what to say. "I hope you know that despite the...ah...financial nature of our relationship, I value you as a friend, and care about you a good deal." He kissed the top of his head and tightened his embrace. Henri hesitated and then squeezed him back, settling himself more comfortably. Tristan discovered that he wanted to offer comfort and kindness to the man that had transformed his life even if he had paid him to do it, because even though money exchanged hands, Tristan couldn't help but feel that there was a real, tangible connection between them. He let his fingers continue to drift through Henri's hair as he frowned at the bruising that marred his beautiful back.

"You are important to me," he whispered against Henri's hair. "If I can help...?"

Chapter 2

SAM CLOSED HIS eyes and held his breath. Exactly as he had hoped.

"It was nothing. Just a beating. I'll be fine."

"Just a beating?"

Sam snuggled tighter. He tried to ignore how good it felt to be held and focused on the fact that whilst he could push his face into Maurice's chest, he didn't have to look him in the eye. "Just a beating." He didn't need to tell him that it was the last beating that pushed him to the edge.

Maurice didn't speak, he just carried on stroking his bruised body.

"I have to tell you something," Sam said. It was now or never. "I have to tell you."

The stroking stopped. "Tell me what?"

Sam took a deep breath. "Well, it might not matter terribly to you, but I am leaving Dante's." Dante's was the name of the club that employed him as a prostitute. Dante was the name of the man that held his life in the palm of his hand and never let him forget it. The man he had to get away from or die. Sam registered the fact that beneath him Maurice had gone completely still.

"When?"

"By the end of the week."

"But it is Thursday already. Where will you go?"

"I don't know. I shouldn't have told you." Sam sat up and ploughed his hands through his hair.

"But I need to know where you are going. How else will I see you? Will I still be able to see you?" Maurice's tone was taking on a desperate note.

"You…I…I won't be able to see you. I…" Sam put his face in his hands. "I beg of you not to breathe a word. I am running away. I cannot face this anymore."

There was a rustle of the sheets as the boy sat up beside him. "I am so, so sorry," he whispered after a long moment's silence, and his voice wavered. "So terribly sorry, I never imagined you would view me in that way. All I can say is you are a remarkable actor. I have been so wrapped up in my own pleasure, my own need for…" He stopped and put a hand over his mouth.

Sam was taken aback. He never imagined that the boy would think that he meant him. How could he even imagine he meant him? He turned so that he could look at him. The misery was back in the boy's eyes, tenfold.

"Not you," Sam said, and meant every word. "Never you." He took the boy into his arms, rocked him, and kissed his temple. "You've been the one thing that makes all this bearable. I love being with you. I love every moment of it. I tried to make them let me only work for you but they wouldn't and I can't afford to live on..." Sam squeezed him again, meaning every word. "Never you."

"I suppose the money that I give them doesn't come to you."

"No. I get bed and board. A roof over my head, clean clothes, and food in my belly. More than most."

"What will you do?"

Sam screwed his eyes tightly shut. "I am going to escape and go to Yorkshire."

"Yorkshire." The boy's voice was breathy. "Yorkshire is an awful long way away."

Sam nodded and risked a glance at him. "I have a cousin there. He escaped from Dante a few months ago. Not many do." Sam smiled at the thought of Harry; settled and free.

Maurice moved out of his embrace and looked at him, his brows drawn into a frown. "What do you mean by escape? Are you not free to leave?"

"No. Dante's make a lot of money from me. I am...popular. Some gentlemen enjoy a firm hand," Sam said, and glanced at Maurice. He flushed. "Others like to experience overpowering a big lad like me. Making me take it. Some get carried away." He glanced over his shoulder at the bruises, then back at Maurice. The owner and his right-hand man think that they can have me whenever it pleases them. He shuddered at the thought of Bill Mosely and Dante. "I can't do it anymore."

"Oh God." Maurice ran his hands through his hair. He had lovely hands. "I've wondered often what your life might be like, what happens to you when I am not here." Maurice looked lost for a moment, then a curiously hard resolve came into those blue eyes, and he spoke the words that Sam had been praying hard to hear.

"Let me help you."

Sam's heart beat fast. This was it.

"I couldn't ask that of you," he whispered, holding his head down.

The boy took hold of his chin and lifted his face so that he could look at him. Sam's heartbeat doubled at the action. Those light blue eyes that often looked shy, shadowed, and miserable were now serious and calm, but still filled with that resolve. "You haven't asked it of me. I offered. I think you should count me as a friend. I know I should like to think of you as such. We have been meeting for over a month now and the fact that I am here—what, two, three times a week?—should tell you that I care for you. A great deal."

Sam could barely speak. He had hoped that he pleasured the man enough to make him want to continue, make him want to set him up in a room somewhere, perhaps as his paramour, or whatever one called a male lover. He hadn't expected a heartfelt offer of friendship.

"Thank you," he whispered, moved and unable to look away.

The boy let go of his face and smiled. "Is Henri actually your name?"

Sam grinned and shook his head. "Nothing so fancy. Samuel."

"Tristan."

The boy stuck out his hand and Sam shook it shyly and asked the question that had been burning inside for a while. "How old are you, Tristan?"

"Four and twenty."

How old are you, Samuel?"

Sam smiled at him. He'd thought him a little younger than himself. "The same, though I will be five and twenty in a couple of weeks."

"Ah, then you have the advantage. I am not five and twenty until the end of the year. You have eight months on me. So how can I help you to get away from Dante's?"

The change in topic made Sam jump and made him realise that although the boy might look younger, might act vulnerable and shy in the bedroom, like as not he might very different out of it as many men were. In fact, he wasn't that young at all. He used his best smile and stroked his thumb over Tristan's hand that still lay in his. "You can't. Not without getting involved and if anyone ever found out and, you would be ruined. You could be hung."

"Why do you need to run away? Why can't you just leave?"

Sam hesitated, shame making his face colour, but he stuck to his resolve to be as truthful as possible, and took a deep breath.

"I owe Dante money. He pulled me out of the gaming hells and paid my debts in return for me working for him. I've done it for nearly a year now and I don't think I can bear it anymore, but the money he loaned me had interest on it and it just grows and grows. I now owe him nearly five hundred pounds. I will never be able to pay it off. Never." The panic in his voice was genuine. At first it had seemed like a capital idea. Saved from his debtors, somewhere clean and comfortable to live, food, and an endless supply of men. What he had not banked on was the depraved nature of many of the guests who visited the club, and the nature of Dante himself and his vile henchman, Bill Mosely. In fact, it was Mosely's return that made him realise that he had to get out if he wanted to stay out of the madhouse.

Tristan's arms came about him again. "What did you do before you worked here?" Tristan asked softly.

"I served in alehouse. The Bucket of Blood in Covent Garden. Wasn't a bad job, but I...I suppose I was greedy. I wanted more, wanted better. I'm good with cards, I can mimic the quality easily, and people seem to like me. I gambled, won, and got...greedy. I knew the stakes were high playing with Dante, but I thought I could win. Thought that I could set myself up for life. I was wrong." Sam hung his head and Tristan squeezed his hand. He was going off script now. He was supposed to be spinning a tale that would make Tristan sympathise with him. He hadn't planned on spilling his pathetic life story. He took several deep breaths and tried to think clearly. Appeal to him. Appeal to the kindness that he sensed in him.

"Now, I only want you," he whispered. It was the truth. The absolute truth. Then he remembered the miserable look in Tristan's eyes when he came in. "Enough about me. When you came I could not help but note you appeared troubled," he said.

Tristan pulled his hand away and fiddled with the sheet over his lap. "You are terribly observant."

"I just think that I have come to know you well." That was better. Sam shifted closer and stroked Tristan's arm. "Do you want to tell me about it?"

Tristan shook his head and smiled sadly. "It's...nothing. Did you really work somewhere called the Bucket of Blood?"

Sam smiled and accepted his avoidance of the

subject. "Indeed I did. They had bare knuckle fights there, so it got messy on occasion."

Tristan smiled back. "How do we get you out of here? Do you have somewhere to go if we do?"

Sam hesitated, but decided not to push Tristan to reveal what troubled him. Instead, he let his smile spread slowly over his face. When he spoke, his voice was a little shy. "I love that you say *we*. I love that you want to help me…I…I think that I love you." Sam held his breath.

The look of unalloyed joy on Tristan's face shook Sam to the core. "Oh, Samuel," Tristan breathed, climbed into his lap, put his arms around his neck, and held him tightly. "Oh, Samuel," he said again. Sam squeezed his eyes shut as guilt bit sharply. He'd guessed that the boy was terribly in need of loving, despite his requests to be taken hard, and he had been right. So right.

Tristan pulled back and stroked Sam's face gently. The look in those beautiful eyes was so tender, so loving, Sam wanted to weep. "I will bring the five hundred pounds. I will come as usual on Saturday, give you the money, and I will find you somewhere to live so that when we get you out you will be safe."

"No, you can't do that. I can't ask that of you," he protested.

"I can and I will." He kissed him on the cheek. "I will find somewhere where we can be together regularly. Where I can visit you…is that what you want? I mean, do you want to continue our association outside of here?" He looked around at the opulent room decked in shades of crimson and purple.

Sam squeezed him tight. "It is what I want. More than anything in the world, I want to be with you."

His words were fervent, and true. He did want to keep seeing Tristan and to have an association with him. His heart thumped painfully in his chest as he wondered if he really did love him. How one earth did a chap know if he was in love? His heart almost stopped completely when Tristan spoke.

"Then I shall make it happen."

TRISTAN HURRIED AWAY from the club, his head ringing. The thought of not seeing Henri…Samuel, regularly made him feel queasy. Samuel. It suited him. His head spun as he walked the pavements, dodged a flower seller, made way for a large, drunken party squabbling over who should sit where in a ridiculously large coach. He held a handkerchief to his nose as he skirted past a sewer and then struck out towards Mayfair. When he reached his townhouse and the door opened he wondered anew whether the footman watched out for him, day and night, waiting specifically to open the door for him when he came home. As usual the huge mausoleum of a house was silent. His boot heels rang on the marble floor and the footman stood by his side ready to take his greatcoat, hat, and gloves. He straightened his coat, smoothed his hair, and made for the study where he dismissed the servants and poured himself a generous brandy. He tossed it to the back of this throat and poured another one and sat down behind his desk. It still felt wrong to sit behind his father's desk, in his father's study, in his father's house. He ran a hand over the glossy surface. In the weeks since his father's passing he didn't know what he would have done were it not for Samuel. He'd never spoken of it, but the man seemed to know he needed more than just satisfaction. Tristan closed his eyes and let his head flop back onto the chair, trying not to think what his father would have said about the thing he was about to do. He sighed and took another, smaller sip of the brandy and, brushing away maudlin thoughts, applied himself to the problem at hand. He was good at problems. Better at problems than people most of the time, but this time, this time he had someone else to consider. Samuel. Samuel. Samuel. He kept saying the name in his head.

The money was no problem at all. The problem was constructing some kind of identity for Samuel so that they could spend time together without arousing suspicion. There was no doubt that he could find rooms for him, somewhere he could visit regularly. God, if he could have his way he would spend every night with Samuel in his bed. He didn't even know what he was offering the man, or what the man wanted in return, but Samuel had said he loved him. He loved him. Him. Tristan. Tristan put his head in his hands as his heart started thundering again.

"What ho, old chap!"

Tristan almost jumped out of his skin. He hadn't heard the door and the footman hadn't made an announcement of a guest. His cousin from his mother's side, Lord Alfred, better known to him as Alfie, stood in the door with his customary supercilious smile on his irritating face; the footman scurried behind him.

"Alfie," he said, holding one hand to his chest. "You scared the life from me." He only saw his cousin in fits and starts because he appeared to lead some sort of dual life. One as a gentleman of the ton, whose sole purpose in life was to irritate him, and another doing God only knew what for the Prince Regent.

"You look like you have the weight of the world on those small shoulders. What's to do, dear one?"

Tristan tried to smile as Alfie walked very carefully across the room, in a manner that suggested he might have overindulged, and slid into a chair in front of the desk. Alfie was ten years older than him. Straight dark hair, dark eyes, dark soul. Even cast away he looked like he had stepped out of a fashion plate.

"Bit of a conundrum I'm trying to work out."

"Glad to be of help. Women problems?"

If only his life could be so simple. "No, not women problems."

"Ahhh," Alfie said and wagged a finger. "Problems of the heart then."

Tristan paused, uncertain of what he meant, and afraid to ask. "You're foxed," he said softly, kindly.

"I am." He looked up, those dark eyes suddenly quite clear. "Don't end up like me, old chap," he said. "Find someone to love even if it is someone you can't be with. Everyone needs someone to love them."

Tristan stared and Alfie dropped his chin onto his chest and laughed. "Have your balls even dropped yet? You don't look a day over eighteen."

Thankful for the change in subject Tristan laughed. "My balls are just fine, thank you." He bowed his head. "Is there someone that you love?"

Alfie stared at the ceiling for a moment then levelled that dark gaze at him. "Yes. Yes, there is. And I can't have them so take heed."

Tristan was taken aback. Alfie had never previously vouchsafed any personal information, so this was a surprise. He noted the fact that he didn't say she, but kept quiet and wondered. He'd been so wrapped up in his own thoughts, his own needs, and his own shame that he had really not considered anyone else. He knew he wasn't the only man to find an attraction to his own kind stronger than any attraction to women. Half of the chaps at school had experimented with each other. Most went on to marry, but he somehow couldn't imagine it, and had certainly never found a woman that he wanted to spend the rest of his life with, or even one that he could imagine bedding. He spent most of his time avoiding them, particularly in London during the season where it seemed that every young woman and every mama was hell bent on matrimony. As he was young, not ugly, wealthy, and came from a titled family, he was unfortunately considered a catch and he had discovered, almost to his cost, that young women could be incredibly devious when it came to securing a husband. His mourning black didn't appear to deter, so he kept himself to the clubs and avoided mixed company where he could. He was lucky in that he did not have a huge family with expectations as to his appearance, but since his father's death he knew that it was only a matter of time before the issue of his marriage and succession raised its ugly head again. He had tentatively decided that he would happily leave the estate to his cousin and his offspring, but looking at Alfie's miserable face now he began to wonder.

Chapter 3

SATURDAY ARRIVED, AND with it, torrential rain. Sam sat in his freezing cold room in the attic, listening to the noise on the roof. It was like sitting inside a tea tin with someone hammering on it. The door opened and his friend Gareth threw himself through in dramatic fashion. Gareth was the man he shared a room with sometimes. Gareth was small, dark, and theatrical to the point where Sam often wondered if he couldn't make a living on the stage. In the brothel, he went by the name of Romeo. It somehow suited him better than the rather pragmatic Gareth.

"Bastards!" he declared. "Bastards. The lot of them." He tossed his long dark hair over one shoulder. His hair was silky and straight and he spent hours brushing it and tending it. His eyebrows were plucked into slender arches, and he made no attempt at all to hide his true nature. He was wonderful.

"Who now?" Sam asked, sipping his coffee.

Gareth held out a hand so Sam gave him the cup. "Thanks, darling." He took a healthy swallow and then handed it back. "Men. Bastards. The lot. Present company excepted," he added, and dropped a kiss on Sam's head. "So, how is the escape plan going?"

"Well. I just need to see if he comes back tonight with the money."

Gareth smiled and sat on the bed. "Do you think he might fancy a threesome?" he said and tossed his hair again.

"You never know." Sam couldn't imagine it. Tristan gave the impression of someone private and quite shy. Sam had made a three with Gareth once before, for a client, and the man was shameless, to say nothing of ridiculously bendy, but there had never really been anything between them other than genuine friendship.

Gareth rolled his eyes and lay down, dropping his head on Sam's lap. "When you are set up, leading a life of luxury, I hope you remember your old friends."

Sam petted his hair. "I will."

"So, is he going to set you up as his mistress? Did he mention an allowance? Will he set you up in Mayfair?" he asked, peering up at him.

"Don't be ridiculous. I'm not anyone's mistress. He just mentioned somewhere where we could meet and be together."

"Bugger." Gareth sighed. "No mention of clothes, jewels? A carriage? Horses?"

"No. Nothing like that."

"I thought he was minted. Are you having second thoughts?" Gareth patted Sam's leg as he looked up at him.

"No, just feeling a bit guilty about deceiving him."

Gareth wrinkled his nose. "How are you deceiving him? You like him, you would be happy to service him, he likes you, and he likes being serviced by you. What's wrong with that?"

"I told him I loved him." Sam felt his face colour.

"Ah. Bit naughty that, but if it gets the job done..."

Sam leaned back against the wall and stroked Gareth's hair. Tristan might not even turn up. Might have decided against it. Somehow he doubted it.

A commotion from downstairs stilled his hand. Gareth sat up and they looked at each other. Their rooms were in the attic but the yelling and banging carried loudly.

"We'd best have a look?" Sam said. "That sounds like Bill Mosely." Bill Mosely was Dante's right-hand man and nobody dared naysay him. Gareth nodded reluctantly. If Mosely was in a bad mood it behoved everyone to keep out of his way, but particularly Sam. Mosely took delight in making Sam submit to him and when he was in a mood, he liked to make it hurt. They crept out of the room and listened. It was definitely Mosely.

"Get back in the room and hide," Gareth hissed as the shouting got louder. "He's foxed. He'll be looking for you. He's had it in for you ever since Harry ran away."

"Oh, Christ." Sam ran up the stairs as he heard Mosely shouting his name. The bastard was drunk. Where was Tristan? It was past the time he usually arrived, but the mistress hadn't been to call him down. He hesitated by his door, but then ran on and dodged into one of the girls' rooms. They screamed and hit him, but when Mosely could be heard bellowing his name they shoved him under the bed and sat on it.

Sam hid and hated himself for doing it. He wanted to stand up to Mosely, tell him to shove it. He pressed his nose into his arm to stop the dust getting up it and went rigid when the door slammed open.

"Where is he?"

"Got a client I think," Charisse said. Sam was sure her name was really Iris, and he thought that was a much prettier name, but they all had stupid made up names. He winced when he heard him slap her, and when she screamed he hated himself even more. The door slammed so he shuffled out. Charisse was holding her head and her friend, Clara, was shouting at Mosely through the closed door. Mosely wasn't stupid enough to mar anyone's face and risk losing the income from providing battered produce, although there was probably a fair few of the clients that wouldn't object. There was a fair few that made their own marks, but they paid extra for that. He took the girl in his arms and rocked her.

She let herself be held for a moment then pushed him away. "You owe me," she muttered.

"I do." He squeezed her arm and slipped out of the room, ignoring Clara's tirade that was now directed at him.

He made his way cautiously to the room where he normally saw Tristan, but when he got there Mosely grabbed him roughly by the arm.

"There you are, you little shit. Where the hell have you been? I've been looking for you. I have need of you."

Sam's heart was hammering. Mosely was as tall and as broad as him. He grabbed Sam's arm and started dragging him to the room where he should be seeing Tristan.

He wrenched out of his grip. "I've got a client.

You'll have to wait."

Mosely's eyes burned. They were dark eyes that sometimes were hard to read, but tonight Sam had no trouble. The man wanted to hurt someone.

"Wait? Wait? Do you imagine for a second that I am going to wait?" he walked towards him, hissing the words as he came until Sam was backed up against the wall, then Mosely's hand was fisted in Sam's hair and he was being dragged. Mosely threw open a door and shoved Sam inside so hard that he fell. He rolled to his feet, hands balled into fists. This was enough. This was the end. He would not be pushed about and abused anymore.

"On your knees." Mosely had one hand on his own cock, rubbing it as he dragged open a drawer with another. He took out a length of chain that made Sam go cold.

"No."

Mosely smiled and unbuttoned his falls to take his cock into his hand.

"No. I mean it. Enough is enough." Sam held out a hand in front of him as if to ward the man off. Mosely probably had fifteen years on Sam, and although Sam was sure he could take Mosely in a fair fight, this was never going to be fair. His only hope was the fact that Mosely had a bad arm. His cousin, Harry, had run away in spectacular fashion last Christmas, taking one of the boys with him and Dante had been beside himself with fury. Mosely had been dispatched to drag him back but had returned not only empty handed, but with a bullet hole in his arm. He seemed to feel that Sam should pay for his inability to find Harry and bring him back.

"Beg pardon, sir, but the gentleman is here for

Henri. The one that pays?"

Mosely's head spun at the intrusion and Sam held his breath. Tolson was the major-domo for the place. The man that kept everything running smoothly like the gentlemen's club it purported to be. In that moment, Sam could have kissed him. He was probably the only person that might stop Mosely.

"Make him wait." Mosely rolled the chain around his fist.

"Send me to him used and he will know," Sam said, praying that greed would win over lust. It also made him wonder how much Tristan paid. His heart was beating in his ears as he waited.

Mosely smiled. He walked over to Sam and stood beside him. He reached out and stroked his face, making Sam flinch. Sam screwed his eyes tight shut as his stomach rolled.

"Then I will watch. I will watch you plough the pathetic little molly. I will watch your every move and I want to see everything that you do. When you have finished, you will come to me and I will chain you to the roof, cuff you, and screw you until you beg for mercy. Do you like that? Do you want that?"

His face was pressed against Sam's. "Yes, I want that."

Mosely shoved him away. "Then move. Don't make the man wait."

TRISTAN SAT ON the chair in the room that they always used and waited for Samuel. He had six hundred pounds in his pocket, and the key to extremely pleasant lodgings not far from his home. His fingers tapped nervously on his leg. When the door opened and Sam finally walked in, his breath came in a whoosh of relief. He stood and went to take the man's hands, but it was immediately clear that there was something wrong. Sam's crystal clear eyes were normally glowing, excited, and filled with passion and focused on him with gratifying intensity. Now, he was glancing around anxiously and Tristan was sure that his hands were shaking a little. He opened his mouth to speak, but Samuel shook his head, almost imperceptibly, and his eyes telegraphed alarm. As always, he cupped his face in his hands and kissed him. Tristan sank into the kiss and wrapped his arms around him. Samuel moved a little and then pulled his lips free and buried his face in Tristan's neck and spoke in the quietest whisper.

"We are being watched...no, don't look, just know we are being watched." He pulled his face back and looked directly into Tristan's eyes and then kissed him again before burying his face in his neck again. "Unless you don't mind being watched, pretend you just want to kiss or something like that."

"What do you want today, my lovely," Samuel said, and pushed his hands through Tristan's hair. Tristan was so hard he could barely function. The thought of being watched was terrifyingly arousing. It was not something that he had ever thought of, but now the prospect presented itself he could scarcely breathe. Samuel must have read something of his excitement because he smiled and there was genuine affection in his eyes.

Tristan cleared his throat. "Lay me on the bed and kiss me. I want you to lie on top of me and kiss me."

"Do you want me naked?" Tristan watched as

Samuel gave the tiniest shake of his head.

"No, I like you clothed. You know that." Tristan smiled and winked as he walked to the bed. He pulled off his coat, which was an effort given how well tailored it was, and laid it on the chair. He pulled off his cravat and unbuttoned his shirt. He could see Samuel watching him and when the man swallowed and licked his lips Tristan swelled even harder. He had no idea why someone would be watching. If they meant to use the information against him it was already way too late, so Tristan decided to put his trust in Samuel, in the fact that the man would not place him in any danger. He took off his shoes, laid on the bed, and opened his legs. Samuel didn't hesitate, he crawled up the bed and laid directly on top of him, lining up their cocks as he did so.

"Like this?" he said in a normal voice. "Am I not too heavy for you?"

"Not at all. I want your weight. All of it. Now kiss me."

Samuel sprawled on top and Tristan lost his breath for a moment. The man was heavy. He coughed and Samuel lifted his chest a little. He stroked Tristan's hair and laid his lips against his. Tristan was lost. Kissing was so terribly intimate. The sharing of breath and taste with another man never failed to stagger him. He allowed himself to be absorbed into Samuel's heat, his mouth, his passion. After a while Samuel gentled the kiss and started nibbling his ear, which made Tristan moan.

"I have to leave tonight. A man named Mosely is watching and he intends to take me once we are done. I cannot stay. If you have changed your mind I understand."

Tristan arched his neck and moaned loudly before kissing his way along Samuel's jaw. "I have money in my pocket and I have rented rooms for you," he whispered.

He felt Samuel go still and then squeeze him tightly. "Keep your back to the wall with the picture if you don't want him to see."

"Won't he be suspicious if we don't do anything?"

"People come here for all manner of activity."

Tristan smiled up at him. "Touch me here," he said loudly, and indicated his nipples. Samuel grinned and kissed his way down to the flat discs and then licked and nipped at each, making Tristan arch and moan again. He kissed his way down Tristan's stomach but pinched tightly at his nipples making him gasp. Samuel came back up and kissed him on the mouth. He unbuttoned Tristan's falls and pushed his hand inside taking firm hold of his cock making him gasp even more.

"Like this?" Samuel murmured.

"More, more," shouted Tristan, throwing back his head.

Samuel stifled a snort of laughter but set about tugging him. He buried his face in Tristan's neck. "Kick up a fuss. Say I'm doing it wrong. Start knocking me about."

Tristan almost laughed. Knocking him about? He luxuriated in the feeling of Samuel's warm hand on his cock for a moment and then pushed at him. "Not like that, you oaf. What are you doing? Why aren't you doing it like you usually do?"

Samuel sat up and ran his hands through his hair. "I'm sorry, my lord..."

"Well, sorry isn't going to make me come, is it? Get off me, you bloody idiot. Get off me." He wriggled free and hoisted up his breeches.

"Come now, do you want my mouth? My cock in your arse?" Sam said in a mock wheedling tone that was frankly hopeless. Tristan could only hope whoever was watching didn't know him very well. Sam leaned closer and whispered, "Say you want a three."

"I want something different tonight," Tristan said, lifting his chin and looking down his nose. "It will take more than you to satisfy me tonight. I want two."

"It will cost you."

"Do you imagine that I care about that? Go. Go and find me another." Tristan waved his hand imperiously. "But kiss me first."

Samuel leaned closer and crowded him with his body. "Run," Tristan whispered. "Run and go to my house." He whispered his direction.

"I can't leave you here." Sam peppered Tristan's face with kisses.

"Of course you can. I'll just kick up another fuss and leave. Tell the footman you have a private appointment with me."

Samuel hesitated and then nodded almost imperceptibly. "I will find just the man for you and together we will give you a night to remember," he said in his dreadful acting voice. The man would never make it on the stage.

"See that you do." Tristan watched Samuel back out of the room. He remembered that he had a part to play so he arranged himself on the bed and stuck his hands in his drawers and rubbed. His cock was completely limp by now. He was so bloody terrified for Samuel. As he lay rubbing himself he saw a flicker of movement from the painting that sat on the wall opposite the bed. An idea struck him.

"What's that?" he shouted, launching himself off the bed, clutching his breeches, and peering up at the painting. There was a definite hole in the black of the woman's dress. "Dear God, am I being spied on? What kind of establishment is this?"

He buttoned his falls and dragged open the door. "Tolson?" he bellowed. "Tolson, get in here now and tell me what the hell is going on. I demand to know what is going on and why someone is fucking well watching me. Get in here now!"

His acting skills were clearly superior to Sam's as there was a mad scramble. A couple of young men he'd seen about before came running, and even a couple of the women who served the clientele. All of them making soothing sounds.

One of the young men, a small dark-haired pixie grabbed his arm. "Oh, sir, we are at your service! Did Henri not suit tonight?" And then he was surrounded by apologetic servants until Tolson arrived to take control of the situation. The staff were dispersed, and Tristan allowed himself to be appeased. He decided against the offer of another prostitute, paid his customary tariff, and made as elegant an exit as possible given the fracas that had ensued. He made it outside and sucked in a lungful of night air before hailing a hackney, praying that Samuel would be waiting for him when he got to the house.

Chapter 4

SAM RAN AS fast as he could. He had left everything behind, not that he had much, but he didn't dare waste a moment. He ran through the streets in the direction of Brook Street in Mayfair where Tristan lived. It was only on hearing his direction that he realised how wealthy his lover must be. Only the wealthiest of families lived in this area. When he arrived at the designated number he rushed up the steps and hammered on the door. It opened almost immediately and he was confronted by a sour faced lackey in a pristine, white wig, who stared down his nose at him.

"I have an appointment with…" he realised he didn't know Tristan's surname. He took a punt. "His Lordship."

"His Lordship is not at home." The man started closing the door and Samuel put a boot in the way and pushed back. "He told me to meet him here. He will be home shortly. I assure you." He was hot, sweating, and breathing heavily. He could hardly blame the man for not wanting to admit him.

"The tradesman's entrance is around the back."

"Well, I'm not a tradesman so I will wait here. Let me in," he said, determined to persist.

"What in God's name is going on?" A deep, cultured voice echoed down the hallway. The lackey stood back and Samuel peered around and saw the most dandyish looking fellow he had ever seen in his life. A good bit older than him, the man was thin, hawkish, and dressed almost entirely in black. His cravat and shirt points were almost to his ears, and a blue jewel glinted in the folds. He had fobs and seals dangling from a waistcoat that looked to be embroidered silver, and he raised his quizzing glass to his eye to observe Samuel with quelling hauteur.

"Gad. What do we have here?"

Samuel straightened. He towered over the tulip, so he took advantage of his height. "I am here to see his Lordship."

The man continued to observe him. He lifted his chin and those dark eyes pinned him. They were alarmingly intelligent. "And which lordship would that be? Hmm?"

Christ. Sam's mind raced along with his heartbeat. "I am here to see my very good friend, Tristan. He asked me to wait for him here as he has been delayed. Somewhat," he added and nodded.

The man raked him from head to foot with the bloody quizzing glass, making Sam feel small. Not many people could do that. He hoped this prancing ninny was a friend of Tristan's. "You'd better come in and wait then," he said, and turned tail.

Stunned, Sam followed. The house was magnificent. It looked as though it had been freshly decorated and there was a gentle smell of beeswax and lemon with a hint of tobacco lingering in the air. His footsteps echoed on the floor, and portraits of ancestors frowned at him as he followed the man into a study. It was huge. In it, stood a large oak desk with a leather chair behind it. The walls were lined with hundreds of books, and a fire burned gently in the grate that was flanked by two comfortable looking chairs. The man indicated one. "Take a seat. Brandy?" he asked as he picked up a decanter and waved it.

"Thank you. That would be most welcome." Sam tried to remember his manners. He had been brought up well, but this was something different again. The room was decorated in shades of cream and dark red. It was warm, welcoming, and comforting. He could imagine Tristan in the room. He could imagine taking him on the thick rug that lay before the fireplace and had to stifle a smile. He took the glass that was handed to him and sipped. Even he could tell that this was brandy of the first order. None of the rank stuff they doled out at Dante's. At the thought of the man Sam shuddered.

"Are you cold?" enquired the man solicitously.

Sam shook his head. They hadn't been introduced, and as the man hadn't offered an introduction, Sam felt that the disparity in social status meant that he couldn't, so he sat quietly and ignored the amused smirk that was now plastered across the man's silly, dandyish face.

Before very long the sound of the outer door broke the silence and moments later Tristan burst into the room. "Samuel. Thank God." He moved forward as though he would take his hands, so Sam jumped to his feet and moved so that Tristan would see the dandy. He did, and pulled up short.

"Goodness, Alfie. What are you doing here?" he said. Sam was fairly certain he was trying for nonchalance, but he failed dismally.

The dandy stood up with a devilish smile. "Tris, my love, at last. You simply must introduce us."

Sam watched the same realisation dawn on Tristan. He had no idea of his last name either, and the bloody dandy knew it.

"Samuel Holloway," he said, and stuck out a hand. The dandy eyed it as though it were a fish.

Tristan's eyes closed momentarily. "Mr Holloway, may I present my cousin, Lord Alfred Barrington? Alfred, Mr Samuel Holloway."

Lord Alfred presented a limp hand. Sam shook it but was surprised at the strength behind it. "Ah, I see what you were asking now when you asked which lord I was looking for." He gave a decisive nod. "Lord Tristan."

The dandy rolled his eyes heavenward and Tristan looked uncomfortable. "Dear boy, he is Chiltern." At Sam's blank look the dandy sighed and gave him a quizzical look. "May I introduce my cousin, Tristan Sebastian Arthur Barrington, sixth Earl of Chiltern?"

"Earl of Chiltern?" Sam echoed weakly.

Tristan rubbed his eyes. "Alfie, be a dear and give us a moment?"

The dandy's eyes were dancing now. He stood and bowed deeply. "Of course, my dear, of course. Mr Holloway, it was an honour to make your acquaintance."

"Likewise," muttered Sam, eyes still on Tristan.

When the door closed, he got up and paced. "You're a bloody earl?"

"I'm a bloody earl," Tristan said, and slumped into the chair the dandy had just vacated.

TRISTAN'S HEART WAS beating so hard he wondered if he might faint. Fainting seemed preferable to dealing with the situation he was faced with. As if his burdens were not already staggeringly heavy, he had just added a complication that could ruin the earldom, and get both of them hung. Not only that, he had waved his indiscretion in the face of his cousin, who was no doubt laughing up his sleeve at that very moment. But then he looked at Samuel. Standing there, tall, strong, dependable, desirable. His hair was awry, and his cravat wilted, but he was exactly what Tristan needed to see. He stood up, walked over to him and put his hands on his lapels for a moment, and stroked gently.

"Are you hurt?"

Samuel's eyes closed momentarily as he shook his head. "No. You came in time. Mosely had me cornered but I got away." He smiled, and tilted his head. "Thank you."

"You are welcome." Tristan hesitated a moment but then slid his arms around Samuel's waist and melted into him when those hard, warm arms wrapped him tight. There was nothing in the world that was better than being held by Samuel. They stood together for a few moments and then Tristan pulled away a little but remained within the circle of his arms.

"Who is Mosely?" he asked.

He felt Sam sigh. "Mosely is in charge when Dante is not here, and that is most of the time. He is a complete bastard." Samuel's arms tightened around him fractionally. "My cousin, Harry, escaped a few months ago. Mosely went after him, but came back with his tail between his legs and his arm in a sling. He's had it in for me ever since." Sam shook his head. "I am afraid he is simply biding his time before he goes after Harry again."

Tristan frowned. "Where is your cousin?"

"He was headed for Scarborough but I don't know if he made it. Mosely isn't saying anything."

Tristan frowned. "That must be a worry."

Sam nodded.

"Will you stay here with me tonight?"

"Here?" Sam said, looking around. "In your home?"

"In my home." Tristan nodded. "Tomorrow I will show you the rooms I have secured for you only a few moments from here. You should be comfortable there."

"Rooms as in more than one room?"

Tristan laughed. "Yes. You will have several rooms."

"Good Christ." Sam rubbed the back of his neck and flushed.

"We will make arrangements for the money to be paid that is owed to Dante. Perhaps you can contact someone from the club and arrange to repay him?"

Sam looked incredulous. "So you will pay my debt, set me up in a room, beg pardon, rooms, and all you want in return is that you get to fuck me exclusively?"

When put like that it sounded sordid and unpleasant. Tristan cleared his throat and chose his words carefully. "Whatever happens between us will be entirely voluntary on both parts. I am not paying for your…your body or your services; I am finding a way for you to live in safety. If part of that includes…being with me then I will be happy. More than happy. If you choose not to, then that will be your choice. It will not be a condition."

Sam stared at him, astounded. Tristan held his breath.

"I will pay you back, every penny," Sam said, and wrapped Tristan up again. "And I want as much of you as you are willing to give me."

Tristan's eyes fluttered closed.

SAM STOOD IN the most beautiful bed chamber he had ever been in. Decorated in shades of blue and gold it was bigger than his mother's entire house had been, and it had been a nice one. Deep, rich carpets, brocade curtains that could be pulled across the chill of the evening, a fire burning, and a bed that looked to be made of feathers with clean, white sheets beckoned. A bed warmer handle stuck out at the side so he knew when he got in the sheets would be warm and aired. He thought of Gareth, Iris, and Clara back at Dante's in their cramped, cold rooms, and wished he could bring them with him. He dipped his fingers in the bowl of warm water that had been brought for him along with a fresh nightshirt. He wouldn't be using that, he wanted nothing more than to feel the soft sheets against his naked skin. He undressed carefully and left the clothing outside the room as instructed. Apparently the servants would make them right for morning. He washed himself quickly and pulled the curtains at the windows back a little to let moonlight into the room. He returned to the bed, pulled the hot warmer out, and slid in between the sheets. He was right. It was truly wonderful. The bed was soft, warm, and fragrant. He closed his eyes and thought about Tristan and what the hell they were going to do next.

Tristan slid into Samuel's room when the household was quiet. The candle had gutted, but Samuel had left the curtains drawn back so moonlight flooded the room. He could see the outline of his body in the bed, hear the soft rhythm of his breathing that told him he was asleep. He drifted to the bed silently in bare feet and stood over him. His face was soft in repose. Gentle. Young. He reached out and caressed his cheek and traced a thumb over his mouth. He moved to leave but Samuel's hand clamped his wrist, surprising him. Tristan looked down into his eyes that were dark in the moonlight, dark and filled with desire.

"Stay." It wasn't a request.

Tristan's knees wobbled and his cock hardened.

Samuel flung back the covers. He was naked and aroused. He lay back, displaying himself and Tristan's breath caught in his throat.

"Take off your nightshirt," he said as he ran a hand over his cock.

Tristan swallowed, hesitated a moment, and then pulled the garment over his head. He stood, waiting, heart pounding as Samuel's gaze travelled over every inch of him. He found himself wishing he were tall and muscled like Samuel, or that he had chest hair.

He always felt small by comparison, but even in the darkness he could see the appreciation in Samuel's eyes, the aching need gathering there and that look, as always, made him feel wanted. He pushed back his shoulders and tugged his own cock and Sam actually licked his lips.

"Get in here." Samuel's voice was a growl.

Tristan let his fingers trail gently up Samuel's naked leg, drift across his hips, avoiding the straining arousal, and then he crawled in, settling himself between Samuel's legs so he could lean down and kiss him. He could feel his heart beat frantically against his own. Samuel kissed him back and then with one swift movement reversed their positions so he had Tristan pinned to the bed whilst he devoured his mouth.

"Do we have oil," he whispered between kisses.

Tristan shook his head. He had only popped in to see if he was settled. "Spit will do," he said, and captured Samuel's mouth again.

Samuel pushed his fingers in his mouth and brought them out wet. He immediately sought and found Tristan's entrance, making him cry out softly, needing more, so much more. Samuel spit into his hand, lubricated his cock, and then pushed inside gently. Tristan squeezed his eyes shut and welcomed the pleasure along with the sting of pain that, as ever, made him feel whole and alive.

Chapter 5

"How long are you staying?" Tristan asked Alfie the following morning over kippers.

Alfie put down his fork and dabbed his mouth with his napkin. "Am I in the way?"

"Don't be ridiculous."

"Dearest boy..." Alfie began, eyes serious for once, but before he could continue Samuel edged his way into the room.

"Samuel," Tristan said, eternally thankful for the interruption. "I trust you had a good night?"

"Excellent, thank you."

"Do help yourself, we're quite informal in the morning despite the surroundings," he said, gesturing to the rather grandiose room. He watched Samuel load his plate with eggs and sausage, take a cup of coffee, and sit down opposite him, casting wary glances at Alfie. The footman left the room, leaving the three of them together. Tristan made a mental note to arrange more suitable clothing for Samuel. The clothes he wore screamed loudly that he was dreadfully out of place.

"Will you be joining us for long?" Alfie said with a wolfish smile at Samuel, his eyes taking in his appearance. Tristan groaned inside.

"No, I must be on my way this morning, but thank you both for your hospitality."

"Do you live close by?" Alfie asked sipping his coffee.

Samuel pushed his food about his plate. "I do."

"Where?"

Tristan watched Samuel stumble and jumped in. "My dear cousin, I have no idea why you would wish to interrogate our guest, but, if it pleases you, Samuel lives in rooms on Half Moon Street." He raised his cup. "Satisfied?" He gave his cousin a pointed look. Alfie looked at Tristan, then at Samuel and then groaned. "Oh, for God's sake, if you are going to carry on in public you need to be a damn sight more discreet."

"Carry on?"

"What the hell are you saying?"

Samuel and Tristan both spoke at once and Tristan could see that the furious blush on Samuel's face clearly echoed his own flush of embarrassment.

"Well, let me look at the evidence. Tristan, my love, you have been in the dismals since your father passed away, God rest his soul. Then suddenly, you are out every other night, have a spring in your step, wince when you sit, arrive flustered hard on the heels of this runaway, and this morning, again, you can barely sit on the chair. Need I say more?"

Tristan was certain that his face had turned the colour of a furnace. He felt as though he was blushing all over his body and that made him angry. "What are you saying? Out with it."

Samuel was on his feet. Tristan stared at him. He appeared quite calm, but something glinted in those unusual eyes. "I think you should stop right there." His tone was hard and directed at Alfie. "I don't think I have ever been quite so insulted, and that you should speak thus of your cousin is shocking." Samuel dropped his napkin on the table. Tristan was open mouthed. Sam always spoke well, but now his diction was cut and precise.

"Are you calling me out?" Alfie said, with infuriating condescension.

Sam hesitated a moment, then smiled. "Perhaps I am."

"And this is exactly what I am talking about. You cannot go about defending his honour," Alfie said, throwing his hands in the air.

"Your cousin is the best man that I know, and yes, I am angry that you would besmirch his name, but I want satisfaction for your insult to me."

Tristan was horrified. "Enough, enough both of you. This is arrant nonsense. There will be no duelling," he said to Samuel. "And I will thank you to keep your opinions to yourself." He stared pointedly at Alfie. "Sit down, the pair of you."

Alfie rolled his eyes and dropped back into his chair. Samuel sat very properly in his.

"Children," Alfie said, his tone conciliatory, but Tristan saw Samuel bristle. "Children. I mean no insult. I am no stranger to the delights of sodomy." Sam looked blank, but Tristan knew he was staring, mouth open again. "I have loved men since I was old enough to know what desire was. I understand, truly I do, but if you are to appear in public you cannot behave like lovers. You cannot leap to defend the other, you cannot betray, by even the merest flicker of an eyelash, that there is anything between you other than manly companionship." Alfie was more serious than Tristan had ever seen him. "Are you presenting him to the ton?" Alfie asked.

Tristan was momentarily speechless. He hadn't thought that far ahead.

Samuel spoke before he could. "No, he will not. Tristan was good enough to lend me his aid when I needed it most. He is helping me now, but it is my intention to repay him."

Tristan stared at him. "You have no need to repay me."

"Yes, I do."

"Samuel..."

"And there you go again," Alfie said, holding up his hands.

Tristan gave up and put his face in his hands.

"Who's the bloody earl here?" Sam demanded, making Tristan look up. "Does he always push you around like this?"

Alfie laughed and for once it was not an unpleasant sound. "Dearest cousin. At least you picked one who has some backbone. Samuel, my dear, I am decades older than our young earl and have spent a lifetime looking on him as a very dear younger brother. Neither of us has siblings, so we have leaned on each other horribly for years. I feel inordinately protective of Tris, and quite resent someone usurping my position so pay me no heed."

Tristan stared, sure he looked like a cod fish with his mouth open and eyes popping.

"That said," Alfie continued, "you must take the greatest of care." He stood up, dropped his napkin on the table, bowed, and made his exit, leaving Tristan and Samuel staring at each other.

"Are we so obvious?" Samuel said with a scowl.

Tristan worried that they were.

SAM WALKED BY Tristan's side the short walk that it took from Brook Street to Half Moon Street. He made sure to keep a discreet distance from him, and walked with his head high looking straight forward.

"You can look at me occasionally; I am sure no-one will divine our secret if you do," Tristan said with a small smile.

Sam glanced at him. He hadn't recovered from the onslaught of 'cousin' Alfie over the breakfast cups. He kept his eyes forward and forbore from comment. They walked in silence until they came to a large property with a beautiful facade. Tristan led him to the solid looking front door and, taking a large key from his pocket, opened it to reveal a grand hallway with a magnificent staircase sweeping upwards. The walls were decorated with portraits and landscapes, and a grandfather clock ticked softly.

"It's quite pleasant," Tristan said, leading him up the staircase.

"Quite." Sam drew in a stunned breath and followed.

At the top of the staircase they paused before a door and Tristan smiled up at him with a glint in his eye before opening it with another key and leading him into what Tristan had described as *gentlemen's rooms*.

"Here we are. I hope you like it." Tristan put the key into a ceramic dish on a polished wood table in the hallway and closed the door behind them. The hallway was dark, with some light spilling through the open doors that led off it. "Come, I will show you around."

Sam followed, quite overwhelmed, as he followed Tristan about. Tristan was clearly excited as he showed him the parlour, a generously sized study, a huge bedroom with a separate dressing and bathing room. The property had small rooms for servants, presumably a valet or a housekeeper or something, and neat kitchens where food could be prepared and all of it was lavishly furnished.

Tristan was talking about hiring a cook, a valet, and a parlour maid, which galvanised Sam. He shook his head. "You will do no such thing. I couldn't bear it. I can cook fine and I can dress myself and tidy. Tristan, this is too much. I was expecting a room, singular; room. Somewhere that I could hide from Dante and Mosely until I decide what to do, a place where we could perhaps spend a little time alone. This is...magnificent...it's too much beyond me. I..."

"Don't say that," Tristan said, coming to stand alongside him. "We can be alone here, it means that we will have somewhere to meet safely, to spend time together. I won't have to worry about you anymore."

Sam looked down at him. He was beautiful through and through and in that moment Sam was certain he did not deserve him. He didn't deserve such unrestrained kindness and generosity.

Tristan smiled, and Sam recognised the glint in his eye. Well, at least there was one thing that he knew he could give in return.

"We should try out the bed," he said with enough growl in his voice to make Tristan's eyes darken.

Trapped 47

"Now." He bent and took Tristan's mouth and let the concerns flow away on a tide of need. He only had to look at Tristan to want him, to need to feel his mouth beneath his, to feel that small, tight, manly body clench with need. Tristan's arms went around him and held him. This was better, this was what they both understood. That heady, pulsating need that drew them together time and time again.

Tristan rubbed up against him and moaned, but then pulled away. "Do you want this?"

Sam smiled at him and pressed his cock against him. "What do you think?"

"Do...do you feel like I am still paying you or do you *really* want this?"

Sam was stunned. "What?"

"I'm...I've never done this before," Tristan said in a rush, pushing his face into Sam's neck.

"And you imagine that I have." It was not a question. Sam pulled away and scrubbed his face. It was bad enough working in a brothel, but at least a fellow knew what the rules were. Here, here he was out of his depth completely. Being a kept man was infinitely preferable to having to service the entire brothel, and dodge Mosely at every turn, but surprisingly, he felt oddly out on a limb and disconnected from everything he knew.

"No, I..." Tristan moved away and went to look out of the window at the street below. "It sounded very straight forward. Find you somewhere to live, and spend as much time as we could together. It only now occurs to me that whilst you would be happy to be out of Dante's you might not want this...with me...?"

Sam was confused. "You risked so much to get me out of there, you have found me a beautiful place to live that is beyond my wildest imagining. You can have anything that you want from me," he said, and waited for Tristan to come back into his arms. Instead Tristan looked troubled. Looked like he did when he came to the brothel when he thought of him as his lordling. He went to touch him, but then thought better. He knew what Tristan liked.

"Hell's teeth, why are we arguing? Just trust me when I say everything is freely given. Here we are, alone, in wonderful rooms with a soft bed. Get in the bedroom. Now. And get your clothes off." He stood with his hands on his hips. Tristan looked at him for a moment and then with a wicked grin scrambled past him to the bedroom. Sam followed, peeling off his own clothes as he went. Tristan was pushing his breeches and smalls down his legs when Sam arrived and his breath caught at the sight of him. Weak sunlight filtered through the window, coating him in warmth. His skin glowed, his eyes were dark, and in that moment, he was everything that Sam had ever dreamed of in a lover, in a man.

"Do we have oil?" Sam asked, walking purposefully to him, kicking off the last of his clothes as he went. Tristan nodded. "Good." He stood before Tristan, stroked his face, and watched those blue eyes flutter closed as he pushed into his hand, and then did what he had wanted to for a long time. Sank to his knees, took hold of Tristan's cock that jutted from his body, hard and wet, and took it into his mouth. He sucked him down, relaxed his throat, and then swallowed. Tristan let out a high-pitched howl as Sam started to suck, lick, and swallow him. Hard fingers were in his hair and Tristan's hips pushed into him. Sam grabbed his arse and started a rhythmic suckling that Tristan picked up on and, gently at first, started thrusting into his mouth. Sam relaxed and let him and watched as Tristan lost all semblance of control and thrust harder. He held him tight and sucked harder when he convulsed and emptied himself down his throat. Sam held him, and took everything that he gave him. Every drop, and then licked him clean. Tristan was doubled over, holding onto Sam's shoulders and panting as though he had run twenty miles.

"Dear...God..." he murmured. "Dear...God..."

"Good?" Sam couldn't keep the smug note from his voice.

"How do you do that? How do you...not..."

"Gag?"

"Yes."

It was on the tip of Sam's tongue to say that it was down to plenty of practice, but decided that was not what he would want to hear. "I don't know." He smiled up at him.

Tristan stood up and pushed his hair out of his eyes with a shaking hand. "Get on the bed."

Sam grinned and did as he was told and Tristan followed him. He pushed him back and Sam went willingly. Tristan took hold of his aching cock and swallowed him. Well, as much as he could without coughing, but then Sam didn't care as he gave himself over to the feel of Tristan's beautiful mouth around him. The pressure built to an unbearable point and as his impending crisis feathered over his skin he pulled Tristan off him. Tristan came away, swiped the back of his hand across his mouth looking utterly debauched, then he took Sam's cock in his sure fingers and tugged. Sam exploded with a yell and let all the joy and happiness he felt at being with Tristan surge through him.

As they lay together tangled on the bed, with Tristan's head tucked on his shoulder, Sam ran a hand down his back to his bare arse and squeezed.

"See. We are wonderful together. We only get in a knot when start thinking and try to talk about things."

He felt Tristan laugh. "You may have a point." He dropped a kiss on Sam's chest. "At least I now know what to do with your mouth if you are talking too much."

Sam shook with laughter. "You do indeed."

They lay entwined together for some time, and dozed in comfortable silence. As they room grew chilly, Tristan pulled up the sheets and they settled themselves again. Sam played idly with a strand of Tristan's fair hair and sighed as Tristan stroked his hip.

Eventually Tristan broke the silence. "You've never done that to me before," he said, and dropped a kiss on Sam's chest.

Sam knew what he meant. "Wasn't sure if you wanted it. You were paying, so you called the tune." He then winced, and cursed himself. Why the hell did he have to remind him. He waited for Tristan to get upset again, and when he scrambled out of his arms Sam's heart sank.

"Tristan, I'm sorry, that was...Oof." Sam sank back into the pillows when Tristan straddled his chest and grabbed his hands to pin them to the pillows by his head.

"You. Are. Talking. Again," he said, punctuating his words with kisses.

Sam grinned. "I also thought you might be a little sore from last night." He reached up and tried to deepen the kisses, but Tristan broke free and shuffled up so he was pinning Sam's shoulders almost with his knees. He was hard again and Sam's mouth watered. He looked up, a little uncertain, but the devilment in Tristan's eyes made him laugh and lunge forward to take him into his mouth. Tristan groaned, and levered himself up so that he could slide in further, and Sam gave himself up to a playful side to Tristan he never imagined existed.

TRISTAN SAT BY the window in White's, sipped his brandy, and willed his hands to stop trembling. Although, in fairness, he was shaking all over. He could scarcely believe what he had done. He had a lover. A male lover. He took another drink. Not only that, but one he had rescued from a brothel and established in one of the most select parts of town. His heart was beating rapidly, making his breathing short. What in God's name had he done? He took another drink and rubbed his hand over his face. What he had done was take control of his dismal life and throw in his lot with a man who loved him. Tristan closed his eyes momentarily and sucked in a deep breath before taking another drink. Samuel loved him. Loved him. Him. He couldn't recall being loved by anyone. His mother, perhaps, but he hadn't really known her, she had died when he was so young. His father had, it seemed, somehow divined his nature and despised him for it. The closest thing to any kind of vague affection came from Alfie, and that was sporadic at best. But Samuel loved him. He suppressed a smile and drained the glass. He admired

Samuel for his courage in saying so because although he was certain that he loved him back, he had not returned the sentiment. He couldn't find it in him to say the words. He wondered if that made him a coward.

Moments later Alfie slouched into the chair beside him, interrupting his reverie.

"Penny for them?" he said, taking a healthy swallow of his drink.

"Sod off," Tristan said, without rancour, and Alfie laughed.

"Can you sit comfortably or would you like to perambulate?"

Tristan closed his eyes and willed the heat from his cheeks away. "Must you?"

"But you make it so easy, my dear," Alfie said, raising his glass. "It truth, I am deeply envious of you."

"Envious of this young whelp?" A hand clapped Tristan on the shoulder, making him start violently. He held onto his composure, horrified that their conversation may have been overheard. He stared up at the man who had interjected. Wallingford. What the hell did Wallingford want with him? The Marquess of Wallingford was an incredibly influential man. Well connected, an intimate of the Prince Regent, and a notorious busybody. Alfie slouched even further into the depths of his chair, and arched an eyebrow at the man, making Tristan want to kick him on the ankle. He had no idea why Alfie had to be so damned provocative.

"Indeed," Alfie said. He took a sip of his brandy, watching Wallingford carefully. "He beat me to the most magnificent filly and has been riding her mercilessly."

It was all Tristan could do not to splutter. He had no idea if Alfie was talking about a horse or a woman, and he was certain that was his intent. Wallingford chortled amiably and positioned himself in the seat opposite. He was a large man, probably of a similar age to Alfie and the kind that made his presence felt the moment he stepped into a room. Handsome in a bluff way, but not to Tristan's taste. The man was too intense, too full of his own self-importance.

"I haven't seen you for quite a while, Chiltern. My condolences on the loss of your father. He was a good man."

"Thank you." Tristan didn't really know what else to say.

Wallingford nodded sagely and at that point Lord Cawley joined them and the conversation turned to horseflesh, a subject that Tristan felt marginally more comfortable with. He joined in, but couldn't help but notice that Alfie was suspiciously quiet. After Wallingford and Cawley had wandered off in search of fresh entertainment, Tristan nudged his cousin.

"What is wrong? Don't you like Wallingford?"

"Not especially. We were at school together. Oxford, too."

"I see."

"Do you, my dear?" Alfie's dark eyes shone.

Tristan stared, open mouthed "Were you..." He gestured vaguely, looking about in case anyone could hear.

Alfie smiled slowly. "Might have been."

"Oh my word." Tristan actually put a hand to his mouth. "I cannot believe you never told me. Wallingford is...." It was the most salacious titbit of gossip he had heard in an age

"My dear boy, how could I?" Alfie stood up and Tristan followed as Alfie gestured towards the dining room and then slid his hand through the crook of Tristan's arm. "You were the most appalling late bloomer. I had to wait and see which side of the fence you would fall. I was reasonably certain you would fall my way, but I had to be sure. I would never have wanted to appall you." He patted Tristan's arm. "You were always my favourite member of the family. I couldn't have borne your disdain."

Tristan was both surprised and incredibly moved by this. He had to concur. Alfie's disdain would have been hard to bear, too. Having something in common, something so personal and desperately secret, was, in an odd way, reassuring and made him feel more connected to his cousin than he had ever been. As they headed towards supper Tristan's heart felt full, and his entire body felt to be tingling with anticipation. He had a lover. A magnificent, lover. And his cousin actually liked him.

"Do wipe that smile off your face, my love," Alfie said in his best bored tone. "People will talk."

Tristan laughed. "Perhaps we should speak of sober things?"

"There is little sobriety in my life, dear one, this will have to come from you."

Tristan shook his head and matched his step to Alfie's. "I met with Millican earlier."

"Good God. You have my condolences."

"Hmm." Was all Tristan could say. Millican was his man of business. A worthy soul, incredibly talented, but dreadfully serious. "He thinks that I should consider selling some of my smaller properties and expend more energy on the most productive."

"Sounds eminently sensible," Alfie said as they arrived at the table.

"He thinks Havering should go."

Alfie pulled a face. "I thought you were particularly fond of Havering.

"I am, but since the tenants left it has fallen into disrepair. It needs a lot spending on it, and the tenant farmers deserve better than I am giving them at the moment."

They paused whilst they were seated and the waiters settled them into their seats and poured the wine that Alfie had ordered.

Tristan took a sip and looked at his cousin over the rim of his glass. "I don't suppose you fancy purchasing it?"

Alfie's lips twitched. "Do I strike you as the kind of man to invest in rundown abbeys?"

Tristan laughed.

"Enough." Alfie waved a hand. "Enough sobriety. Let us return to our previous topic."

Tristan shook his head. "Which was…?"

A wicked smile lit Alfie's face. "About whether or not you would like to sit…or walk around a little more."

Chapter 6

SAM SAT IN the parlour of his new home tapping his fingers on the table. One leg set to jiggling, so he stood and paced a little. It was getting late and he hadn't seen sight nor sound of Tristan all day. He had explained that he had obligations to attend to so Sam had agreed to entertain himself. He had walked the parks, investigated the delights of Bond Street, made a mental note to see if he could gain admittance to Gentleman Jackson's boxing emporium, and eaten a splendid pie in a chop house. He kept himself well away from his usual haunts. Was this what a gentleman did all day? Went to shops, clubs, and paraded around? It sounded like a life of wonderful, idle luxury but after only a few days Sam was feeling not only distinctly out of place, but surprisingly lonely. The silence in the beautiful but huge apartment became oppressive. He was used to being constantly surrounded by people and animals. Chatter, laughter, arguments, and general noise were a constant part of his existence. He was used to sharing not only every moment, but every space that he had and it has ever been thus. Here…here there was no-one but himself for company. He was also terrified that at any moment Dante or Mosely would locate him, so was forced to keep away from the places he was familiar with, his friends, or anyone that might be connected to his old life. He felt the need to be constantly on his guard. He was wondering how to broach the subject of the money that he owed Dante with Tristan when the door sounded and he came into the room. Sam paused and looked at him. His blue eyes were bright and shone with a good humour that was the complete opposite to the way he used to look when he arrived at Dante's. A smile curved his lips as he walked purposefully across the room, took him into his arms, and kissed him thoroughly. Sam smiled into the kiss, wrapped his arms around him and for a long moment they simply kissed. Breathing together, moving together they were one.

Tristan pulled away long enough to smile at him. "Hello," he whispered. There was no sign of the miserable looking boy who had rescued him from the brothel.

Sam touched his nose to Tristan's. "Hello."

"What have you been up to today?" Tristan pecked him on the lips. "Have you eaten? My odious cousin has departed for the evening, so you would be more than welcome to join me for supper."

"Wouldn't you rather eat here? We could eat naked." Sam waggled his eyebrows.

Tristan laughed and kissed him again. "What would we eat? You don't have a cook yet."

Sam squashed an entirely unreasonable feeling of

irritation. "I can cook, you know. I just need to buy some food." At Tristan's arched eyebrow he gave in with a sigh. "As you please." He hadn't meant for Tristan to employ people to care for him. A room to live in and be safe would have been more than enough.

"Come, we will eat and then pop back here and coze the evening away."

"I need to work out a way to repay Dante." Sam had been reluctant to raise the issue of money, but the longer he held off paying Dante the worse it would get, and the likelihood of him finding him grew. Dante had connections throughout the entire ton, and would use them to get at him, of that there was no doubt.

"Of course, we must see to that. And while we are on the subject, would you take this?"

Sam looked at the parcel wrapped in paper and tied with string that Tristan had extracted from his coat pocket, and took it cautiously. "What is it?"

Tristan shrugged. "Pin money?"

Sam's chest seized. "Pin money?" He stared at him. "Tristan...Tristan, I am not your wife," he said as gently as possible.

"Of course not." Tristan stroked his face briefly, "but you need money for day to day expenses. I have arranged for my tailor to visit tomorrow to arrange a new wardrobe for you and..."

"Tristan...Tristan," Sam insisted as the man rambled on about formal wear, day wear, cravats and the like.

"What is it?"

"I don't need all of those things. I will not be moving in circles that require formal attire, I will only need a few items, and I might even be able to get Gareth to bring my clothes from the club."

"Oh. I thought you might like some new things."

He looked so crestfallen that Sam felt guilty. "Of course I would like new things, of course I would…" He shook his head. "Forgive me?"

Tristan tilted his head to one side and smiled. "We are talking again."

Sam paused, and then laughed aloud. Tristan laughed along with him and it was a little while before they set off to his town house.

OVER DINNER TRISTAN brought up the subject of the money that he owed once the room was cleared of footmen. It was odd eating with Tristan in his home as one's conversation had to stop intermittently as servants moved silently in and out. Fortunately, it was an informal supper so there were no footmen stood behind them. To say the meal was informal when they sat at an alarmingly large table covered with, what Sam considered to be, very ugly silverware, was a bit of a stretch.

"How can I get the money to Dante for you?" Tristan said, as he cut up a piece of chicken. "I have it, but I am not sure of the best way to convey it."

"I can get a message to my friend Gareth. He works for Dante and he could get the money to him safely." Sam speared a piece of buttery potato and popped it in his mouth. It was divine. "Then, I think you should go back as a customer."

Tristan's fork hit the plate with a clatter. "What? What are you talking about?" His eyes were wide and shocked.

Sam chose his words carefully. "I am worried that

Dante will associate my disappearance with you if you stop attending."

"You want me to..." he gestured vaguely with one hand. "With someone else?"

"Good lord! No," Sam said, shocked. He stared at his plate for a moment, the thought of someone else with Tristan was discomfiting in the extreme.

"Well, I don't want to either," Tristan said, and Sam enjoyed the frostiness in his tone and the pinched mouth expression.

"I have been thinking about this, and I think you should go and ask for me. When I am not available, obviously, ask for Gareth. His working name is Romeo." Tristan was staring with his mouth open so Sam continued. "Gareth is my friend. He knows about you and how I feel about you. If you tell him why you are there he will understand. You will be able to pass the money to him and he will give it to Dante."

"I see." Tristan licked his lips. "What if they are spying on us again?"

"It's a risk, but if you just ask to be kissed again they would accept that. Many men come to the club just to be held and kissed. Nothing more."

"Really?"

Sam nodded. "Really. Some people are dreadfully lonely."

Sam's chest ached when Tristan immediately dropped his gaze to look at his plate.

"Very well. I will go tomorrow as usual."

The footman came back at that moment so conversation became mundane and Tristan chatted about people that Sam didn't know, and Sam talked about people that Tristan didn't know, and they smiled awkwardly at each other.

Trapped 61

❖

TRISTAN STOOD IN the alley outside Dante's club, tucked discreetly away off St James', and pulled his evening cape closer around him against the cold fog. He adjusted his hat and then rapped on the door with his cane. Moments later the door opened and he was invited in. The club was high quality. It catered to the tastes of a wide variety of people but, on the surface, it was a small, quiet, respectable gentleman's club where a man could have a peaceful meal and conversation with friends and engage in a spot of gambling. In reality, it was a place where a man could have his wildest fantasies satisfied. He strolled into the main room and headed for his favourite chair, and Tolson appeared as if by magic.

"My lord, how good to see you. I was afraid you might have been offended by our little...problem at your last visit."

"Well, if I am honest, I did give it second thoughts."

Tolson nodded sagely. "Will sir be requiring a private room tonight?"

"I will." Tristan wondered if Tolson could hear his heart beating, it was hammering so hard against his ribs.

Tolson disappeared and returned with the brandy decanter and left it by his elbow. He sat in silence for some time, no-one bothered him, but then no-one ever did. There were not from his usual set here, not that he had many friends to speak of, and he would have been shocked to the back teeth to see any of them, so he simply watched until Tolson came back to escort him. Tolson stood back and allowed Tristan to enter the room where he had met Samuel, loved

Samuel, and rescued Samuel. It was their room.

"Sir?" Tolson broke his reverie. "I am afraid Henri is no longer with us."

"I am hardly surprised." Tolson looked relieved and opened his mouth to speak, but before he could do so Tristan jumped in again. "There was a young man that night. Small, long dark hair. I fancy I have had my fill of brutish types."

Tolson nodded, his tall frame bending slightly. Tristan settled himself in the chair to wait. He remembered the first night he had come to Dante's. He had almost run before Samuel arrived, but when he did, when he walked through the door, tall, broad, and impossibly handsome, Tristan had known he was lost. Irretrievably.

Moments later the door opened again, and the young man walked in. He was roughly the same height as Tristan, but looked younger. Long, straight shiny dark hair swirled about his shoulders, and Tristan could have sworn he had some black liner around his dark eyes making them stand out. He pouted and put a hand on one hip. "Are you familiar with the house rules?" he asked. His voice was curiously husky.

"I am."

"How can I serve?"

"I want to kiss."

Tristan found he was shaking as the young man sauntered over to him, stood before him, and looked him up and down. He lifted a hand and trailed the backs of his fingers down Tristan's cheek, slid his fingers along his jaw, and then kissed him. It was an exceptionally good kiss. Expert, practiced, and calculating. Tristan returned the kiss in half-hearted fashion, feeling like he was betraying Samuel. The kiss was good but the man felt wrong, tasted wrong. Smelled wrong. He pulled away. "Lie on the bed with me."

The man smiled and took his hand. They climbed onto the bed together, and Tristan lay on his back with the man over him. He pulled him closer. "I have a message for you."

The man kissed him softly and ran a hand down his chest. "Do I get to fuck you whilst I listen to it?" he said.

"No. You get to listen and pretend."

Gareth pouted. "But you are so pretty." He ran his hand to his stomach and Tristan tensed. Gareth leaned down and kissed him again and then ran his hand further down his body and took hold of his cock through his breeches. Tristan was mortified to find he was hard. He ran his fingers through Gareth's hair and then gripped hard making him wince and pull his mouth away.

"Listen to me," he said in a low voice. "I am here for Samuel. Nothing more. You will listen to what I have to say and go. I do not want your services or your tricks. Understood?"

Gareth paused, gave him a squeeze, and then released him. "As you wish, it's your blunt."

"It is. Now listen."

TRISTAN ARRIVED AT Half Moon Street feeling distinctly guilty. Samuel was waiting for him, those grey green eyes worried.

"Safely delivered." Samuel met him halfway across the hallway with a kiss. Tristan decided that he could get used to having someone to come home to, someone to kiss him when he walked in.

"Bless you," Samuel whispered against his mouth.

Tristan's scalp prickled and he pulled away. "I should tell you I had to kiss Gareth."

Samuel smiled at him, a lopsided smile with a twinkle in his eye. "Did you now. I would have liked to see that."

Tristan was certain his jaw fell open. "What?"

"Did you do more?"

"Well…he…touched me." Tristan watched Samuel's eyes grow hooded and dark.

"Where?"

His voice had a hint of a growl that lit a fire in Tristan's belly. Emboldened, he took Samuel's hand and place it on his iron hard cock. "He touched me there."

Samuel squeezed him hard making him gasp. Tristan moaned softly. "Bastard."

Tristan's heart thundered. "He wanted more," he whispered. "He wanted to fuck me."

"Did you let him?"

"No. Not without you there to watch."

Samuel's breathing hitched, his eyes darkened, and Tristan felt as though he would come if Samuel so much as rubbed him. Samuel moved closer so his face was a hairsbreadth from Tristan's. "Clothes off. On the rug. Now." Tristan watched as Samuel strode away, presumably to fetch the oil. Tristan dragged his clothing off and was dragging his shirt over his head when he returned.

"All fours."

Tristan was aching all over. He knelt and heard Samuel moan, then the soft scent of oil filled the room, and Tristan's heart stopped when Samuel leaned over him and kissed the back of his neck. He was unspeakably aroused and Samuel's instant need to claim him after his encounter with Gareth made him feel ten feet tall. This handsome, wonderful man wanted him. Needed him. Loved him. Tristan moaned as Samuel kissed his way down his spine, running his hands down his sides, making him twitch. When Samuel reached around him and grasped his cock, Tristan moaned aloud.

"Tell me what you want," Samuel said, moving to kiss the base of his spine.

"Anything. Whatever you want to do to me," Tristan said. He meant it. He had told Samuel what he needed in the brothel, but here, now he wanted Samuel to be a part of their lovemaking, not just at his beck and call. He wanted Samuel to know how different the relationship could be.

Something occurred to him. He glanced back over his shoulder and Samuel kissed him softly.

"Do you want me to fuck you?" Tristan asked. "I know we always did it this way at the brothel because that was what I asked for. I need to know what you want. What you need."

He watched Sam's face carefully and saw the surprise, swiftly followed by a wicked smile. "I would like you to fuck me one day, but today I need you." He slid his hand down and let his fingers drift down Tristan's crease, making him shiver. "I want to claim you. Mark you. Make sure that you are mine."

"I'm yours. God, I'm yours," Tristan said, his voice almost hoarse with need. He let out a long, harsh moan as Samuel took his balls and squeezed them gently.

"Lie on your back." Samuel pushed him and arranged him on the rug. Tristan looked back at him, puzzled.

"I've changed my mind; I want to do it looking at you. I want to see your face when I fuck you."

Tristan's heart squeezed. They had never done it this way before but when Samuel settled between his thighs and lined their aching cocks up, his breathing faltered. Samuel leaned in and kissed him. It was a long, searching kiss that demanded everything Tristan had and he gave it freely. Samuel broke free to rub oil over himself and then pushed Tristan's legs back so that he could ease into him Tristan's heart felt so incredibly full. Samuel had never said that he loved him since that day in the brothel, and he still felt guilty for never saying them back, but when Samuel held him this way he knew in his heart that he was loved. Samuel pushed in hard, stealing his breath, and then pulled out, only to plunge back and then Tristan simply held on. True to his word Samuel watched him as their bodies came together and it was almost too intense to bear. Samuel's eyes drifted closed, and his face contorted as his thrusts grew ragged. He dropped his head onto Tristan's shoulder and slid a hand between them to take Tristan's cock and within moments they both erupted, shouting and clutching as they exploded into one another and for a moment had no idea where one ended and the other began.

A FEW DAYS later, Tristan watched Samuel parade in the new clothes with a tight feeling in his chest. He really did look every inch the gentleman. Those shoulders, those thighs. He shook his head.

"You look splendid," he said, walking over to twitch the set of his coat. His waistcoat was a soft green that made his eyes look even greener. Tristan tilted his head to one side and considered. Jade. He needed jade. Perhaps a cravat pin...

"Beg pardon?" He stared at Samuel, who had been speaking.

"If you keep looking at me like that these clothes are not going to stay on long."

Samuel was grinning at him and Tristan felt himself blush. He was so relieved that Samuel liked the clothes.

"I like your new hair," he said. Tristan's valet had done a superlative job in taming Samuel's curls into a fashionable a la Brutus.

Samuel rubbed a hand through it. "Do you? You don't think it's a little...dandyish? Something that Alfie might have done?"

"Definitely something Alfie would like to do but he has such straight hair it would never take."

Samuel laughed, and then stood upright. "My lord," he said, with a deferential bow of just the right depth. "How might I be of service?"

"Very good," Tristan said, bowing in response. "You would easily pass as a gentleman." Samuel didn't respond, he just smiled. Tristan closed the distance between them and took his hands. Sometimes he worried that Samuel would become bored of him. Truth be told, he felt like that frequently. They didn't mix in the same circles so they spent little time together out of the bed chamber and wonderful though that was, sometimes Tristan felt he wanted more. Felt Samuel wanted more, but he couldn't for the life of him fathom out how to do that. If he'd been a woman he would have begged for his hand, married him, and by now they would have been setting up home with a mutual group of friends with whom they would socialise. Tristan had several times over the last few days pondered the possibility of discreetly introducing Samuel to some of his friends. They could conjure up a reasonable explanation for his presence, and for his lack of town bronze, he was sure.

"Do you think…would you like…" He tried to find the words. "I worry that you may become bored here alone. You do look quite the gentleman; I think we might be able to introduce you to some of my set. We could probably attend my club together without attracting too much attention, I don't really attend balls and whatnot." He was warming to the idea now. "We could concoct a background for you that would be eminently believable—what?" The look on Samuel's face brought him up short.

Samuel was looking sad. "That would be wonderful. I would love nothing more than to enjoy some company, some society, I wasn't always a whore, you know."

Tristan was shocked. "I'm sorry, I didn't mean to infer that you…"

"It wouldn't work."

"Don't say that. We could invent a wonderful story for you."

Samuel was rubbing his ear. "Tristan, it would only work until we bumped into someone who uses Dante's and recognises me. They would not only know what I was, they would know what you are, too. You would be ruined."

"No, I wouldn't. They wouldn't be able to say any-

Trapped 69

thing without incriminating themselves."

"But they would know. I couldn't do that to you. I couldn't bear it that people might look at you differently because of me."

Tristan was quiet for a moment. "Then you must spend some time with your own friends. Surely the threat from Dante will have disappeared? He had his money so you might be able to go back and see them."

Samuel's mouth twitched, then he smiled. It was a roguish smile and his eyes danced. "I might do that. It has been an absolute age since I saw them. I'm not sure about Dante, but if I was careful...?"

"Just over a week actually." Tristan tried not to be irritated at the excited expression on Samuel's face. He was talking as though he had been parted from them for an eternity.

Samuel reached out and touched his face briefly. "Thank you for thinking of me."

Tristan felt like a cad for his irritation. "I want you to be happy here."

"I am. Let me change out of these and I will get you something to drink. I have cake. I went shopping," he said with a wide smile.

Tristan watched as he disappeared into the dressing room. He had made some enquiries about staff for him, but Samuel steadfastly refused. It did mean that they had somewhere to go where they knew they would not be interrupted, though.

Samuel returned looking more casual and disappeared into the kitchen so Tristan followed and watched as he moved about boiling water and preparing a pot of tea. He got two plates out and opened a tin that contained a large cake. Tristan peered at the confection. Samuel cut two generous slices.

"Where did you get it from?" Tristan asked. It looked delicious.

"How do you know I didn't make it?"

Tristan was startled. He had assumed that when Sam said he had been shopping it had been to buy a cake.

"Did you?"

Sam rolled his eyes. "Of course not."

Tristan shook his head and laughed. They settled back into the study with tea and cake and Samuel grinned at him over the rim of his teacup. "I'll wager you never made your own tea before," he said.

Tristan had to admit that he had not. They ate in silence for a little while until Samuel spoke.

"So, how long have you been an earl?"

Tristan paused and put his cup down carefully. "Six weeks."

Samuel's eyes widened. "Six weeks, but that's…"

"When I started coming to see you? Yes. That's right." Tristan kept his eyes on the cake for a moment, but glanced up quickly to see Samuel's reaction.

Sam shook his head and sent him a sympathetic smile. "No wonder you looked bloody miserable all the time."

Tristan had to laugh. "I had no idea I was so transparent."

"Your eyes were sad."

Tristan looked at the cake again and held onto his composure.

"Were you very close?"

"Not at all. I am fairly sure he knew about my preferences, and…well, let's just say we were not close. He was in the process of arranging my marriage when he died."

Samuel put his cup down and came to kneel by Tristan's chair. "Are you to be married?"

Tristan put his own plate down and brushed a crumb from Samuel's lip. "No. Fortunately she had no real desire to marry me either, so we called it off quietly."

"Do you miss him?"

Tristan had to think about that. "Not so much him: as I said, we were never close. My mother died when I was small, I barely remember her, and I rarely saw my father when I was growing up." He thought for a moment and then was struck by a truth that he hadn't really realised before. "I miss the idea of him though. I miss having someone to call on or turn to if needed. We weren't close, but at least he was there. Now there is no-one. Just me. I sometimes feel…adrift." He was surprised at how true that was.

Samuel tugged him out of the chair, and when he stood was engulfed in his warm embrace. Tristan sighed and closed his eyes. Samuel always knew what he needed. He held on and wondered how he could miss something that he never had. His father had always been completely peripheral to his life.

"What are you thinking?"

Tristan laughed. "How do you know I am thinking?"

"I can hear your mind working. It's worse than talking, you know, thinking."

Tristan pulled back to look up into Samuel's sparkling blue green eyes. Eyes that were filled with love.

Chapter 7

SAM PROPPED ONE arm behind his head as he lay in the bed with Tristan curled beside him. Two weeks. They had been together for two weeks, and Sam was beginning to feel he was getting to know Tristan a little beyond the bedchamber. The more he got to know him, the more he liked him. Liked his kindness, his generosity, and quiet sense of humour, but found that alongside that there was a steely backbone coupled with an intensity that was sometimes surprising. His lover was a man of principle, notwithstanding the fact that he was lying in bed engaging in entirely illegal acts. Tristan's life was extremely busy, despite his being an aristocrat and all. Sam had fondly imagined that they would both while away the days together, but apparently earls had substantial responsibilities and sometimes they seemed to weigh heavily. By contrast, Sam's life was one of idleness. Very comfortable idleness crammed with every conceivable luxury, but idleness nonetheless.

Being a gentleman of leisure had its advantages, but Sam had reached the conclusion that he really needed some sort of work. All Sam had to do was sit about and wait for Tristan to call. Admittedly, he was visiting almost every night now so that was extremely pleasurable, but Sam had the oddest feeling that his life was on hold. If a man did not need to earn a living, what did he do? What was his purpose? Tristan had given him a home, clothes, food, money, and everything he could ever want and he felt ridiculously ungrateful when he thought of the lives most of his friends lived, but there it was. He tried to imagine what his family would say, what his father would think. He didn't have to imagine too hard. His family were reasonably comfortable, but his father was an exceptionally hard working man. He would expect nothing less from his sons. Sam discovered that even though he had no contact with him anymore he could often hear his father in his mind.

Tristan moved and settled himself a little more comfortably so Sam kissed him gently on the head. He'd been in touch with Gareth and arranged for him to visit, so he was looking forward to the latest gossip from Dante's. He was also considering seeking Gareth's advice on possible employment because he couldn't quite imagine what he might do. He was able bodied, strong, could read and write a little, but whatever he did needed to fit in with the life Tristan had set up for him. He couldn't imagine any kind of work fitting with the life Tristan was forging for them, and in all honesty, he couldn't see Tristan liking the idea at all. Quite plainly, gentlemen did not work. He sighed and shifted and Tristan tightened his grip on him, making him smile and drift his fingers over his shoulders. It really was the most wonderful feeling being in bed with him and feeling safe.

"Are you thinking up there?" Tristan said, his voice muffled by the blanket and Sam's chest. He peered up. His fair hair was awry, eyes sleepy, and with a little stubble on his chin he looked wonderful.

Sam peered down his chest at him. "I was thinking how lovely you are."

Tristan laughed. "You are growing soft."

"No, I am not," Sam said with a laugh, and pressed his morning erection into Tristan's hip, making him laugh even more.

"Surely you can't go again," Tristan said, kissing his chest.

Sam shook his head. "Probably not, but my cock doesn't realise it yet."

They laughed and kissed, and Sam wondered if perhaps he might, but Tristan was exhausted. They had been up half the night but Sam didn't seem to be able to get his fill. He doubted he would ever have enough of Tristan, there was something about him that had wormed its way into his heart, and Sam suspected that he was there to stay. He wanted to say something, something heartfelt, romantic even.

"I...like you. A lot."

That wasn't quite as romantic as it sounded in his head, but the look on Tristan's face was reward enough. He wondered how to broach the subject of work in a way that would garner the same result.

"That kind of thinking I can live with," Tristan said with a soft smile. "I like you a lot, too. An awful lot." He wriggled a little until his face was level with Sam's and then kissed him gently.

"Many happy returns," he whispered.

Sam grinned. He had remembered his birthday? "Thank you." He kissed him back and they lingered a little while before Tristan pulled away.

"Wait there," he said, and threw back the covers and bounded out of the bed, stark naked, and disappeared through the door. Sam settled himself against the pillows and waited. After a little while he returned, balancing a tray. Sam sat up a little and viewed the contents. His heart melted a little.

"Just so you know I am not completely helpless; I have made you tea." Tristan put the tray on a small table by the fire.

"Tristan..." Sam was touched.

"Not only have I made you tea, but I have made you toast, as well." He pulled the cover off a plate with a flourish to reveal several slices of slightly burned bread dripping with butter."

"That's..." He was lost for words.

They pulled on robes and sat before the fire eating toast and drinking the tea that Tristan had made and Sam felt complete. Whatever worries he had seemed unimportant for the moment. He had everything he needed right in front of him.

Tristan wiped his mouth with his napkin and then put his hand in his robe pocket and pulled out a small, flat box. It looked to be made of velvet. Sam's heart thumped a little.

"Here. This is for you. Just a small token from me to the man who has made me enormously happy in a way I never thought that I could be."

Sam felt himself flush. He went and knelt by Tristan's chair, and took the box gingerly. He ran a thumb over it.

"Open in," Tristan said.

Sam opened the box. Inside, nestled in more velvet, was a cravat pin set with a stunning emerald. He stared at it.

"I thought it might go some way to matching your eyes." Tristan sounded awkward, endearingly awkward, so Sam closed the box and pulled him into his arms.

"Thank you," he whispered. "It is beautiful. I have never owned anything so beautiful."

Sam didn't know what to say. He couldn't imagine ever daring to wear it. That Tristan had spent so much more on him was...He swallowed.

"I am glad you like it," Tristan said. Sam held him tighter. "I meant what I said," Tristan whispered. Sam just nodded, his throat too full to speak.

SAM ANSWERED THE knock on the door with anticipation. He opened it, and there stood Gareth. Resplendent in a vibrant blue coat and a frothy white cravat, his long dark hair made him look exotic. He had been itching to see him for days, ever since he sent the note.

"Gad. You open your own front door? And there I thought you had an earl at your beck and call."

"Shut up." Sam pulled him into the hallway and enveloped him in a hug. "Good to see you, although I should probably plant you a facer."

"My dear boy, why would you want to hit me?"

"For kissing my man, touching him?"

Gareth laughed into Sam's coat. "That was ages ago. He was so terribly uptight. I had to do something lest he faint dead away." Gareth pulled away still smiling. "He is dreadfully prudish. I can't quite imagine him being enough for you." Gareth patted Sam's backside.

Sam ignored that taunt and ushered Gareth inside. He headed for the kitchen and Gareth followed.

"Many happy returns," Gareth said, and waved a letter at him. This arrived for you."

Sam's heart jumped. "Is it from Harry?"

"I have no idea, you had best open it. It came in a very roundabout way through Iris, so I suspect it is. He will know that Mosely will be waiting for him to contact you."

Sam ripped open the unfamiliar seal and scanned the words quickly, smiling as he did so.

"I have to burn it when I have read it, but he is safe. He has met someone. Someone wonderful, he and Julian are settled and happy and safe." He looked up with a huge grin on his face.

Gareth smiled and came to peer around him to see. "Good to hear."

"He's worried though. Apparently, his new lover bested Mosely twice. Shot him and knocked him out and had him flung in gaol for Christmas, so he is expecting another visit from him anytime, possibly one from Dante."

Gareth sighed. "He's right. I can't see Mosely letting that go. Dante is livid by the way." Gareth twitched his shoulders in a small shrug. "Harry, Julian and now you."

"Can't help that, but I don't want him taking it all out on Harry."

"He knows where Harry is?"

"By the looks of it." Sam looked at the address on

the letter and memorised it. He stoked the fire in the range and reluctantly fed the letter into it. He didn't dare keep it in case someone read the fact that his cousin was in love with a wonderful man. He smiled as the flames consumed the missive.

"Well, what is he going to do?" Gareth's eyebrows were almost in his hair.

"It sounds like they know he might return but they are ready for him."

"Must be miserable just sitting and waiting for Mosely or Dante to descend."

Sam was forced to agree, however the kettle boiled so he lifted it with a cloth and filled the pot.

"Could I send a reply through Iris?"

"I don't see why not. If you pen something now I will take it with me."

Sam nodded. "Come on. Tea and cake in the study whilst I write."

Sam carried the tray and then poured.

"Answering your own door, writing your own letters, and making your own tea? Samuel, my man, you are failing dismally as a kept man."

"Hush. Eat some cake."

Sam scratched out a note to Harry in his awkward hand. Told him that he was safely away from Dante and Mosely, but thinking he might like to visit Scarborough soon to see him. A plan began formulating in his mind as he blotted and folded it, then hunted for a seal. Once done he handed it to Gareth, who placed it ceremoniously in his pocket. If he could go and stay with Harry for a little while, just until things had settled, and then he could try and work out how to create a life that could involve Tristan without him feeling like a bloody ladybird. The

Trapped

one thing he couldn't imagine though, was a life without Tristan in it.

They both tucked in to large pieces of cake and chatted around mouthfuls. "Seriously though, how are things developing?" Gareth asked. "It was definitely a stroke of genius cultivating the boy."

"It wasn't hard to do." Sam had known from the start Tristan was special; different. He'd known that what passed between them was more than just sexual congress. That was what had prompted the notion that he might help him get away, because he might have cared as much as Sam did, but he wasn't going to admit that to Gareth.

"I'll bet. He is quite pretty, but seducing an innocent in a brothel to persuade him to set you up in the lap of luxury was a masterly. Every whore's dream. How much does he give you? Those clothes look outrageously expensive, too." He gestured with his cake fork.

"I have no doubt they were outrageously expensive, as are the rooms I now live in." He looked around at the opulence and then picked up on part of Gareth's observation. "How on earth do you seduce someone in a brothel?"

Gareth rolled his eyes and helped himself to more cake. "You take a miserable looking, terrified little boy in search of his first cock, fuck him until he screams, take him in your arms, and hope that he falls for you."

Sam winced a little at his words.

"Well, isn't that what you did?" Gareth's eyes were sparkling with laughter. "And you told him you loved him." Gareth shook his head in mock appreciation, pointing at him with his fork again. "I had no idea you were so manipulative, my darling. I take my hat off to you and your cleverness."

"For God's sake..." Sam's voice tailed off. A movement by the door caught his eye and what he saw stopped his heart dead in his chest. It exploded back into action, slamming so hard against his ribs it made his head swim.

Tristan stood there. Immobile.

Hands hanging by his sides; face the colour of cold porridge. His beautiful eyes were...Sam had to look away from the expression in them. He scrambled to his feet so quickly he overturned the table with the tea, making Gareth shout.

"Tristan..." he began, but Tristan held up a hand.

Sam looked helplessly at Gareth, who for once wasn't mincing or smirking. "Lord Chiltern," he said with a small, tense bow. "Pay no heed to my foolish words. I am merely jealous of my friend's good fortune."

In a blink, Tristan regained his composure and his reply was delivered in a bored drawl. "I am sure you are. After all, I am every whore's dream."

"Tristan, please," Sam said, holding out a hand. "Let me explain. Please."

Tristan stared at him for a moment, then turned and walked away. He closed the door behind him quietly. The click of the latch however, sounded like a rifle shot in the silence that he left behind. Sam turned to Gareth and they exchanged horrified stares.

"You need to go after him. Christ, did you see his face?"

"Stop it," Sam whispered.

"He *really* loves you. It's not just...Oh, Sam, I am so sorry." Gareth put his hands to his mouth.

"You only spoke the truth." Sam pinched the

bridge of his nose. It was the truth. Not quite so blunt, or so sordid, but he did set out to seduce Tristan. He did want a way out of the brothel. What he hadn't banked on was actually falling in love.

TRISTAN STOOD IN the hallway of his home, his back pressed against the door. He closed his eyes. The man's words kept racing around his mind. How unutterably foolish he had been. How unspeakably stupid. Shame and humiliation washed over him again, making him feel dizzy. At the same time, he was wracked by a sense of loss so deep it made his chest feel as though it were about to crack wide open. He pressed a hand there and tried to breathe. He made his way to the study and poured a brandy. He stood by the fire a moment or two and then crumpled into a chair still clutching his glass. He wondered if he might cry, but he felt too numb, too bruised, too hollow.

He had no idea how long he had been there when the door opened and Alfie walked in.

"What the hell are you doing hiding in here?" he asked in his own inimitable fashion. Tristan couldn't speak. "Trouble in paradise?" he asked. Tristan just sat. Alfie came closer and peered down at him. "Tris?" This time there was no drawl in his tone, no teasing light. "Tris, what is it? What has happened?" Alfie reached down and took the glass carefully from him. He looked up at Alfie's face. The face of his childhood friend. He had to blink several times.

"Bit of a shock. That's all." He ran his hand around the back of his neck and tried desperately to think.

"I take it this is about Holloway?" Alfie sat opposite him and was staring at him. When he cared to make the effort, Alfie had the most penetrating stare of anyone he knew.

"Don't stare."

"Then tell me what is wrong with you. You look like someone stole your last sixpence."

Tristan smiled. "Not quite that bad. I just discovered that...Samuel is not quite the man I thought he was." He had to swallow a couple of times before he could continue. "It would appear that I may have been taken for a fool." It hurt to say those words, and it almost undid him. He rubbed his chest again as the crushing pain worsened. He felt so humiliated, so foolish.

"I'm sorry to hear it. I had just popped over to see if the both of you would like a little escapade, but perhaps this is not the right time. Is it all over?"

"Escapade? What on earth are you talking about?"

"A few...likeminded people are taking a jaunt to the country for a few days. I thought perhaps you and Holloway might like to join in. I thought he seemed sincere. It looks like I was wrong." He sounded faintly surprised that he might be.

It would have been just what Samuel needed. A little company, a little fun. Tristan pinched the bridge of his nose.

Before he could respond a commotion in the hallway interrupted them. Samuel burst into the room, followed by an agitated footman that Alfie quickly dismissed.

Tristan stood up as Sam strode over and gripped his arms. "Tristan, please let me explain, please listen to me."

"Unhand me."

"Tristan..."

"I said unhand me." Tristan threw off Samuel's hands forcibly.

Samuel stumbled back, clearly shocked. He closed his eyes for a moment and then opened them. "Tristan, I am so sorry that you overheard that. Gareth is...well, he overstates things and exaggerates."

"I didn't hear any contradictions."

"Can we speak alone?" Samuel cast an awkward glance at Alfie, who was watching the whole drama with unconcealed interest.

"Alfie, be a dear?" Tristan said.

Alfie smiled. It wasn't a pleasant smile. "Of course, my love. I shall be within calling distance if the brute cuts up rough." He sauntered from the room. Samuel balled his hands into fists and glared at his retreating back. He then began pacing. His hand kept going to his mouth where he rubbed and pulled at his bottom lip. "I need to explain something. I need to...Oh God, what a mess."

"Indeed. I shall be interested to see how you explain what Gareth said." Only years of ruthlessly masking his feelings and his nature allowed Tristan to remain reasonably impassive.

Samuel looked tortured, but his next words floored Tristan.

"It was all true."

"True?" The words came out as an incredulous whisper. He had expected emotional denials, explanations, excuses, appeals, but this?

Samuel nodded, rubbed his mouth again, and then let his arms hang by his side. "Would you sit down? It's a bit of a story."

Tristan knew he should throw the man out, but found himself sitting. Samuel sat opposite him and leaned forward with his elbows on his knees looking at him intently.

"Go on, then."

Samuel pulled at his lip again. "I told you I wasn't always a whore."

"You did."

"Well, it's true. My family is reasonably well to do. Not anything like you, but we had a nice home and a good life. I am the youngest of six children and I had a happy childhood. My father was incredibly strict, but my mother loved me." He paused, but Tristan didn't speak. He just watched. "When I was sixteen my father found me in the stables with our neighbour. He was older than me, quite a lot older than me. I was…big for my age. He liked me, he liked…well, he liked me." He cleared his throat. "My father walked in as I was ploughing his arse."

Tristan watched those beautiful grey green eyes darken with the memory. "Save to say I was beaten and thrown out. He spared me by sending me away. I was to leave and never go back, leave and make my own way in life and to repent of my sins. I left with the clothes that I stood in and nothing more. My mother managed to sneak me a few shillings from her pin money, but that was it."

"What happened?"

"I ended up in London where I discovered that honest work was scarce and finding somewhere to live almost impossible. I got some work at a couple of inns, where I found there were a multitude of lonely men who would pay good money to have a strapping young lad. That's when I caught Dante's eye and he introduced me to a whole new world. He gave me clothes, a home, paid for me to gamble in the club; men..." Samuel closed his eyes. "Eventually I owed him all the money that you paid him. Gambling and interest. By the time I realised what he was doing it was too late. I was trapped. He did it to Harry, Gareth, all the others. He lures them in and traps them."

"I see."

"It was supposed to be safe. I got fed and clothed, only I was never safe from Mosely." Sam's gaze was fixed on the floor.

"Go on."

"I've been there almost a year and I am sick to my soul. Sick of pandering to the whims of old men who think that because they are paying the club they can do whatever they want, treat you like dirt. So when you came, and you wanted me, it was like...it was like a real person wanted me. You were so kind, so real, so..." He paused and shook his head. "I wanted you. I adored you. I counted the days to each visit, and I knew you liked me in return. I had no way out, no hope of escaping and Mosely's demands were becoming more and more..." He was gesturing with his hands, and his eyes beseeched for a moment and then he went still. "Everything Gareth said was true. I was trying to get you to take me out of Dante's. I was hoping that you would like me enough to want to make me exclusively yours. The day that you got me away Mosely was chasing me around the house like a madman. You were wonderful. Just wonderful."

"You said you loved me. Was that a lie?"

"I...no...yes...I..."

"I will take it that you don't."

Samuel got off the chair and knelt between Tristan's knees. Tristan wanted to touch him so badly and hated himself for his weakness.

"Tristan, I adore you. I desire you like I have never desired anyone, and I want to be with you more than anyone. I am miserable without you, and I want nothing more than to be with you. If that is love, then I do love you, but I admit I said it in Dante's to coerce you. I am so sorry for that. So sorry." He moved to take Tristan's hands but he pulled away. He didn't dare allow Samuel to touch him.

"You want me to leave, don't you?" Samuel's voice was dull.

"Go back to the apartment. The rent is paid until the end of the month. You may continue to use it."

"I...thank you. Tristan, I..."

"Nothing has changed. I pay for you and in return I can have you whenever I like." Tristan averted his eyes from the shock on Samuel's face. He couldn't quite believe those words had come out of his mouth. He was shamed by them. But even more shamed by the realisation that whilst he couldn't give Samuel up, neither could he give him any inkling of what was in his heart. It was the best he could do. But he couldn't look at Samuel as he said it.

Chapter 8

IT WAS ALMOST a week before Tristan came to visit. Sam had just about given up on him ever coming back, and it has been the most miserable few days. He couldn't bear how badly he had hurt him, but couldn't see how he could ever fix it. He had tried being as honest as he could, tried explaining, but all he had managed to do was turn Tristan from a shy, loving man into a cold aristocrat. He wasn't sure if Tristan would ever come and visit him again. He had been out a few times, but then worried that Tristan may come when he wasn't in, so a few days had been spent waiting. Sitting, waiting, and worrying until he felt he could wait no longer. He had put all his belongings into a bag, left the things that belonged to Tristan, and started to plan. On his jaunts he had located a small, reasonably affordable room near Lincoln's Inn Field that he could rent using some of the money that Tristan had given him. He knew he couldn't do it any other way, but he bought a small book and wrote in it everything he had taken from Tristan, and worked out how much he owed, with every intention of paying him back even if it was likely to take years. He had packed the most practical clothes and left the elegant things behind. It hurt to leave the emerald cravat pin because it had been a gift, but he knew in his heart he could not take it.

Sam had almost everything arranged, his bag packed, and the key to the room in Lincoln's Inn Field in his pocket, when the door slammed and Tristan walked in. Sam was shocked. Anxious and shocked.

Tristan was pale and tense. Since his escape from Dante's he had become accustomed to Tristan's blue eyes sparkling with love, good humour, passion, and affection. Now he could read nothing. His face was a blank, aristocratic mask that conveyed nothing but supercilious boredom. Those eyes that had followed him eagerly now looked through him.

Sam's mouth was dry. "Hello." It was hardly an original greeting but Sam didn't have the faintest notion of what to say. Where to begin or what to do.

Tristan just nodded. He stripped off his coat and gloves and threw them on a chair.

"Have you eaten?" Tristan said. For the first time in their acquaintance Sam was uncomfortable in Tristan's company. Was this how it was going to be?

"I have eaten. Thank you."

Then I suggest we get down to business." He strode in the direction of the bedroom, leaving Sam with his mouth open. He followed, eying Tristan warily.

Tristan pulled his way out of his coat that was terribly tight-fitting, and then unwound his cravat. "As I am funding your living expenses I will not pay you for each visit. If you need more money you only have to mention it."

His words were like a punch to the gut. So that was how it was going to be. He was going to treat him like a whore. Funny, but Tristan was the only man who had never made him feel that way even when they were in Dante's. This was it. Tristan coming in and demanding that he service him. Sam's heart squeezed tight and he found it hard to speak. "Is that it then? That's how we are now?"

"Isn't that what you wanted?" Tristan undid his shirt and pulled it over his head, revealing all those lovely, tight muscles that made Sam quiver, only this time they didn't.

"No."

Tristan unbuttoned his falls and pushed out of his breeches and stood naked. Cock jutting. Demanding. "Get on with it. You know how I like it."

"Please don't." Sam's voice was low. He couldn't bear it. Couldn't bear that he had hurt Tristan so much he would do this.

Tristan simply went and laid face down on the bed, and looked away from him. Sam hesitated, started to undress, but then remembered that Tristan liked it when he was clothed. He climbed on the bed and looked at the lonely figure laying there. Looked at the curve of his spine that was just perfect and blended into that luscious backside. He had very little body hair, just a faint dusting of blond a bit like down. Sam sighed, ran his hand down the full length of that beautiful spine, stroked the softness of his arse, and then bent to kiss him. He kissed the dimple at the base of his spine, kissed each buttock, and felt them quiver. He trailed the backs of his fingers down his thighs and then kissed the backs of his knees.

"What are you doing?" Tristan's voice was muffled in the pillow.

"Kissing you. Remembering you." He kissed his calves and then slid his hands over Tristan's feet. He had small feet for a man and there was something a little bit boyish, a little bit innocent about them. He moved back up the bed and kissed between his shoulders and watched his skin quiver a little at the contact and then ran his hands over each arm and kissed the apples of his shoulders.

Tristan pushed up onto his elbows, eyes looking a little unfocused, hair awry. "What are you doing? Get on with it."

Sam took that beloved face between his hands and kissed him on the mouth. He wasn't surprised when Tristan didn't kiss back. He kissed each eyelid.

"Tristan, you are the only man that never made me feel like a whore even when I was one. You never treated me badly, in fact you were always considerate and kind. And I loved you for it. I will not allow you to do this to yourself or to me, as much as I care, as much as I adore you." His voice was starting to waver so he paused a moment. "Let's leave it with all those lovely memories, happy moments and..." He dipped his head and worked to keep his voice under control.

He looked back up to find Tristan watching him, mouth slightly open. "What do you mean, remembering?" He was beginning to frown.

"Remembering every lovely inch of you." Sam got up off the bed and went to the tallboy where he had stored his already packed his things. "I am going to go before this turns into something that it shouldn't."

Trapped

Tristan sat up and ran his hands through his hair. His cock lay soft against this thigh. "What are you talking about?"

"I think you know." Sam checked his pockets and then smiled. "I owe you so much money I don't have a hope in hell of paying you back. There's the money for Dante, the rooms, the clothes…" Sam sighed and felt embarrassed. "I have kept some of the clothes, just a little of the pin money you gave me to keep me going, but as soon as I find work I will start to repay you. I swear I will." He pulled the book out of his pocket and waved it. "I've written it all in here so don't think I will forget."

He put a number of bills on the bedside table which was the remainder of the pin money, along with the velvet box that contained the emerald pin. He had wanted to keep that so badly; so very badly. He kissed the top of Tristan's head and then left before he lost control. He heard Tristan shouting and fumbling about getting into his clothes, so he just closed his eyes and walked faster into the night.

SAM SETTLED BACK into the most comfortable chair in his room and sighed. Room, not rooms. The accommodation he had found was sparse, but reasonably comfortable and affordable on the money that he had kept from Tristan. It had a large bed, a table with two chairs under the window, and two armchairs along with a somewhat rickety assortment of furniture and utensils. The landlord had eyed him with suspicion, but the payment of two months in advance apparently smoothed over any misgivings he might have had. The next plan was work. At least he had decent clothing that would allow him to seek reputable work, although he couldn't for the life of him think what he might do.

A knock at the door broke him out of his reverie.

"Dinner." Gareth held up a bag and from it emanated the tantalising smell of meat pie. Sam smiled and opened the door wider to let him in. He found plates and crockery and invited his very first dinner guest to take a seat. "Good to see you," he said, and poured them each a small glass of wine from a bottle he had purchased earlier.

"You, too. Slightly less opulent than your last abode though." Gareth took the glass and raised in a toast.

Sam touched his glass to Gareth's. "I know. I wish I could say at least it is mine, but it's his money paying for it at the moment."

"So what are you going to do?" Gareth took a drink.

"Work. I need to work and get myself out of this stinking mess honestly."

"Did he kick you out?"

Sam shook his head as he chewed a mouthful of warm, savoury pie. He put his fork down. "No, he wanted to continue, but I couldn't stomach the terms much as I want him."

Gareth frowned. "What terms?"

"Cold, impersonal...like you would behave with a whore." Sam pulled at his bottom lip for a moment and then picked up his fork again. He stabbed a piece of meat. "He used to look at me like I was made of gold. Like I was sent from heaven just for him. Like he couldn't believe that we were together." He put the meat in his mouth and chewed for a while, then put the fork down again and rubbed his eyes. "Then, after he found out about my plan he laid face down on the bed and told me to get on with it."

Gareth was staring at him. "Well, given that he had rented you the most beautiful suite of rooms, bought you a magnificent wardrobe, and still given you more money than most see in a lifetime, couldn't you have just fucked him?"

"No."

"How often did he visit?"

"Well, I left before he could establish any sort of routine, but in the brothel, it was three times a week."

Gareth was still staring. "And it was good?"

"Very."

Gareth gave him a look. "So this chap, who is an earl, offers you a magnificent home, clothes, money and a good, safe fuck three times a week and you throw a tantrum and walk out because he doesn't *look* at you right?" Gareth's voice was getting more and more high-pitched. "Have you got bats in your attic?"

Sam tried to laugh. "I know it sounds ridiculous." When put like that it did. "If I didn't care about him I could do it. But..."

"But you care about him?"

Sam pushed the pie around on the plate and nodded. "So much."

Gareth's fork clattered on the plate. "God's knees, you soft sod. It's all just a game. Play it right and you live in the lap of luxury with a man you care about and enjoy fucking. Mess it up and like as not you will end up selling your arse in a shitty brothel again, taking every stinking toff that thinks because he's paying for it he can do whatever he likes to you, and you just have to take it."

Sam looked at Gareth sharply. "It isn't a game

with Tristan, it's different. If I didn't care so much I would take what was on offer but I find that I can't. Don't you think that I have had this self-same argument with myself? Take the money and just fuck him?"

"Different? Different? You really do have bats in the attic my friend. There is nothing different about this. It is a transaction. A transaction between a rich sodomite and a poor sodomite. They have the upper hand and we dance to their tune. I wager within a week he is back at Dante's looking for another poor sod to ream his arse for him and won't give you a second thought." Gareth pushed back his chair. "In fact, I might offer myself as your replacement. He was damned keen for me to kiss him and fondle his cock for him even though he was supposed to be having something going on with you." Gareth threw his napkin on the table and stood up.

Sam was open mouthed.

"Did he admit I had a good feel? Did he tell you it wasn't innocent? I'll wager he didn't."

"He told me immediately. He told me all about it." Sam toyed with his fork. "He apologised." Sam smiled and remembered how aroused they had both been at the thought of another joining them. How open and honest Tristan was, how...he stopped that train of thought and looked straight into Gareth's dark eyes. "There are some men you can just fuck and have a good time with, and then there are those that will take your heart and your soul and leave you raw. Tristan leaves me raw. I can't fuck him and know he thinks that I am worthless. It's as simple as that." Sam surprised himself with the outburst. He had never thought of it like that before. Never needed to because there had never been anyone whose opinion mattered to him. He had discovered that what Tristan thought of him mattered a great deal.

Gareth seemed to droop a little and the fire went out of him. "You poor bugger," he said. Sam was inclined to agree.

TRISTAN REGRETTED ALLOWING Alfie to drag him to White's the moment they arrived. It was full of people who had consumed far too much brandy, cigar smoke, and gossip. Wallingford emerged out of the crowd, giving him a friendly nod.

"Chiltern, my boy. Good to see you again."

Tristan nodded and smiled at him and the group of men that appeared to be assembling to take a trip to the theatre. He declined an invitation to join them and managed to retreat to a corner and disappear behind the pages of a newspaper. He would have been hard pressed to even say which newspaper it was, but it served as a barrier between him and the rest of the world. The butler had placed a large glass of brandy at his elbow and he was working his way through it. Sometimes being in mourning had its advantages. He decided that he would continue with his black armband as long as he could.

Alfie had been nattering on about eating, but Tristan doubted he would be able to get anything past his lips. All he could think about was Samuel and how he had been taken for a fool. An absolute fool. Gareth's words rankled more than he could ever admit. He had been far too perceptive and his summation of the situation far too close for comfort. He felt like an idiot. He had tumbled head over ears into lust with Samuel, that was all. Putting him up in rooms had been stupid, and expecting anything from the liaison other than gratifying sexual congress was equally stupid.

But acknowledging his stupidity didn't stop the pain that ripped through him every time he thought of lying in bed with Samuel; didn't stop him craving his touch.

"Chin up," Alfie said as he slid into the chair beside him. "You will have the gossips betting on what is putting that look on your face in no time." Tristan smiled. He was probably right. The betting book in White's was infamous and the club members likely to bet on anything and everything.

"What do you think the gossip would be?"

Alfie stared up at the ceiling for a moment, fingers steepled beneath his chin, and then grinned. "That you have gambled your last farthing and are about to leap into matrimony with the richest debutante on the circuit to recoup the family honour whilst keeping six ladybirds on the go, such is your legendary stamina."

Tristan actually laughed and Alfie's answering laughter was not unkind. He glanced around and they were quite secluded so he leaned closer to Alfie's chair and spoke in a low voice.

"Have you ever bedded a woman?"

Alfie's eyes widened and he looked around swiftly, then pulled his chair a little closer. "Yes. Have you?"

Tristan shook his head. "I have wondered about marriage. I feel I should at least make some effort to continue the line, but I feel it would be unfair to any woman."

Trapped

"You would not be the first, or the last, to take a wife but keep a man on the side."

"Seems very wrong."

"I would agree."

Tristan shook his head. "I was relying on you to carry on the family line."

Alfie laughed and waggled his eyebrows.

Tristan sobered. "I am glad I can talk to you about this. It has been killing me for years."

"I suspected for a while. I'm sorry I didn't speak out sooner." He glanced over at Tristan. "Do you want to tell me what happened?"

Tristan picked at his thumbnail. "I found out it was all a plan. He planned to seduce me to get me to help him escape."

"Escape from where?"

Tristan looked up with a sigh. "Dante's."

Alfie's eyebrows shot up. "He's one of Dante's boys?"

Tristan nodded. "You know of Dante's?"

Alfie rolled his eyes. "Of course I do."

A rather uncomfortable thought struck Tristan. "Have you ever…ah…did…?"

"Dear lord, no." Alfie looked horrified. "I have no interest in whores, never have had. I said I know about it, not that I had used it. Fear not, dear one. I never tupped your beloved."

Tristan groaned and covered his eyes.

"But if he was one of Dante's boys you really did do him a favour. I've heard some rather chilling stories on that score."

"Didn't you hear what I said? He tricked me into believing that he cared for me to persuade me to pay his debts, set him up in rooms, and bring him into my life." Tristan lowered his voice as it was beginning to rise. He looked around but no-one appeared to be paying them any attention. "He betrayed my trust, he betrayed my feelings for him...He *lied* to me," he hissed.

Alfie's gaze was steady. "What did he lie about?"

Tristan scowled. "Well, he...he told me he was leaving Dante's. He was covered in bruises he had been beaten so badly and I said I would help."

"You saw the bruises?"

"I did. They were quite dreadful." Tristan was lost in the memory of the awful marks that had marred Samuel's skin. "There is a man there who hurts him. The day we got him out the man was chasing him and trying to...well, I think he was trying to rape him." The words came out low, and shocked Tristan. He had never quite thought about it like that. But it was what it was. Samuel stood in constant danger at Dante's. He looked up at Alfie. "What do you mean, chilling?"

"Did he ask you to get him out?"

"Well, no. He told me he was going to run away but he did it in such a way that I felt compelled to offer assistance."

"Did he ask for the rooms and the clothes?"

"Well, not really. He was shocked at the apartment. He said the thought I meant room, singular, probably in a rough area. When I gave him money he tried to give it back and was quite uncomfortable about it." Tristan recalled Samuel's reaction to the pin money.

"Has he asked for gifts? The last man I set up asked for a carriage and pair and a wardrobe. When he started talking about a pianoforte I had to draw the line."

Tristan was beginning to feel queasy. He picked at his thumbnail some more. "No. He said he didn't want clothes. Offered to try and get his back from the club." Tristan drew in a breath. "He got quite emotional when I gave him a cravat pin for his birthday, but he left it behind." The pin was in his pocket. He had meant to return it to the jeweller but hadn't got around to it.

"Did he ever turn down your advances? Claim a headache?"

Tristan's voice was a whisper. "Never." Quite the opposite.

"Well, my darling boy, I suspect that you have some thinking to do. Do you think he cares for you or is just worried about losing his rooms and your money?"

"I told him he could stay until the end of the month, but he has gone already."

"Tris." When Tristan couldn't look up at him, Alfie spoke again. "Tris, look at me."

Tristan looked up. Alfie's eyes were concerned. "That boy was in a state when he came to the house. Those were the actions of a man afraid of losing something precious. Did he try and lie his way out of it?

"No. He was painfully honest." Tristan's hands were trembling. "Have I made a mistake?"

"Darling, only you can answer that."

Tristan took a long drink from his brandy glass and let the heat spread through his body. "I really don't know him terribly well."

"He's the man who warms your bed. Do you need to know him?" Alfie arched an eyebrow at him and smirked.

"I…"

"He is there when you need him and if he services you well…what is the problem? He's handsome, clean, and willing. And if he did play on your sympathies a little it shows he has ambition and intelligence. Qualities I find quite admirable in a man."

Tristan drained his glass. "I may have overreacted."

"May?" Alfie drawled.

Tristan stared into his empty glass. However right, or sympathetic Alfie might be, he couldn't quite bring himself to tell him that what hurt most was he had believed Sam loved him. It was that betrayal that hurt the most because it made him feel foolish and unutterably stupid for thinking that someone might actually love him.

"So where is he now?" Alfie asked as he signalled to the waiter to refresh their drinks.

"I don't know."

"Did he go back to Dante's?"

Tristan sighed and rubbed his neck. His head was pounding. "I don't know. I doubt it."

"So you couldn't put it right even if you wanted to."

Tristan closed his eyes. God, Alfie could be so... "No. I couldn't."

TRISTAN SAT IN the bedroom at Dante's in the same chair as he had waited for Samuel many times. He adjusted his cravat and shifted uneasily. It had taken a lot of thinking to get him into Dante's, days in fact, and he was far from certain that this was the right thing to do. The only thing that he knew he needed was to speak to Samuel. Speak to him when they had both had chance to calm down. Well, he was probably the one that needed to calm down. Hard on the heels of that thought was the possibility that Samuel had forgotten him and moved onto something or someone new.

The door opened and Gareth came in. "Good evening, my lord," he said with a slight bow.

Tristan stood up and cleared his throat. "Good evening."

Gareth stared at him for a moment, considering, and then crossed the room to stand before him. His movements were sinuous, but his eyes were speculative. "How might I serve you this evening?"

Tristan recognised the words. Samuel had said them to him the first time that he had visited. It hurt to think that was simply what they all said.

"I would like to know where Samuel is." He let the words sit between them.

"He is safe."

Well, that was something. "Where?"

"I am sure that if he wished you to know he would have sent word. If he has not, I can only assume he would prefer not to see you."

Tristan closed his eyes for a moment and then pinched the bridge of his nose. "So you do know where he is?"

"I do."

"I need to speak to him."

"I'm sure you do but I don't think he wants to speak to you." Gareth's eyes were angry. He stepped closer and Tristan had to force himself not to move. The man stood only as tall as he did but there was a restless energy about him that made him feel larger. His dark eyes glittered. "He told me what you did to him."

Tristan felt the colour flood his cheeks. He stood his ground and lifted his chin. "He played me for a fool. I was angry and I think I was entitled to be."

"How? How did he play you for a fool? By being a whore? By wanting a better life? For wanting you?"

Gareth raked him with a contemptuous look. "He's a good man. He shouldn't be in here." He ran a hand around the back of his neck dislodging the long dark silken sheath that was his hair. "It was killing him."

"Where is he?" Tristan reached out and touched Gareth's arm. "I need to see him. I need to explain, to apologise...I..." He dropped his hand. "I thought that he was simply using me and felt like a fool. I felt like a fool for laying my feelings bare, for...well, for so many things."

Gareth's hard gaze lingered on his face for a moment and then something shifted. His voice dropped to the merest whisper. "He is in grave danger. Dante wants him back and what Dante wants he usually gets, largely because Mosely makes it happen. I will tell you where he is, but you must take the greatest of care." He moved closer and took Tristan's face between his palms and whispered again. "And now, my friend, we must make this look convincing." He touched his mouth to Tristan's and then kissed him. Tristan kissed him back but kept his eyes open and was surprised to find Gareth's eyes were slitted open, as well. He was good at kissing, Tristan found himself aroused again, but it wasn't like kissing Samuel where his entire body and soul felt to be engaged. This was pleasure. Pure and simple, not offering up your soul as he did when he kissed Samuel.

They pulled apart and Tristan was faintly gratified to see that Gareth was breathing heavily.

"Get on the bed," Gareth said.

Tristan lay on his back and Gareth loomed over him. He was positioned with his back to the painting and put his face close to Tristan's. "Listen carefully," he said as he dotted kisses about Tristan's face.

Chapter 9

THE FOLLOWING DAY, Tristan found himself sitting with Gareth in a hackney travelling to a small boarding house in a rougher part of the town, but not one of the worst. Tristan looked around as he dropped down from the carriage and felt faintly relieved. At least he wasn't living the rookeries. He paid the man and waited for Gareth to get out. They walked around a little, Gareth pausing to look in the occasional shop window before nodding to Tristan and disappearing down a back alley. Tristan followed. After several twists and turns they arrived on a small, quiet street and Gareth opened a door and slipped inside.

"Do you think we were followed?" he said as Gareth headed towards the stairs.

"I don't think so, but I don't want to lead anyone to him. Mosely is a nasty bastard. He doesn't care to be thwarted."

As they climbed the stairs a crash followed by

shouting from above halted them both.

"What's that?" Tristan said, gripping the bannister and staring upwards.

"Oh fuck," Gareth whispered and then tore up the stairs like a madman. Tristan ran after him, heart pounding. Gareth paused at a door on the top floor. It was slightly ajar and the commotion was coming from within. Gareth kicked the door hard and ran in shouting. Tristan followed and was confronted by the sight of two men in the room. One throwing things about, the other standing over Samuel's prone body and hitting him with a cudgel. Tristan heard the roar that came from his throat as he launched himself at the man. He leaped on his back, locking his arm around the man's throat squeezing as hard as he could, whilst Gareth beat the other about the shoulders with a large brass candlestick. The man grappled with Tristan for a moment and then flung him off. Tristan was all too aware that he was sadly lacking in any experience with real fighting, but he was damned if he would stand by and allow the brute to hurt Samuel. He scrambled back to his feet and ran at him, wrapping his arms around the man's middle and pushing him to the floor. He could hear the other screaming for them to get out, and when the man in his grasp caught him with a blow to the jaw, making him see stars, he realised they were making a run for it. He wanted to give chase, but wanted to see to Samuel more.

He dropped to his knees by him, closely followed by Gareth, who was breathing heavily. "Samuel?" he whispered.

Gareth rolled Samuel gently over. "Hey, hey, old

thing," he crooned softly. "It's safe now. You're safe now." There was no movement and no response.

Fear gripped Tristan. Hard and brutal.

He pushed Gareth aside and took Samuel's face in his hands. Eyes closed, unmoving. He couldn't see a wound, but then Gareth dragged his arm from behind him and his coat was covered in blood. They both stared stupidly until Gareth put a hand to the back of Samuel's head and it, too, came back coated in blood.

Tristan pushed his fingers into Samuel's neck, frantically searching for a heartbeat. It was there. It was strong. He managed to breathe through the fear that strangled him.

"Go and get my cousin."

"Who the fuck is your cousin? He isn't going to listen to me. You go. I will take care of him."

"I am not leaving him."

"You have to. He won't die."

"How do you know?"

"I won't let him. Go. Now."

Tristan hesitated and then tore out of the building. He ran until he found a hackney. The driver took one look and sprung the horses all the way to Mayfair. Tristan fell out of the cab when they arrived at Alfie's door. Threw coins at the man, told him to wait, and scrambled up the stairs of Alfie's house. He didn't even knock. He staggered into the hallway, slipping on the polished tiles.

"Alfie! Alfie! Where are you?"

The butler bustled into the hallway looking deeply affronted. "My lord." He bowed. "Lord Alfred is in his chamber. He is not yet dressed…my lord…?"

Tristan ran past him and up the stairs until he located Alfie's room and barrelled through the door.

Alfie was standing in his shirtsleeves as his valet slid his waistcoat on for him.

"Good God, Tris?" he shrugged his valet's hands away and did up the buttons himself. "What are you doing haring about at this ungodly hour?"

"It is past noon," Tristan panted. "I need your help." He looked pointedly at the valet and Alfie flicked his fingers and the man left.

"Sit."

"I can't. I need your help. Samuel has been injured. Someone hit his head. He is bleeding and unconscious. I need you to come you will know what to do. You served in the army. You saw injured men. I am afraid to get a physician in case I give us away…"

"Show me." Alfie was pushing his arms into his coat and Tristan had to help, it was so well fitted.

"I have a hackney waiting outside."

GARETH STILL HAD his arms around Samuel in exactly the same spot as he had left him. He was still crooning softly, and Samuel was still unconscious.

"Let me." Alfie moved Samuel so that he could lay him on the floor and examine him. Alfie may have all the hallmarks of a dandyish fop, but during the wars against Napoleon he had fought valiantly and spent time as a medic tending to the wounded. There was no-one else that Tristan would have trusted to look at Samuel. Alfie ran his hands all over him, and then pulled up his shirt revealing bruises and contusions. He felt his pulse and opened each eye carefully.

"Concussed I would say, but otherwise appears in good shape. What happened?" He looked up at

Tristan and then ran his eye over Gareth, who was looking shaken.

"We don't know. Might I introduce Gareth…" Tristan looked at Gareth, conscious that yet again he was introducing a man to his cousin without knowing his name.

"Scott. Gareth Scott." He held out his hand.

Tristan completed the introduction.

Alfie took Gareth's hand, shook it for a moment, and then returned his attention to Samuel. "We need to get him to bed."

"We can't stay here," Gareth said. "They might come back for him."

Tristan knelt by Samuel's side and ran his hand gently over his hair, and then down his face. Gareth surprised him by gripping his shoulder and casting him a warning look.

"Don't worry. Alfie knows."

Gareth stared for a moment and then nodded.

"I am presuming you do, too?" Alfie said with an unreadable look in Gareth's direction. Gareth nodded, chin in the air. "We need to take him out of here and get him somewhere safe," he said.

"Get him to my house," Alfie said. "We will drag him in and make it look as though he is foxed."

Tristan gathered up everything that belonged to Samuel that wasn't ruined, thrust it into a bag, and then between the three of them they got him down the stairs. Samuel started moaning softly as they did so and never had Tristan been so pleased to hear someone groaning.

"Shh, love. Nearly there," he whispered. Samuel opened his eyes a moment and there was a look of such relief, such trust, that Tristan had to look away.

❖

Every inch of his body hurt. Sam peeled open an eye as he tried to make his feet work. He found himself being bundled into a hackney, and the only thing that kept him from passing out again was Tristan's firm arm about him. His head lolled because his neck appeared to be too weak to hold it up.

"Come on, old chap." Tristan's voice broke through the fog and he felt him stroke his cheek. "Chin up. Have you safe in a trice."

"Wha...wha..." Sam tried to unglue his tongue from the roof of his mouth. "Wha' happened?" His head wouldn't work any better than his mouth.

"Don't you remember?"

Sam didn't really want to remember so he let his eyes close and leaned into Tristan's warmth, feeling thankful that he was there.

He was being dragged upstairs. Sam tried to lift his feet but the pain exploding in his head made it hard. He heard someone calling him a lazy sod and tried to give them a piece of his mind, but his mouth wouldn't work properly.

Tristan. Where was Tristan? He had to warn him, couldn't let them get to him. Couldn't let Mosely anywhere near Tristan.

"Tristan! Tristan!"

"He's calling for you," Alfie said.

Tristan was off the bed in Alfie's guest room before he was fully awake. He staggered a bit but grabbed the bedpost. "Is he awake?"

"Not really, but he is getting himself agitated and that can't be good." Like him, Alfie was still dressed, but his hair was messed and his cravat wilted. "Though I confess I will feel happier about him when he wakes up."

Tristan rubbed his eyes and followed. Samuel was in the guest room and they were taking turns at watching over him. He had wanted to stay the whole time, but had finally allowed Alfie and Gareth to share the burden on the proviso that they called him if Samuel so much as moved. He hurried down the dark corridor, and on hearing Samuel call his name in a state of high agitation he broke into a run. His stockinged feet padded soundlessly on the carpet.

"I'm here," he said, sliding onto the bed beside Samuel. "Shh, I'm here." He took the man's hands and rubbed them. "You are quite safe."

"You have to get away. They are coming for you. Mosely is coming for you." Sam's eyes were still closed but his brow was furrowed and his head thrashed on the pillow. "Tristan! Tristan!"

"Hush now. I am here with you so I am safe. We are all safe."

Samuel subsided into the pillow and closed his eyes still muttering. Tristan stroked his head.

Gareth came into the room yawning. "What was that?"

"He said they were coming for me."

All three men looked at each other. "Is this Dante's men? Mosely?" Tristan asked of Gareth.

"I'd lay odds."

Alfie arched an eyebrow. "What in God's name would they want with Tristan?" he said to Gareth. He then turned to Tristan. "Do they know who you are? Have they your direction?"

Tristan shook his head. "No, I have been careful to remain anonymous." His heart was beating fast.

Gareth pulled a face. "I hate to tell you this, but I guarantee that Dante and Mosely know who you are, and are perfectly aware of where you live."

"Wonderful," muttered Alfie, running his hands through his hair.

"Gareth, you should return," Tristan said. "They might realise you are gone."

Gareth flicked his hair over one shoulder. "Too late for that. The men who attacked Sam are Moseley's men. They recognised me and probably you, too."

Alfie made an exasperated sound and let his hands flop to his sides.

Gareth glared at him. "The problem is, Sam's cousin ran away at Christmas, and Mosely was sent to get him back. He failed. If Dante realises that Sam is gone, and now me..." He shrugged.

"I have no connection at all to Dante so we should be safe here," Alfie said.

"Well, I am not going anywhere," Tristan said. "If Dante works out the connection between us and wants to come here we will be ready for him. Damned if I am letting the man chase me away. Samuel needs to rest. We are staying here."

"The other thing is..." Gareth hesitated and then continued. "I am afraid Mosely has something of an obsession with Sam. That was one of the reasons he ran when he did. Mosely is not a good man. He's a bastard through and through." Gareth rolled his shoulders and then spoke again. "When Harry Wilson got out he managed to get one of the children out with him, too. Mosely was furious. I heard Dante was apoplectic."

"Children?" Tristan frowned. "What do you mean, children?"

Gareth looked at Tristan, over to Alfie, and then back to Tristan. He cleared his throat. "Some of the clients like them young."

Tristan went cold all over. "I see," he whispered.

"If Dante finds out that Mosely has lost another then…" he shrugged.

Alfie crossed his arms over his chest. "I still don't see what the hell this has to do with Tristan. This chap Mosely would have nothing to gain by coming for the Earl of Chiltern."

Gareth tilted his chin at Alfie. "He will think that the Earl of Chiltern has an awful lot to lose and it wouldn't surprise me in the slightest if Mosely didn't fancy making up the lost income from a spot of blackmail."

"Bastard tries anything like that and…" Alfie said. Tristan place a hand on his sleeve, halting his tirade.

"Alfie, we just need some time for Samuel to recover. How long will it take?"

Alfie controlled himself with some difficulty. "It depends when he wakes. If there are no ill effects, a day or two."

"What kind of ill effects?"

Alfie looked away.

"Alfie?"

"Well, injuries to the head are tricky. Mostly, one wakes up with a raging headache, but I have seen men wake and forget who they were. I have seen people apparently recover only to die…" He shrugged. "I can't say."

Tristan's heart squeezed so tightly in his chest that it was hard to breathe.

"I see."

"I think we need to lock all the doors, just in case, and get some rest." Alfie moved with brisk precision.

"I agree. I am going to stay with Samuel. I suggest you two rest." Both men left with some reluctance, and Tristan slid into the bed with Samuel, Alfie's words ringing in his ears. He was damned if he was going to lose him either to Mosely or to a head injury. Samuel stirred as he settled himself beside him.

"Tristan?"

"I'm here."

Samuel dragged open his eyes, but they were unfocused. "Stay away from Mosely," he whispered. "You must stay away..."

"Shh." Tristan stroked Samuel's cheek. His head was bound with a cravat, leaving tufts of dark hair sticking up out of the top. His face felt warm. "Hush now. You are quite safe here. We all are."

"Jus' keep away from him. Promise."

"I promise," Tristan whispered and stroked his face again until he settled. When he appeared to be sleeping naturally he moved silently from the room and returned to the parlour where Gareth and Alfie appeared to be having words.

"Is aught amiss?" he asked and both shook their heads.

"I think we should get away somewhere," Gareth said, planting his hands on his hips.

"I am not running away." Tristan couldn't see how going anywhere would help, but then he realised that Gareth was probably in the same position as Samuel. Beholden to Dante, owned by Dante and wholly without money.

"Please don't worry, Gareth." Tristan closed his

eyes and rolled his shoulders. "I will make sure you are safe and provided for."

Gareth stared at him, and Tristan braced himself for the rejection, the prickly show of pride, kicking himself for speaking without thinking.

"Damned right you will. You got me into this, so it's your responsibility to get me out of it. And to make sure I have enough blunt to live."

Tristan opened his eyes wide. Well, that was direct.

Gareth walked over to him and put a finger under his chin. "Do not mistake me for Sam. I will take everything that you offer and more." Those dark eyes were disconcerting, but Tristan held his gaze.

"I will not run away. I will…"

"Oh, for crying out loud will you listen to yourselves," Alfie said, and pulled at Gareth's arm, moving him out of Tristan's way.

"Do you recall the invitation I extended for the house party this weekend?"

Tristan halted with a frown, nodded.

"Why don't we go there?"

Tristan hesitated.

"We are not running away; we are simply taking up the offer of a weekend of likeminded company."

He had a point. Whilst he was not prepared to run, he could see the sense of getting Samuel away until he was well enough to deal with the situation himself, and Gareth was right, he did have a duty to him.

"I suppose we could," he said.

"Likeminded company?" Gareth said.

Alfie tugged his ear and then turned to Gareth. "The weekend is a gathering of likeminded individuals; you would be welcome to come if you feel that your position within the club has been compromised by helping my cousin."

"I think we can safely say I have been compromised," Gareth said, casting a sly glance in Alfie's direction.

"You can pose as my guest," Alfie said, surprising Tristan.

Gareth stared at him, chin in the air. "Is it a molly house?"

"Good God, no. This is a gentlemen's weekend at the home of Lord Overdale where a few of us will meet for a weekend of gambling and sport on the face of it. There is nothing sordid about it, I assure you. It is merely an opportunity for men of our...persuasion to have time where we can act as we please and not have to look over our shoulders every moment, not have to guard our expressions at all times."

Tristan watched the exchange with interest. He also wished he had known that this kind of party existed. It would have made life significantly more tolerable.

"You appear to be assuming that my nature is the same as yours." Gareth tilted his hips slightly and put a hand on one. It was a ridiculously effete gesture and Tristan had to smile, particularly as his oh, so smooth cousin was looking a little flustered. "Are you asking me as your partner for the weekend?"

Tristan's eyes were bouncing from one to the other, he was fairly certain his mouth was hanging open.

"I am suggesting that we all go somewhere safe. The exact arrangement can be decided upon later. I am merely suggesting that you stay with us out of interest for your safety given your efforts to protect my cousin. Take it or leave it."

Gareth straightened, tossed his long shiny hair over one shoulder, and walked sinuously across the small distance that separated them and stood before

Alfie. Alfie stood his ground and didn't move an inch. There were almost nose to nose.

"Thank you," said Gareth, his voice low and husky. "Your concern is touching." He blinked slowly, leaned forward, and touched his lips to Alfie's and kissed him gently. "I think I would rather like to be yours for the weekend." He flicked Alfie gently on the cheek with one finger and then turned back to Tristan. He rubbed his hands together, changing demeanour and tone completely. "Right. Let's get cracking. We need proper togs for this outing. I for one am not turning up looking like a country bumpkin. He strode over to Tristan. "We are much of a height and build, perhaps you could loan me something?"

Tristan smiled. "It would be my pleasure," he said, watching Alfie, who was flushed and touching his fingertips to his lips.

Chapter 10

AFTER A SWIFT visit to Tristan's house, the bags were packed and loaded into a carriage. Samuel had enough outfits still at the house for a weekend away, and Gareth was suitably outfitted for the excursion having raided Tristan's wardrobes. The doors were bolted, staff alerted to the possibility of intruders, and Tristan worked out that they had a few hours before setting off, so he made sure that his guests had all they needed and then bade them goodnight.

He took a deep breath and headed in the direction of Samuel's room. He needed to stay with him through the night to make sure that he didn't take a turn for the worse. Alfie had terrified him and he wasn't prepared to take any risks. He crept into the room, feet soundless on the thick carpet. The fire was burning low in the grate, casting a soft shadow over the room and as the door clicked closed, Samuel moved. He groaned and rubbed his eyes.

"Fuck," he muttered.

Tristan moved to stand by the bed. "How do you feel?"

"I have a headache and I feel as though I have been trampled. By horses. Large ones." He shifted a little and put a hand to his head. "What the hell happened?"

Tristan had to breathe evenly and force himself not to gather him up into his arms. He was awake. Awake and lucid. That was something, but Alfie had said that sometimes men did that and then died. He didn't know what he would do if Samuel died.

"Mosely sent his men to find you. Gareth and I arrived just as they were beating you…" Tristan stopped and took another deep breath. The memory of that moment would haunt him for a long time. "I thought you…I thought they had killed you. Do you remember Gareth?" he said, and then cleared his throat.

Sam moved his hand and stared at him. "Of course I remember Gareth. What were you doing at my rooms? What are you talking about?" Samuel said, after considering him for a moment, squinting a little at him in the firelight.

Good question. "Sorry, just something Alfie said about men with head injuries waking and not know who they were."

"I know who I am. How did you find me?"

"I went to Dante's to find Gareth to see if he would tell me where you were. I wanted…needed to talk to you."

"I see."

Silence ticked between them. Samuel closed his eyes and massaged his temples.

"We have decided that the best thing to do is to go away for a little while. Wait for all the fuss to settle and then we can decide how best to get you away from Dante's safely. You and Gareth."

Samuel opened his eyes. "Gareth?"

Tristan nodded. "Do you mind if I sit?" he said, gesturing to the edge of the bed. Samuel shook his head and moved his legs so Tristan perched there. He wanted to take hold of Samuel's hand but didn't.

"I had to get help for you. I was terrified you were going to bleed to death. Alfie was a medic in the war. He's a soldier, so Gareth stayed with you whilst I ran and got Alfie to help."

"I thought you didn't want anything to do with me," Samuel muttered, picking at the sheet by his chest.

"I never wished you harm."

Samuel kept his eyes on the sheet. "Go on."

"Well, between us we got you here, but then realised that Mosely now knows that Gareth has run away and that I am involved…it's all getting rather messy."

"I'd say."

"Well, the thing is I felt quite strongly that we should stay here and not be forced to run away but I can see the sense in finding somewhere to let you recover, somewhere we can think and decide what to do."

"I see."

"Alfie has an invitation to a house party this weekend, it's for men of a certain persuasion, and we think it best if all four of us go. Gareth will pose as Alfie's guest, although they do seem a little tight already."

Samuel's eyebrows raised at this and he smiled a little. "Really?"

Tristan grinned. "I think so."

"Are you matchmaking?"

Tristan laughed and was relieved when Samuel laughed, too. The laughter subsided into an awkward silence.

"Where is this house party?"

"Lord Overdale's country house. It's not too far away, and apparently it is a small gathering of men like us." At Sam's raised eyebrows Tristan smiled a little. "Where men can relax and not have to guard every look, every word. I had no idea such parties existed."

Samuel just smiled. Probably at his naivety.

"So it seemed like an ideal opportunity to give us a little time to think."

"That's decent of you, but there is no need. I had letter from Harry, my cousin who ran away? I can go there." Samuel shifted and closed his eyes. "I will be safe there."

Tristan swallowed and nodded, keeping his face straight. "I see."

"If you don't mind me keeping the money that you gave me a little while longer, it will buy Gareth and I tickets for the stagecoach."

"Well, let's decide in the morning. I suspect Gareth and Alfie are rather looking forward to it."

"Well, let them go." Samuel's voice was getting low and sleepy.

"You need to sleep." Tristan cleared his throat. "I am going to stay with you to make sure that there are no ill effects from the blow to your head."

Samuel shifted and opened his eyes with some effort. "Stay?"

"Yes," Tristan said, but when Samuel just stared he backed down. "Do you want me to go?"

Tristan sat unmoving until Samuel shifted. "Samuel?" he prompted when there was no reply.

"Sam. Just call me Sam. And yes, you should go."

Tristan sucked in a deep breath, surprised at

how much that hurt, and then stood up. "If that's what you want."

Sam let out a groan. "Oh, for God's sake stay then, but I am in no fit state to fuck you."

Was that what he thought of him? Tristan's chest squeezed so tight it was hard to speak. "I never expected you to."

Sam grunted, put an arm over his eyes, and threw back the bedding at the side of him with the other. "Get in then, if you are staying."

Tristan removed all his clothing except his shirt, and climbed in beside Samuel...Sam. He lowered himself onto the pillow and pulled up the coverlet, taking care not to touch. He could hear Sam's regular breathing, feel the warmth from his body, catch the scent of him on the sheets. He closed his eyes and wondered if there was any way at all to repair what stood between them. Wondered if he *wanted* to repair it. He didn't speak or move until Sam's breathing slowed, his arm fell onto the bed and he began snoring softly. Only then did Tristan realise that they had never simply slept together. He edged closer until he could put his hand on Samuel's... Sam's chest, feel the soft rhythm of his breathing, and then closed his eyes.

"GET YOUR ARSES out of bed, you lazy sods." The covers were ripped away, leaving Sam groaning. Beside him, Tristan sat bolt upright and grabbed the covers to his chest. Sam peeled open his eyes and had to smile at Tristan's shock. It wasn't even as though they were naked. Both wore rather respectable night shirts although Sam's was rucked up, giving Gareth a bit of an eyeful. He tugged it down.

"I'm injured. You should never shock an injured man, particularly if he has a head injury. You could do irreparable damage." He rubbed his eyes and yawned. "What time is it?"

"Do you *mind?*" Tristan said, with centuries of aristocratic breeding oozing from every outraged pore of his body, despite the fact that his fair hair was sticking up at all angles and his eyes were clogged with sleep.

"Well, it might have been more fun if you'd both been in the altogether," Gareth admitted with a saucy grin.

"You are far too bloody jolly. It's not even morning," Sam said, adjusting his position and wondering if he should attempt to sit up.

"It's five-thirty. Alfie has everything packed and we are ready to go. Breakfast will be in fifteen minutes. Alfie has held his valet off until you get to your room and make it look as though you slept there rather than with sleeping beauty here."

"Alfie?" Sam said with a raised brow.

"Apologies." Gareth laid a hand on his chest and sketched a brief bow. "Lord Alfred."

Sam groaned and held his head. "Oh, God. You've fucked him, haven't you? Haven't you?"

"You wound me," Gareth said, nose in the air.

Sam struggled to a sitting position, feeling his head swim alarmingly as he did so. "And you don't think that this whole thing is complicated enough without that? You need to get back to Dante's before he starts looking for you, as well. We can't just gallivant off to the country. We are not toffs like these two with more money than sense, we have to earn a living. We have to go back to the lives that we have and find a way to deal with Dante that doesn't involve him killing us."

Gareth made a derisory sound and flicked his hair over his shoulder. "It's too late for that. By now Dante and Mosely know that you are involved with Tristan, they know that I have run away, too. We can't go back."

"Well, I am not going on this jaunt you all cooked up," he said, holding onto his pounding head and wishing he could think clearly.

"Excuse me?" Tristan's aristocratic affront was now focused on Sam, who sighed and held his head again.

"What?"

"More money than sense?"

"I mean no offence, but…"

"We really don't have time for this, ladies. Of course you are coming with us. Up. Now." Gareth patted Tristan on the shoulder and sallied out of the room, leaving Sam to deal with a bristling Tristan.

Sam closed his eyes and held onto his patience. This was turning into a farce. "I am afraid that if I embroil you in this any further you will be hurt. Your family reputation, your reputation…That's all." He held out his hands in a silent plea for understanding. "I cannot go through with this plan. I cannot involve you, Alfie, and Gareth in this. Mosely's quarrel is with me. Let me deal with it.

"You involved me when you planned to trick me into getting you out of Dante's." Tristan's mouth was thin and a muscle ticked by his temple. "You involved me when you accepted my hospitality. You involved me when you lied to me. I *am* involved. We are all involved. Now we need to get dressed and get moving."

Sam put his thumping head in his hands. He simply didn't have the energy to argue.

AGAINST HIS BETTER judgement, Sam found himself en route to some wretched house party, crammed in a swaying carriage with Alfie, Tristan, and Gareth. All three were dozing, but his head hurt abominably, and the swaying was causing all kinds of nausea, so he simply stared miserably out of the window. How in the world he was going to get away from Mosely, God only knew. Was he to spend the rest of his life running from the man? He had now involved Gareth and felt partially responsible for him, too. Both had a living to earn, not like Tristan and Alfie. He looked at Tristan. He was frowning in his sleep. Those fair brows were drawn together and his lips were turned down at the corners. Gareth was leaning against the side of the carriage, arms folded and mouth open and Alfie was slumped so far down that his knees were getting in the way. Arms folded, he apparently slept peacefully, but Sam wondered if he was asleep at all. He peered out of the window again. They had to be almost there. If they weren't, he was sure he was going to embarrass himself. Almost as if he had read his thoughts, Alfie opened one eye, glanced out of the window, and then heaved himself up and stretched.

"Almost there."

Thank God. Sam nudged Tristan, who muttered and attempted to roll over. He shook his shoulder, making him start. Gareth let out a loud snore and startled himself awake. All four men stretched as much as possible in the confined conditions, but Sam, who stood a good few inches taller than them all spread out the most.

"Tell me again who our host is?" Tristan asked as he adjusted his clothing and smoothed his hair.

Alfie pulled his gaze from the window. "Lord Overdale. You must know him. Bit of a philanthropist. Does a lot of work with children, foundlings and the like. Raises a lot of money for good causes. I'm fairly sure he has spoken in the house about it."

"I seem to recall the name. I am sure I will know him when I see him. Anyone else I am likely to know?"

"I wouldn't know."

The house came into view. It was large, opulent, and nestled into the hillside. Surrounded by leafless trees, it basked in the late afternoon sun with rays bouncing off the windows.

"Pretty," remarked Gareth, leaning over Sam's legs to get a better view.

"I need to get out of here. Quickly." Sam shifted so he wasn't quite so squashed.

"Right-ho." Alfie opened the door as they drew to a halt in front of the enormous house. It was constructed on a symmetrical plan, three storeys in warm sandstone with a huge entrance nestled beneath magnificent pillars, long and straight.

There was a flurry of servants who arrived to help them down and carry their luggage, and then a large man came out of the door raising a hand and shouting in greeting.

"Chiltern! How damned good to see you, my boy." He came down the steps and pumped Tristan's hand, bowing as he did so. "Honoured that you would stoop to visit my little party. Honoured."

Tristan smiled and bowed slightly in response. He looked unruffled, calm, and had that aristocratic tilt to his head, to the way he held himself, and Sam couldn't tear his eyes from him. There was nothing of the shy boy about him now.

"You are too kind. I hope you don't object to a party of us arriving?"

"Indeed not, indeed not. You are all most welcome. Most welcome. Your cousin was kind enough to send word of your arrival with a rider in advance, so we are prepared, all prepared."

They all bundled out and shook themselves. Tristan made the introductions. Overdale bowed and shook hands with all of them and then ushered them into the house. Sam could hear voices inside.

"We are all settling in at the moment and dinner will be at eight. If you require refreshment at any time, just ring for the servants and they will be only too pleased to accommodate you."

All the men nodded and smiled as they looked around the opulent entrance way that was filled with paintings of all manner of clocks and ornaments. A plaque with a deer's head on it, antlers and all, stood over a huge, stone fireplace that probably once housed a massive spit. The floor and staircase appeared to be made of marble and boot heels rang out as they walked. Footmen appeared to guide them silently to their rooms, but before they moved away a door opened a little way down one of the corridors off the hallway and two young men came out. They were smiling and laughing and didn't notice them. They set off walking down the corridor, away from them, the taller of the two took hold of his friend's hand. Sam watched as they walked away hand in hand. As if it were nothing, as if it were perfectly natural thing to do in a country house. Two men, hand in hand. He glanced over at Tristan, who seemed to be having a similar thought. He smiled up at him and he looked a little emotional.

They followed the footmen and assured their host that they were perfectly well catered for. Sam found himself in a beautiful room that overlooked the parkland at the back of the house. There appeared to be an adjoining room and when he opened the door he found Tristan.

"Our rooms are linked," he said, quite unnecessarily.

"Indeed." Tristan was watching him. "How are you feeling?"

"Dreadful. I am going to sleep for a little while."

Tristan nodded, but looked uncomfortable. "When you have rested, I think we should talk."

"Really? Talking rarely gets us anywhere."

Tristan laughed, a soft huff of a sound. "I know, but I think there are some things we need to clear up. We have a few days now where we can talk a little…if that's what you want?"

Sam rubbed his aching temples. "Tristan, the last time I came anywhere near you it was…"

"I was angry," Tristan said, interrupting. "I was angry. You played me for an absolute fool so I think I had every reason to be."

"I didn't play you for a fool…I didn't…You weren't…" He closed his eyes. He couldn't even think straight. Moments later he dragged them open. "I need to sleep. We can talk later if you wish."

Tristan hesitated, and for a moment Sam thought he might argue, but then he nodded and gave a tight smile as he made to leave.

"Sleep well."

When the door closed behind Tristan, Sam removed most of his clothes and flopped onto the bed. He felt vile, but most of all he felt hopelessly at a loss as to what to do. He felt completely out of his depth with the company they were about to engage with. A house full of aristocrats, respectable men with lives he could only dream about, and him. A whore. A prostitute. A man who had tricked his client into helping him escape the clutches of a madman who now pursued them all. He put an arm over his eyes. He hadn't realised Tristan was titled when he'd begged him for help, hadn't realised how well connected he was and now…well. He swallowed. How stupid to fall in love with a man who was so far above him, so beyond his touch. He might make a fair play at it, but he would never be respectable enough for Tristan to be anything other than his kept plaything. And not only that, he had hurt him abominably, put him in danger, and now his head hurt so damned much he couldn't even fuck him. He felt even more stupid when tears pricked behind his eyes.

Chapter 11

SAM SUFFERED THE services of a valet and stood unmoving as he was helped into his coat. He was beginning to get used to seeing himself in the mirror looking every inch the gentleman. Here, he would probably pass as respectable, even taking into account the sickly pallor of his skin. If only his head would stop pounding, and his stomach would settle, he would probably enjoy an evening of playing the gentleman with Tristan by his side. But every movement made his head ache.

A knock came at the door and the valet left as Sam welcomed his visitors. Gareth and Alfie came in, both looking startlingly handsome. Gareth looked, as always, fabulously dandyish in his borrowed clothes. Starched shirt points stood high, but not too high that he couldn't move. Wearing evening black, he looked sharp and elegant. Gareth's hair had been drawn back into a queue and he looked quite the exotic gentleman. Alfie looked sombre, but there was something a little dangerous about him. Sam couldn't help but note that the two of them exchanged glances frequently. He was about to speak when the adjoining door opened, Tristan walked in, and Sam's breath left his body. Just like the others he was dressed soberly, but with such elegance. His cravat was simple but perfect. A sapphire blue pin nestled in the folds. His waistcoat was shades of silver and grey and as he slid his watch into his pocket he smiled politely at the room.

"Gentlemen. Should we dine?"

"At last. I am starving." Gareth adjusted his borrowed waistcoat of green and gold and set his shoulders back. Sam watched as Alfie rolled his eyes and Tristan smiled. Tristan seemed to be avoiding looking at him.

"I'm not terribly hungry. I still feel a little out of sorts," Sam admitted. It was the truth. He felt like death. His head ached. Even his eyeballs hurt.

Alfie crossed over the room to stand before him. He reached out and lifted first one eyelid, then the other. "You look fine. Avoid too much wine and eat lightly. Another good night's sleep should help."

"Thank you, doctor," Sam said with a smile. Alfie raised an eyebrow.

They left the room and made their way along the corridor. As they did so, Tristan fell into step beside Sam.

"You do look rather pale. If you'd rather stay in your room I can arrange for a tray to be brought to you."

Sam looked down at him. He looked so somber. "I will be fine," he said, and slid his hand around Tristan's to squeeze it briefly without looking at him. "Thank you. I don't deserve it." Sam held his breath and waited, but Tristan didn't speak so he let go of his hand.

"I appreciate everything that you have done," he added, trying again.

Tristan looked up at him, and Sam met his unreadable gaze. "Would you ever have told me yourself?"

Sam thought about that for a moment and then smiled a little sadly. "On our fiftieth anniversary when you would be too old to leave me."

Tristan was staring at him but his expression was unreadable. "So, you saw this as a long term thing?"

There was something in his voice that made Sam's stomach tighten. "Who knows," he said, thankful that they had reached the dining room. He didn't know if he saw it as long term, he didn't even know if two men could have anything long term. He sighed as his head started to pound again.

TRISTAN WATCHED SAM carefully. He wanted to ask him more about how he saw them. He had been surprised when he had alluded to them being together forever. He hadn't thought about that. He hadn't thought about the long term at all, he had been too enamoured of Sam to see anything but what was in front of him, but Sam had apparently had plan. A long term plan.

As they arrived at the dining room, Tristan was torn between bracing himself and bursting with curiosity every time he thought about who might possibly be at the party that he knew. To think, all this time, people that he called friend might have been sharing the same dark secret.

They walked in, and Tristan could see that there were easily a dozen men there, drinks in hand, just talking. Or so it seemed. When Tristan looked carefully he could see that some men touched each other, lingering over touches in a way that would be entirely unacceptable in any polite society. More than one couple exchanged glances that were frankly adoring. Nothing overt, nothing lewd, just men talking with men but not hiding how they felt. Tristan's heart beat rapidly as he swiftly counted the number of familiar faces. There were four that he recognised, but none that he would call friend. The men that he knew stared for a moment, but then smiled and lifted their glasses in acknowledgement. That was all, just a friendly gesture. Tristan was rooted to the spot momentarily, but moved when Sam put a hand in the small of his back and urged him forward. Lord Overdale welcomed them and made introductions. Tristan had to smile at Alfie and Gareth, who played their parts admirably. Gareth was incredibly confident, witty, and with Alfie at his side they charmed most of the company. He and Sam were able to relax a little in their shadow. There was a moment when his breath caught as Gareth smiled at Alfie and touched a finger to his cheek. Nothing happened, no-one paid the slightest attention, and he breathed again.

"It's remarkable," he said a little while later to Sam, who had gravitated to his side.

"What is?"

"Being able to talk freely, look at you without fear that someone will discern my feelings..." His words trailed off as Sam was looking at him oddly. Sam looked at him a moment longer and then cast a glance around the room. "Doesn't really look much different to me. They are not exactly fawning over each other as they might in the brothel."

"Well, a gentleman would never indulge in public displays of affection, even if he were with a woman, so why would it be any different for gentlemen who are together. All that is needed is a look, or a touch, but in the rest of society that might be enough to arouse suspicion. Here, it is not."

Sam nodded and took a sip of his drink and looked out over the crowd when he spoke. "I'm not a gentleman so I wouldn't really know about that."

Tristan debated about how to respond for a moment, but then took the plunge. "If I overreacted to what I heard, I apologise."

Sam's head snapped around and those beautiful, crystalline, grey green eyes were wide.

HE'D APOLOGISED. SAM kept glancing at Tristan, who sat on the opposite side of the dining table. He had apologised if he had overreacted. Sam thought about that for quite some time. Had he overreacted? Probably not. In his shoes, Sam doubted that he would have ever been able to get over what had heard. Guilt still ate at him, but he doubted he would ever forget the look on Tristan's face after he had overheard his and Gareth's conversation. He was without doubt the bigger man. Sam watched him. He was smiling at something his dinner companion had said whilst picking up his glass of claret. He took a sip, put the glass down, and patted the corner of his mouth with his napkin. He was beautiful. Through and through. He was what Sam knew he could never be no matter how much he might play the game. He was a gentleman. He was respectable.

Sam played with the food on his plate. His head was a thumping mess and his stomach was still queasy. He managed to eat some of the chicken and a potato, but his stomach was tightening ominously so he put his fork down and took a sip of the water in the glass beside his wine.

"Not hungry?" the man beside him said.

"Not terribly. The food is quite delicious though."

"Overdale always puts on a good spread." The man had introduced himself as Garforth. He was older than Sam by a good few years, but still very attractive with a hint of silver in his dark hair.

"Have you been here before?" Sam asked, taking another sip of the water.

"Several times. One of the few places where a chap can relax and indulge his senses."

"Indeed."

"Are you attached?"

Sam glanced up and found Tristan's eyes fixed on him. His face was tense, his shoulders braced as if waiting for a blow. Sam didn't have a clue if Tristan wanted to be thought of as attached to him or not. But he had apologised. He had suggested he might have overreacted and last night he had got into bed with him and cared for him.

He smiled a little at Tristan, whose breath seemed to hitch.

"I am attached," he said, turning back to Garforth.

"Then I am happy for you." Garforth raised his glass in salute to Tristan, and Sam watched patches of colour rise in Tristan's cheeks as he raised his glass in return.

"Are you attached?" Sam asked, taking another sip of his water.

"No." Garforth looked at his plate, smiled, and then looked back up. "I don't really believe in attachments. I am more a..." He paused, tilted his head, and then looked directly at Sam. "More of a connoisseur. Happier to sample all the delights and rare treats Overdale will have on offer rather than settle for one."

"Then I am sure you will have a pleasant evening," Sam said, looking at the men around the table. There were some quite attractive men seated around, some he recognised from Dante's.

"Should you change your mind, or decide you might like to sample a different dish..." He glanced over at Tristan with a warm, appreciative look that made Tristan flush even harder and Sam was hard pushed not to laugh. He had met many men like Garforth, but he would have wagered his last farthing that Tristan never had.

"You are most kind. Should we decide to expand our culinary horizons then you will be the first to know." He lifted his water glass in salute. Garforth glanced at Tristan again and then laughed lightly.

SAM DRAINED THE last of the water in his glass. If he drank the wine, he had no doubt he would be ill. He hated feeling so weak. The rest of the meal was interminable. He pushed pudding about his dish and accepted more water when Tristan summoned one of the footmen. They were too far from each other to converse easily. He drank more water and rubbed the back of his neck and fidgeted as the port was passed around. He needed to stand up and get some air quite urgently but he didn't want to draw attention to himself, or to Tristan for that matter, so he held firm and accepted the glass. He didn't dare drink it, so he just touched it to his lips a few times.

As they continued to chat, the guests around them shifted and as their host stood to repair to the parlour, Sam felt a sense of relief that was almost dizzying. Garforth stood to one side to allow Sam to move first, and managed to stroke his arm as he did so. Sam barely took any notice of it, but caught Tristan's expression from the corner of his eye. He was clearly unhappy. Sam thought to offer some sort of reassurance, but he felt too ill to try. If he could just get through the next hour or so before he could go to bed and sleep he would be pleased.

As they filed out slowly Tristan appeared by his side. "How are you feeling? You look quite unwell."

Sam smiled tiredly. "I feel like death, truth told. How are you bearing up?"

Tristan shook his head. "You should excuse yourself and retire. You had a nasty blow to the head, to say nothing of a shock."

Tristan took his hand briefly and squeezed it. Sam returned the pressure with another smile. "I might do that."

They made their way to the parlour, following the rest of the guests and Sam felt better just having Tristan beside him. He felt oddly proud to have him there. He was so at ease in this environment, so effortlessly elegant. He wished he felt better so he could enjoy the evening more and not be a complete burden. He wasn't much use to Tristan in the state he was in.

"I never knew parties like this existed," Tristan said as they ambled along.

"I've never been invited to one either," Sam said, and glanced sideways to find Tristan looking up at him. They shared a smile.

"It's good to know that people can be civilised about things rather than lurking around in back alleys and molly houses." Tristan laughed a little as he said it.

"Safer, too," Sam said, thinking of the raids that had taken place in London over the last few years. He looked down as his feet as they walked on the deep red carpet. "I'm glad we are speaking again," he said quietly.

"Me, too." Tristan didn't look at him, he stared at the carpet, too.

They walked the rest of the way in silence until they reached the parlour and all of them wandered in. The room had been set up for cards and several members of the group were arranging themselves in groups.

"Do you play?" Tristan asked.

Sam looked around the room. "I've no taste for it. I prefer to keep hold of what little money I have. This is how I got into difficulty in the first place."

"Of course. I'm sorry."

Tristan moved closer, making Sam's heart beat faster. He could feel the warmth from his body. "Let's retire," he said softly.

"What about…" Sam nodded to the rest of the room.

"I somehow doubt they would care."

Sam had the strongest urge to gather Tristan up in his arms and hold him tight. To bury his face in his neck and feel his arms around him. He settled for reaching out and touching the back of his hand briefly.

"I will go up."

They stared at each other for a moment until Sam tore his gaze away and set off in the direction of his chamber. God, but he needed to sleep.

TRISTAN WATCHED SAM walk away across the enormous hallway and set off up the grand staircase. He looked unutterably weary and Tristan couldn't help the worry that set up inside him. Alfie's words kept coming back to haunt him, the comment about men with injuries to the head apparently recovering only to die later. The thought of a world without Sam in it made his chest seize painfully and put some perspective on their argument. He swallowed a couple of times and went in search of Alfie. He found him in a corner engaged in conversation with Gareth. The pair looked quite animated and Tristan had to smile. He had never seen Alfie work up enthusiasm to overcome his fashionable boredom with anyone before. He took a glass of champagne from a passing footman and went to join them.

"Where's Sam?" Gareth asked with a small frown.

"Retired. He looked ghastly. I will be following him shortly."

Alfie took a sip of his drink and nodded. "He didn't look the best. He needs to rest and take care of himself."

Tristan bit his lip. "You said that sometimes men recover and then..." He gestured with his hand, not even wanting to say the word aloud.

Alfie grimaced, understanding perfectly what he meant. "I have seen it but only rarely. Forgive me, I shouldn't have worried you like that."

Tristan shook his head. "I'd rather know. I will keep an eye on him tonight."

Gareth knocked back the remainder of his drink and popped it on a table. "Well, gentlemen, I am simply exhausted. I fear I must retire immediately."

Tristan watched as Alfie's gaze drifted from the top of Gareth's head to his toes. "As you wish, my dear." Gareth walked across the room away from them, and Tristan could barely conceal his smile as Alfie's gaze followed his every step.

"Are you smitten, dear cousin?" he said, once Gareth was out of sight. He expected a witty rejoinder, but Alfie looked surprisingly serious as he stared out over the space that Gareth had recently occupied.

"He is...interesting." He shook his head and turned to Tristan. "How much does Sam's past concern you?"

Tristan had to think about that. He pursed his lips, then took a sip of his drink. "It does bother me, but not enough to make a difference to how I feel."

"So you have forgiven him?"

Tristan scratched his ear. "I am trying to."

Alfie looked as though he might say more, but his eyes widened, and he nudged Tristan and nodded to the door. Tristan followed his gaze, and his jaw almost dropped. Overdale was crossing the room in long strides, holding out a hand in greeting to the man who had just walked in. Wallingford.

"God's knees..." Alfie's whisper echoed exactly Tristan's thoughts. There was a momentary hush in the room, and then a buzz of interested chatter. At first, Tristan thought that they were simply as shocked as he and Alfie were, but then it became clear that the buzz was excited chatter. He exchanged a glance with Alfie, but he looked as nonplussed as Tristan felt. Wallingford looked around the room, and when his gaze fell on them, he smiled and headed in their direction. Wallingford was an imposing man. Large, fair haired, with an air of complete confidence about him.

"My dear boys, how good to see you." He shook hands with them both and then looked around the room. "I had wondered if one day I might see you here."

Tristan felt uneasy. He smiled and nodded, but said nothing.

Alfie's eyelids were lowered slightly, and he looked around the room, too, in a typically bored fashion. "I must confess, I had wondered exactly the same thing," he said with a faint smile at Wallingford.

"Well, I am glad to see you, I must say. We should talk more but I have some arrangements to see to if we are to have our entertainment this weekend." He nodded to Overdale over the room. "Until tomorrow," he said with a nod of his head, and walked away from them chatting to people, touching some, as he went.

"What do you make of that?" Tristan said.

Alfie shook his head and pulled in a breath. "I have no idea, but I don't think I like it above much."

Tristan had to agree. Wallingford's presence made him feel distinctly uneasy. "I am heading upstairs," he said to Alfie, and finished the last of his drink.

Chapter 12

TRISTAN HURRIED ALONG the dimly lit corridor back to their rooms, deep in thought. Up until Wallingford's appearance, the weekend had seemed like a good idea. The people present were anonymous enough not to give pause, but Wallingford was different. Tristan couldn't think of any reason for him to be present that didn't benefit him in some way. He was beginning to think that perhaps he should have let Sam visit Yorkshire to recover, as it didn't appear that anywhere was safe at the moment. He had hoped that the weekend might give them some opportunity to talk and resolve the issues that stood between them. He still felt guilty when he thought about how he had treated Sam at their last meeting, how he had tried to reduce their relationship to a monetary transaction, and he couldn't even begin to imagine how Sam must have felt. The question that he was grappling with was, could he continue in some kind of relationship with Sam knowing he had lied about loving him. Knowing that he didn't love him.

He arrived at his door and paused. Had Sam been well he was fairly certain that they would have fallen into bed and made up. As it was, they seemed reliant on talking to patch things and they had agreed some time ago things went wrong when they talked. He sighed and let himself in. The bed had been turned down, a candle burned by the bedside and the fire was banked so the room was reasonably warm. The adjoining door was firmly closed. He undressed himself, having left his own valet at home. He had politely declined when offered the service. He pulled a modest nightshirt over his head and hesitated.

On a practical footing, and putting the question of feelings to one side, he needed to see that Sam was recovering and well. He ran a hand over his hair, took a deep breath, and tapped on the adjoining door and walked through.

Two candles burned casting a soft glow over the room. Sam was in bed, in his own nightshirt, with one arm flung over his eyes. He raised it to peer at Tristan.

"Is anything amiss?" he asked, as he struggled up onto one elbow.

"Everything is fine. I was just a little concerned about you so thought I would come and see how you are faring."

"Oh." Sam lay back and put his arm over his eyes again.

Tristan faltered. It was not an encouraging response. "I was going to suggest that I spend the night in here with you until you feel better. Alfie tells me that head wounds can be tricky."

Sam kept his arm over his eyes and licked his lips. "If you like."

Not encouraging at all.

"I'm still too ill to fuck," Sam said, without moving his arm.

"I know that." Tristan spoke evenly and held back the words on the tip of his tongue. Did Sam really think that was all he was interested in?

"Well, in that case..." He let the words trail away so Tristan took it as agreement and slid carefully into bed beside him so as not to jostle him and make his head worse.

SAM'S HEART THUDDED heavily in his chest and his head thumped along with it. What the hell was he to do? He wanted nothing more than to fall into Tristan's arms, beg him for forgiveness, and let him hold him. He wanted every part of him. Wanted to be part of his life. Wanted, wanted, wanted. He moved his arm away from his eyes and looked over at the man who lay beside him, but not touching him. Tristan's eyes were open and he appeared to be looking at the canopy over the bed. He could feel the warmth from his body; catch the scent of his skin. He wanted to beg him for forgiveness and ask if they could begin again, but he knew in his heart that anything like that would not only be impossible, but foolish to boot. What he needed to do was get out of Tristan's life and let him go back to his life as a peer of the realm. By embroiling Tristan in the sordid cesspool that was his life he had endangered him in ways that he never could have imagined.

"I'm sorry," he said, his voice was a thread in the darkness.

Tristan turned to look at him.

"So am I."

Sam wasn't sure what Tristan was apologising for. "I should be feeling more the thing by morning. I will slip away. I have endangered you enough," he said.

Tristan didn't move. He stared at him; unblinking. "You don't need to."

"I do. I never dreamed that anything like this would happen. If I had thought for a moment that by asking you to help me I would put you in harm's way, I would never have done it."

"Well, you did and I am here." Tristan turned his head to look at the canopy again. "We should sleep."

Sam nodded. He wanted to touch Tristan so badly it hurt. Wanted him to pull him over so he could lay his head on his chest, listen to his heartbeat and let it lull him to sleep, but Tristan rolled on his side away from him. Sam closed his eyes.

TRISTAN AWOKE IN the early hours with Sam moving around the room.

"Are you feeling unwell?" he asked as he peered through the gloom.

Sam slid back into the bed, bringing the cold with him and Tristan could feel him shivering. "No, just needed to piss," he said as he crawled in. "And to have a drink. My mouth feels like sawdust."

"How is your head?"

"I don't know. I'm still asleep."

Tristan smiled in the darkness and took a gamble. "Do you want to come over here?" He held up an arm. Sam hesitated, his expression unreadable in the dark, but then he shuffled over and squirmed under Tristan's arm to lay his head on his chest. He wrapped an arm about his waist, and threaded one leg between Tristan's. Tristan pulled the coverlet up about Sam's ears and then let his arms close about him. He buried his nose in his hair as he let sleep claim him again.

SAM AWOKE WITH a start to find himself alone in the bed. He blinked and moved experimentally. He definitely felt better. He stretched expansively and yawned and then peered around, but Tristan was nowhere to be seen. The bed was still warm so he couldn't have gone far. Sam considered getting up and finding him, but was saved the effort when Tristan came back through the connecting doors. When he noticed him he paused and smiled tentatively.

"Good morning. How are you feeling?"

"Much better. Thank you." He wanted to say thank you for holding me in the night but remained silent.

Tristan nodded as he walked to the bed. He wore only a nightshirt and Sam could tell he was erect beneath it and his entire body was filled with warmth. He swallowed.

"I have a proposal." Tristan stood beside the bed. He looked resolute.

That startled Sam. "I see," he murmured, not sure of how to respond. He waited.

Tristan cleared his throat. "I propose that we put everything behind us for a couple of days. Dante, the club, what I overheard; everything."

Sam frowned. "What will that achieve?"

"We have a rather unique opportunity to just be ourselves. We don't have to hide from anyone, worry about anyone…we can relax…" Tristan looked down for a moment. "Can we just be Tristan and Sam? Two men who like each other, desire each other and, for a couple of days, don't have to hide how they feel?"

Sam's entire being yearned to say yes, but he didn't know if he would have the strength to say yes, spend days being together, and then walk away from him as he knew he needed to. He was trying to work out what to say when Tristan spoke again.

"Please."

Sam's throat closed up. He had to swallow a couple of times. How could this beautiful, aristocratic man be pleading with him after what he did. After the mess that he had landed him in?

"Tristan, I want you more than you can know but…I shouldn't. I should let you go back to your life." He shook his head, unsure about how to go on.

"Do you want me now?"

"I…"

Tristan reached over his head, pulled his nightshirt over his head, and stood before him. Naked. His beautiful, leanly muscled body was taut in the pale morning light and the sight of him aroused made Sam's body flush all over again and lose whatever sense or will he possessed.

He threw back the covers and pulled off his own nightshirt, revealing his own arousal. He saw Tristan hitch a breath and run a hand over his balls and stroke his cock.

"Why don't you bring that in here?" Sam said. His

voice sounded husky even to his own ears.

"Are you sure? Are you up to this?"

"Why don't we find out?" Sam spread his legs, allowing Tristan to climb in between them. He moved, but Tristan put a hand on his chest and made him lie still.

"This is just us. Me and you. Sam and Tristan. Nothing to do with money, nothing to do with anything other than the fact that you are a beautiful man and I want you. Do you want me?"

Sam melted at the thread of uncertainty in Tristan's tone. He hadn't realised how unsure he felt, and supposed that when you were paying for someone you never quite knew if they wanted you or not. He sighed. "I want you," he said. "I want you so very badly."

Tristan leaned forward and caged Sam's body with his arms, leaving Sam breathless. In their encounters he usually took charge, but he laid back and let Tristan's mouth find his. They kissed. Softly at first, but then Sam was reaching up to deepen the contact. It felt like coming home. Tristan lifted up after a while, smiled, and then plied soft kisses down Sam's throat, his chest, and then bit softly at his nipples, making Sam moan and writhe beneath him. He remained still as Tristan worked his way down his body and as he reached his navel and dipped his tongue into the indent, Sam closed his eyes and went to take himself in hand, but Tristan caught him and held his hand back. Sam was panting now. Back arching, waiting, needing. Tristan nibbled and kissed the soft skin beneath his navel and Sam cried out and threw his head back into the pillow. By the time he could feel Tristan's warm breath tantalisingly near his cock, he knew he was about to explode.

"Tris, please, please." Christ, he was begging, but when Tristan's warm mouth closed over him he groaned loudly at the sheer pleasure, the intensity of sensation as his tongue slid around his shaft, as he licked and then sucked him down hard. Tristan cupped his balls and rolled them gently as he pleasured him. Sam knew he wouldn't last so he pushed at his head. Tristan immediately pulled off, sat up, spit in his hand, and took both their cocks together and, laying on top of him pumped them hard. He pushed himself up on one arm and Tristan looked into his eyes.

"Come for me," Tristan said, and those words, coming from his beautiful lordling, sent him over. His whole body contorted with the wave of unadulterated pleasure that pulsed into Tristan's hand, shouting as he did so. Tristan followed him into the abyss with a hoarse cry. They clung together, breathing hard. Sam wrapped his arms around Tristan and kissed the dampness of the skin on his shoulder. Tristan burrowed into him, not seeming to mind the sticky mess between them. Sam sifted his fingers through Tristan's hair and kissed him again. How in God's name was he ever to give this man up?

Chapter 13

SAM'S APPETITE APPEARED to be returning. Tristan watched as he wolfed down a pile of sausage and eggs. His colour was better, and his eyes had regained that incorrigible sparkle that had been missing. Tristan wondered if any of this was down to their activities during the early morning. He usually took a passive role in their encounters, but this morning had been remarkably satisfying. Taking control of their loving, and hopefully being able to take control of their lives was perhaps what he needed to do. He glanced around the room and was relieved that breakfast appeared to be a quiet, informal affair with people drifting in and out, and after a little while they found themselves alone for a moment.

"Are you familiar with the Marquess of Wallingford?" Tristan asked.

Sam frowned. "I've heard the name, but I don't know him." He shook his head. "I might know him by sight," Sam said as he applied marmalade to another piece of toast. "Why do you ask?"

"He turned up last night. Just after you had retired. It was a bit of a surprise."

Sam paused with the toast half way to his mouth. "Why?"

Tristan hesitated himself and thought for a moment. "Well, he is terribly well connected, influential…a shocking gossip." Tristan shrugged. "Not the sort of chap one would expect to find here."

Sam grinned and took a huge bite. When he had swallowed, he wiped his mouth with his napkin. "Point him out to me and I will tell you if he has ever been to Dante's. I'll wager he has. All the toffs go there."

Tristan ignored the flutter of unease in his stomach. "Ah…do you recognise some of the people here?"

Sam swallowed, stared at his toast, and nodded.

Tristan wanted to ask if he had…

"I have never bedded any of them though. None of them were clients of mine."

Tristan's stomach unknotted. Marginally. "That's… good to hear."

Sam sighed and rubbed the back of his neck. "Now do you see why I could never come to the clubs with you?"

Tristan nodded.

They ate in silence as the room filled up again. When Sam pushed his plate away, Tristan put his fork down.

"The weather looks quite pleasant. Perhaps we should take a walk. It might help clear you head."

Sam gave a polite nod and gestured for them to leave. As they walked out Tristan watched Sam studiously ignore the occupants of the breakfast room and sighed.

❖

THEY HAD NOT walked far when Tristan heard a shout from behind and turned to see Alfie pursuing them with Gareth beside him.

"Good morning," Alfie said as he reached them.

"Good morning. I trust you had a good night?" Tristan said the words without really thinking but then flushed at the scorching look Gareth exchanged with Alfie.

Sam saved him from having to offer a response by speaking over whatever Gareth was going to say. "We are heading out for a walk. What are your plans?"

Alfie raised an eyebrow. "Should you not be considering what needs to be done to get you out of this mess?"

Sam's jaw jutted and his eyes narrowed but he maintained his smile. "Yes. That is exactly the plan. However, I see no harm in a walk. I need to clear my head. It might be a good idea to have these discussions away from the house, too?"

Alfie nodded. "Do you want to talk now, or are you two…enjoying the sunshine together."

Tristan thought it best to intervene. "Alfie, we are merely walking off breakfast. We will be back at the house before too long. Would you like to talk then, or join us on our walk?"

Alfie smiled. Slowly. "We will leave you to, ah, enjoy the sunshine."

"Thank you." Sam's tone was pleasant but firm.

Alfie and Gareth disappeared and Tristan and Sam walked.

"Your cousin is an irritating man." Sam said, quite pleasantly.

Tristan laughed. "He is the most annoying creature that I know, but he is family. And when everything went to hell he was there to help. He came and made sure that you were not going to die, he helped us to get away, he brought us here..." Tristan glanced at Sam.

Sam shook his head. "As I said. Annoying. Nothing worse than being beholden to an annoying man."

Tristan laughed, and as Sam laughed with him something relaxed a little between them. They walked in a more companionable silence for a while. When they reached a large ornamental pond with a seat positioned to take advantage of the magnificent view Sam motioned for them to sit. Tristan was pleased when Sam took his hand as they placed themselves side by side.

"It's so unfair, isn't it?"

"What is?"

Sam turned in the seat so that he could better face Tristan. "Unfair that I can't court you."

"Court me?" Tristan was taken by surprise. "If anyone were to do the courting it would be me."

Sam's lips twitched as he evidently tried to suppress a smile. "No, it would definitely be me."

Tristan laughed aloud. "I thought we agreed that for today we would be equal."

"We did. We did," Sam said.

"We truly are an aberration, are we not?" Tristan looked out over the landscape.

"Don't ever say that. We are...all that is wonderful." Sam leaned over and kissed Tristan on the mouth. "I just wish it could last."

"And why can't it?" Tristan kissed Sam back.

"Well, there are all manner of reasons."

"Name them." Tristan turned so that they were

looking at each other.

Sam tilted his head to one side. "Well, you have money and a high-ranking position, and I don't have either of those things."

"I don't see that as a barrier." Tristan was firm.

Sam hesitated and pursed his lips. "Well, and please don't take this badly, but that's easy for you to say being the one with all the money and position."

Tristan frowned. "Why is that a barrier? It worked before. All you need to do is come home once we have sorted out this mess with Dante and Mosely."

"With me living in accommodation you paid for, wearing clothes you paid for, eating food you paid for, and me waiting on my own all day to see if you are going to call in to be fucked?"

Tristan felt as though someone had drenched him in ice cold water. Was that how he viewed their arrangement? He stared at Sam for a moment and then looked away. "I had no idea that was how you saw us. I thought that was what you wanted when you asked for my help."

"I thought so, too, until I realised that I actually do have some pride." Sam tilted his head and then stroked Tristan's cheek. "I think it hit me when you offered me pin money as if I were your mistress and it dawned on me that that was exactly what I was. Your mistress. Someone to keep tucked away, out of sight."

"I'm sorry I made you feel that way. It was never my intention." Tristan knew his tone was stiff and probably accusatory but he didn't seem to be able to help it.

Sam reached over and took his hand. Tristan held on tight.

"And now, not only did I drag you into my sordid world I have put you in danger. Grave danger."

"There are no rules for this kind of relationship," Tristan said, holding tight to Sam's hand.

"Yes, there are," Sam said, looking at him. "The law has plenty of rules about it. So does the church."

"Not those kind of rules," Tristan said. "The kind of rules that men and women have. Courtship rules."

"Tristan." Sam paused, his head down bent. "There are no rules so we must make it up as we go on, but we know that this can't last. Don't we?"

"Of course." Tristan looked away as he said it.

"I'd like to have this weekend because you want me. Not because you are paying me, but because you want to be with me. Just as you said."

Tristan's heart hurt. He realised that as he tried to breathe in. Realised it as he tried the lie in his head. "Just for this weekend then," he said. "We will just have this weekend."

Sam's smile widened as he reached into his pocket and pulled out a vial of oil. "Have you ever been fucked outdoors?"

Tristan stared, and then doubled up laughing and wondered if it was hysteria.

Tristan wriggled and brushed in the region of his bare arse. Sam peered down his nose at him. "What are you doing?"

"Something was crawling on me," he muttered.

Sam brushed his hand over Tristan's beautiful backside. The one he had thoroughly taken only a few minutes prior. "Better?"

"Hmm. I suspect laying naked in the grass sounds better in theory than it is in practice."

Sam was inclined to agree. He was freezing cold and damp but hadn't wanted to spoil the moment.

"Perhaps we should dress?" Tristan said.

They got up awkwardly, brushing grass and twigs from each other's semi-naked bodies as they did so. Sam took the opportunity to run his hands all over Tristan's taught muscles again and was surprised when his cock started to fill. Tristan bent over to retrieve his clothing and Sam trailed a finger lightly over his crease, making him jump and turn around. Sam looked down at his groin and then up at Tristan and waggled his eyebrows.

"Good Christ, man, you are insatiable." A look of pure delight crossed Tristan's face and he immediately dropped to his knees in front of Sam and took him into his mouth, making Sam shout with surprise and delight and Tristan laugh with his mouth full. In moments Sam was convulsing down Tristan's beautiful throat and shouting aloud. Sam's heart was thundering as he grabbed Tristan and rolled him to the ground, both of them laughing, but when Sam found Tristan's cock and took it into his own mouth, Tristan moaned and tried to push him away, but it didn't take long to have him shuddering his own release. They lay entangled in the grass again, hearts thundering.

"I think," Tristan said, panting, "that we are back to where we began."

Sam laughed and held him tightly and then kissed him hard.

"You taste of me," Tristan said, running his tongue over his lips.

"And you of me." Sam kissed him again and then licked his own lips. They laughed and rubbed noses.

"I had no idea this could be fun," Tristan said after a moment, as he pulled back so he could look into Sam's eyes. "Sexual congress always seemed such an intense, serious business."

Sam smiled at his innocence and kissed the tip of his nose. He was so proper. So gentlemanly. "This is why it is best that we make things up as we go along rather than abiding by rules set by society."

Tristan shifted so that he could look at Sam. "Very true. We should set our own rules."

"Then we shall do that." Sam squeezed him.

"Perhaps we should write a guide for gentlemen who love gentlemen," Tristan said with a grin.

Sam's chest tightened as he wondered if he realised what he had said, but decided that perhaps he was reading too much into his words.

Chapter 14

LATER THAT EVENING they congregated in Alfie's chamber, at his request, and sat sipping brandy.

"I trust you had a pleasant day?" Tristan said.

Alfie grinned. "I did indeed. You?"

Tristan was sure he flushed. He didn't think he had words to describe it so he just nodded.

"Sadly, we must now focus on reality as I would like to be able to return to my life without fear of some madman attempting to dispatch one of us," Alfie said with irritating pragmatism. He looked first at Sam and then at Gareth. "So, my lovely young gentlemen, remind me. Exactly why is this man attempting to kill you?"

Tristan opened his mouth to speak, but Sam raised a hand and gave him a look so he subsided.

"Dante took me from the gambling hells where I had made a mess of things. I owed money. He paid my debts and gave me a job in Dante's. I was paid to satisfy gentlemen so that I could pay off my debt to him."

"My cousin paid your debt to Dante. Why does he still want you?"

Sam put his head in his hands. "There could be few things." He rubbed his face and tugged on his lip. Tristan recognised the gesture. "A cousin of mine ran away from Dante's and took one of the boys. Bill Mosely is in charge, and got it in the neck when he returned empty handed." He looked over at Gareth, who nodded his agreement. "If I disappear, too, Mosely is in deep trouble. Added to that," Sam said, and then hesitated. "Added to that I appear to be a particular favourite with both of them." He stared at the carpet as he spoke and Tristan felt cold all over. The kind of cold that seeps into the soul. Just what had Sam had to endure in that place? What did all of them endure just so men like him could...he couldn't even finish the thought.

"Fortunately, we rarely see Dante, but Mosely in particular appears to be obsessed with me. More than I imagined. That's one of the reasons why I needed to get out. He is...unpleasant."

Gareth made a snorting sound and threw his hands in the air. "The man is a bastard. He forces himself on the unwilling and he is a sadist. He enjoys inflicting pain and humiliation and Sam bore the brunt of it for long enough."

Tristan remained frozen. Sam's face was now a dull red as he glared at Gareth. "That's enough," he snapped.

"No it isn't," Gareth said, standing and pacing the room. "He will never let you alone, he sees you as his and he won't let you go. Of that, I am certain."

Tristan watched as Sam put his head in his hands again and then look back up at Gareth. "Couldn't we have left this until tomorrow? Couldn't we have had just one more night feeling like normal people?"

"We need to decide what to do," Gareth shouted. "We have all put our heads on the block for you, now we need to decide how we keep ourselves safe."

Sam surged to his feet. "I will *tell* you what we are going to do," he shouted back. "I am going to leave you all here and travel north. I will get as far away as I can and begin a new life so that you can all return to yours. I need to go where he cannot find me. It is the only way." He ploughed his hands through his hair. "I have had a letter from Harry. I can go to him for a while until I get on my feet."

Tristan was on his feet, too, as the words tumbled from his lips. "Like hell you will."

Gareth was shouting at Sam and Sam was yelling back.

Alfie put his fingers in his mouth and whistled loudly, shocking them all into silence.

"Gentlemen." His tone was soft. Low.

Tristan had to swallow several times and clear his throat against the emotion that threatened to overwhelm him before he could speak and when he did his voice was raspy with emotion. "I do not think it is necessary for you to run away. I want you to consider staying with me. We could leave together and..."

"Tristan," Sam said, his voice a soft moan, "Tristan, you are the Earl of Chiltern. You cannot just disappear. You have a life, a position in the Lords, a responsibility to all your people; your estates." His eyes were sad. "You are more trapped than most."

Tristan felt as though a lead weight crushed his chest. He struggled for something to say but Sam continued.

"I adore you," he said softly. "I adore that you saved me, I adore that you looked after me but we both knew that this was temporary, we both knew it couldn't last." He moved and cupped Tristan's face with his hands and then kissed him full on the mouth. In front of Alfie; in front of Gareth. Tristan squeezed his eyes shut and clenched his jaw. "Let me leave," Sam said softly, still holding his face. "Let me leave tomorrow and find somewhere safe."

Tristan began to speak, but Sam placed a finger over his lips. "Shh." He looked down at Tristan and when he was satisfied he wasn't going to speak, enfolded him into his arms. "We still have tonight," he whispered. All Tristan could do was wrap his arms tightly around him and hold on.

TRISTAN STOOD IN his nightshirt. He was really coming to hate nightshirts. He could still hear the low hum of conversation from Sam's adjoining room so he waited until he was alone before going through. He supposed the staff were all aware of the nature of the liaisons between the gentlemen visitors but he was not going to parade himself in front of them. He heard the door close, and silence fall, so ran his fingers through his hair and took a deep breath. This was his last chance to persuade Sam to stay, or allow him to travel with him until they could work out a way to see each other. He simply could not accept that Sam would leave tomorrow and he would never see him again; he just could not. He closed his eyes and prayed that he would be able to find a way to persuade him. As he made for the door he was stopped by a tap at the main door to his room. Puzzled, he changed direction and opened it. A small boy stood there in a nightshirt. Barefoot, gripping both hands in front of him.

"Good evening," Tristan said, as he couldn't think of anything else to say. He had not seen any children in the time they had been there and couldn't imagine what this one wanted, or even where he had come from.

"Sam sent me to you, my lord."

Tristan frowned. "Beg pardon?"

The boy twisted his fingers together and pressed one bare foot on top of the other. "Sam sent me to you. As a special treat."

"A special treat?" Tristan was trying to process what was being said but failed.

The boy swallowed. "I can suck you if you like."

Tristan went cold from head to foot and then colour exploded over every inch of him. Indecision gripped him for a moment, but the misery on the child's face won. "Won't you come in?" he said to the boy as gently as he could. The misery in those young eyes deepened, but he followed him. He closed the door behind them. "Tell me you name," he said.

"Ollie."

"Well, Ollie, there is someone that I would very much like you to meet."

The child raised eyes to him that were weary. "Oh," he whispered. "Is there two of you then?"

Tristan couldn't speak. He knew without even having to think that Sam would never be involved in anything like this, and the fact that the child had been sent filled him with fear and horror. He went to the adjoining door and opened it.

"Would you join me in here a moment?" he called.

There was a muffled thud from the room and then Sam came through the door pulling off his nightshirt as he went.

"I have a guest," Tristan said pointedly, and Sam cursed and pulled the garment back on.

"Dreadfully sorry," he said, and then scowled first at Tristan and then at the boy. "Who are you?"

"Sam sent him," Tristan said, and watched Sam go very still. "Sam sent him as a special treat. His name is Ollie." Tristan put a hand on Ollie's shoulder, but the boy flinched so he removed it. Tristan watched the emotion play over Sam's face and found he wanted to weep.

"How old are you Ollie?" he asked the boy after a moment.

"How old would you like me to be?"

Tristan closed his eyes.

"Right." Sam said, sounding decisive. "Let's get a few things straightened out." He bent and picked the boy up and sat him on the edge of Tristan's bed. "I'm Sam, and I certainly didn't tell you to come here."

The child's eyes widened with horror. "I'm sorry, I…"

"No, no, don't worry. As I said, my name is Sam, and this is my friend, Tristan. You understand the way of the world and the way of things between men I take it?"

"Yes." The boy's voice was a thread.

"Well, Tristan and I are very attached to each other. We both like men, not boys. You are safe here."

The boy just stared.

Tristan sat beside him. "If we send you back, what will happen?"

"They will give me to someone else."

"Well then. You must stay here until morning," Sam said, with cheery pragmatism. "Have you eaten?"

The boy shook his head. "I only get to eat when I have done what they tell me."

Tristan nodded. "Then we will arrange for some food to be brought to the room."

Ollie stared at him with confusion, and just the faintest touch of hope. "Really?"

"You two get acquainted, I will go and arrange food." He ruffled the boys head.

"I will ring for service from my room," he said to Tristan and disappeared, leaving Tristan alone with the child.

"So, how old are you really, Ollie?" he asked, sitting beside him at a careful distance.

"Twelve."

"And who really sent you?"

The child fidgeted. "Bill Mosely, but please don't tell that I told you that, please."

"Word of honour," Tristan said, and drew a cross over his heart. "Well, at least that's that sorted." Tristan smiled at him but inside his heart was thumping and his head racing. Bill Mosely, here?

"Are you really a lord?" Ollie said, glancing up at Tristan.

"I am. Actually, I'm an earl," Tristan said with a small smile.

"Do you know the king?"

"I have met him on occasion, but I don't think I could claim him as a friend."

"Do you live in a palace like this?"

Tristan scratched his head. "I do rather. Where do you live?"

"I live on a farm. It's just a little way from here on

Trapped 163

the way to Hinton. Do you like men then?"

Well, that was direct. Tristan licked his lips and rubbed the back of his neck. "I like Sam," he said, by way of qualification.

"Is he good to you?"

"Very," Tristan said softly, and felt as though his heart might physically break. He couldn't believe he was having such a conversation. The boy was still a child, so youthful, and to have such knowledge was beyond bearing. How in God's name was he going to send him back?

"What are you going to do with me?"

"Let's wait for Sam to come back and then decide, hmm?"

The child nodded and fiddled with his nightshirt. Thankfully, the door opened and Sam came back through bearing a tray balanced on one hand.

"Here we are, a feast fit for a king," he said, and placed the tray expertly on a table.

"Well, he's an earl so that's good," Ollie said, jumping from the bed and scampering barefoot after Sam.

Tristan followed. The tray held what looked like chicken sandwiches, some apples, and a huge pile of macaroons with a cup of milk.

"After you," Ollie said, eyes wide and hopeful.

"We have eaten. This is for you."

Ollie stared at Sam as though he couldn't quite believe him.

"It's true," Tristan said, with an encouraging smile.

The child sat and picked up a sandwich, looked at both Tristan and Sam, who nodded and then he fell on the food.

Tristan drew Sam to one side. "What are we going to do with him?"

"Let him fill himself up then he can have my bed and I will share with you."

"And after that?" Tristan was staring at the boy.

"After that he comes with me. I've never seen him at the club before," Sam said

Tristan put his hands in his hair and held tight. "He said Bill Mosely sent him. Said he lives on a farm nearby."

Sam's eyes widened and then he groaned softly. "Bastard must keep children close by for when Overdale has a gathering. Overdale must have connections with Dante's. Damn and blast it."

"I think we need to find out where he is, and more to the point, what he is going to do. I can't imagine this is a coincidence. How the hell does he know you are here?"

Sam scratched his head. "I think we might need to get out of here sooner than I thought."

Tristan pinched the bridge of his nose. "Who was the chap you talked with at dinner on the first night?"

Sam looked to one side a moment and then grimaced. "Garforth. Asked if we wanted to spice things up. Asked if we wanted to try a different dish."

"Bastard," Tristan muttered. "Absolute bastard. He must be involved with Mosely. What does he think we are, for crying out loud?"

"Well, that's fairly obvious," Sam said, rubbing his face.

"The absolute bastard," Tristan muttered, his ire rising by the second. How dare the man.

"Climb down off your high horse. It's not that uncommon."

Tristan couldn't believe what he was hearing. "Not uncommon?" he said, staring at Sam. "Not uncommon?"

Trapped 165

Sam scrubbed his face with a hand. "No. Some men…" He shrugged.

Tristan's head was racing and the thought that hit him shocked him to the core. "Alfie said that Overdale runs charity organisations for orphans," he said. "Do you think that he uses them in this way? Is this why he has orphanages?"

"It wouldn't surprise me," Sam said.

"What in God's name?" Tristan was beside himself.

"Are you arguing?" a small voice said, interrupting them.

Tristan whirled to the see the child staring at them with wide wary eyes.

"I'm sorry," he said. "That was appallingly rude of us. Please, eat your meal." He managed a relatively normal, reassuring tone, but inside he wanted to scream.

Ollie picked up a macaroon half-heartedly and nibbled the edge of it, watching them carefully. He had carefully portioned the food, and appeared to have only eaten half of it.

Sam went and sat beside Ollie and gave him a huge smile. "Well, Ollie, my friend. We need to talk."

Tristan sat on the bed and watched Sam with the boy. He was wonderful with him. He immediately put him at ease, and his accent changed slightly, losing the cut diction that he used when they were together so that he sounded a little more like someone from the market.

"Do you have family?" he asked him.

"Just a brother. He's only ten."

"Does he work the gents, too?"

Ollie nodded and put the macaroon down half-eaten.

"I used to work the gents like you do."

Ollie stared at him.

"It's true. I had to do things that I was told to do, even when they were horrid."

Ollie's eyes filled with tears and his chin wobbled. "I hate it," he whispered.

Tristan clamped a hand over his mouth when Sam's eyes watered a little, too. "I know. I hated it, too," he said to the boy. "You said that Bill Mosely sent you?"

Ollie nodded.

"Is Mosely here now?"

"No. He is coming back for us in the morning."

Sam glanced at Tristan over Ollie's head.

"Why don't you sleep in here tonight? Tristan will share with me so you will be quite safe. I am leaving in the morning. I am going to travel north to get away from Mosely. Will you consider coming with me?"

Ollie's eyes were wide, his mouth open. He swallowed. "I can't leave my brother."

"Then we will get him and bring him, too. Is he in the house? How many of you are there?"

Ollie nodded staring at Sam with something close to worship, but tinged with enough doubt to make Tristan's heart ache. "Arthur is here. I think there is just the two of us tonight, but more will come tomorrow. Can I save this for Arthur?" Ollie pointed to the sandwiches, an apple, and the macaroons that he had saved.

Sam took them and wrapped them carefully in a napkin and put them beside the bed. "Of course. Do you know where he went to?"

Ollie nodded, but before he could say anything more there was a sharp rap on the door, which then opened and Gareth, Alfie and a small boy that bore a striking resemblance to Ollie tumbled through and slammed the door behind them.

Tristan thought he was beyond being shocked, but apparently he wasn't.

"Arthur!" Ollie jumped off the bed and ran to his brother.

"So you got one, too?" Alfie said, rubbing his chin.

"This is bad," Tristan said. "There is something most peculiar going on here. How well do you know Overdale?"

Alfie pulled a face and shrugged. "Not terribly well, but well enough to get an invitation."

"Have you been here before?"

"No."

"Have you ever been offered..." Tristan gestured in the direction of Ollie and Arthur

"Never."

All four men looked at each other, and then at the two young boys huddled together. Tristan's head was spinning.

"He said Bill Mosely sent him," Sam said to Gareth.

Gareth closed his eyes momentarily. "Dante," Gareth said. "I'll wager he is not far away if Mosely is here."

"Well, if he is here, why not just come and have it out with us?" Tristan said. "Why play games?"

"Because that is what he does," said Sam. "This is exactly the kind of thing that he would do."

"Then the man is deranged," Tristan muttered, pacing a little.

"I think we established that," Sam said, and then turned to the boys. "Arthur, your brother saved you a sandwich and a macaroon," he said, going to the bedside table and picking up the napkin containing the food. He held it out and Arthur's face lit up.

"Thank you," he said with a smile at his brother and Sam.

"Why don't you two eat this up whilst we talk, then we can get you settled in bed. You must be tired."

Arthur looked at Ollie, who nodded, and both boys clambered on the bed and set about finishing the food. Tristan was beside himself. Both boys were small and thin, with huge dark eyes in pale faces. How many of these children were there? What in God's name were they to do with them? He watched as they polished off the last of the macaroons, and then sat looking up at them. Waiting.

Again, Sam stepped into the breach. "Right-ho," he said. "Time for bed. Do you need to use the chamber pot?"

The boys giggled and shook their heads.

"Are you sure? Right. Well, in that case, you two bundle up in here and we will be just next door." He pulled back the coverlet, plumped the pillows, and stood back to let them get in. Once they were in place, he tugged the sheets and blankets up around their ears. The children looked terribly small in the big bed, huddled together in the middle. Sam reached over and ruffled both dark heads and twitched the blankets. "Sleep tight. Don't be afraid to shout out if you need us." He set two candles by the bedside, threw logs on the fire, and then gestured for the other occupants to repair to the adjoining room. Tristan watched as he winked at both boys. Ollie did a creditable wink in return, Arthur squeezed both eyes shut in a parody of a wink, making Sam laugh kindly. Tristan's heart felt too full for his chest. He had to turn away and walk through the door.

❖

SAM LEFT THE candles burning for them because he remembered only too well being afraid of the dark, and then locked the door to the outside corridor. He wedged a chair under the handle just in case, and to offer some reassurance to the children that he believed their fears.

Sam gave them one last wave and then went in search of Tristan and the others. He pulled the door to a little, but left it open as he had promised, and turned to face them. Alfie, ever the dandy, appeared bored as he leaned against the fireplace, but Sam wasn't fooled. Gareth sat on a chair looking wary, and Tristan. Tristan was curiously unreadable.

"I think they are quite settled," Sam said, postponing the arguments that he knew were about to come.

"What time is it?" Tristan surprised him by asking.

"One thirty," Alfie said, shutting his pocket watch with a click. "Why?"

"I think we need to get out of here. I don't like this at all, and I wouldn't be surprised if Dante wasn't here somewhere." Tristan was calm. Frighteningly calm. Sam had expected him to be in a temper. He could have handled that.

"I agree. I need to get on the road as quickly as possible. This simply speeds things up."

"It could, of course, simply be Overdale overstepping the mark," Alfie said from his position by the mantel.

"Well, it seems far too coincidental to me and the boys said that Mosely sent them." Tristan said. "I think we all need to get out of here, and take the boys with us. We need to find out if they have any parents, any family anywhere, and if they do not, then..." he said, and then shrugged.

"You can leave together, but I need to make arrangements to travel north," Sam said. He rubbed the back of his neck. "Gareth, I think you should come with me."

Tristan stood stock still and arched one eyebrow. "*I* am coming with you." His voice was hard and implacable. Every inch the aristocrat again. Sam picked up his valise and started filling it with his things.

"You know you can't."

"I can damn well do as I please and I am not leaving you to look after two children unaided whilst a madman pursues you. It will not do."

Sam had to turn away from Tristan. He couldn't afford to let him see how deeply those words affected him. He picked up the envelope that contained the remainder of the money that Tristan had given him. He quickly counted the notes and decided that it would be plenty to get him and the boys settled somewhere until he could find work.

"Are you going to Harry?" Gareth asked.

"Who the hell is this Harry that you keep talking about?" Tristan's face was pinched and angry.

"I explained who Harry is," Sam said. "Yes," he said to Gareth. "Go and get your things."

"Come," Alfie said, pushing away from the mantel and holding out a hand to Gareth. "Let us leave these two to argue in peace. We can gather your belongings."

Gareth stood up and patted Sam on the arm and followed Alfie from the room, leaving Sam and Tristan alone. Sam braced himself.

"Do you mind if I keep this money?" he said, waving the envelope.

"Of course you can keep it. You can have every blasted penny that I have."

Sam wanted to say *come with me* so badly. Wanted, wanted, wanted. But he could want all he liked, he could never ask Tristan to give up his life for him, and that was what it would amount to. He piled the rest of his things back in the valise and put the money on top, and then stood fingering the paper. He gave it a pat and then turned to Tristan.

"You know, I had planned on giving you the seeing to of your life tonight, but I don't think I can perform with an audience." He nodded to the door that stood ajar. To his immense relief, Tristan smiled. It looked like he tried very hard not to, but it crept out.

"Let's not fight," Sam whispered. "I couldn't bear to fight with you again."

Tristan came and stood before him and put one hand on his chest. "I am not going to fight you. Let the boys get a little sleep and then we will make a move."

Sam put a hand over Tristan's and then pulled it to his lips and kissed it, then they were in each other's arms, holding tight. Sam buried his nose in Tristan's neck inhaling the very essence of him, remembering him.

He felt Tristan swallow, and then he pulled away, turning his head to one side as if to hide his eyes. Sam let his hand linger on his shoulder until he moved away.

"We should get dressed," Tristan said. "Can't go into battle in a nightshirt." His voice was thick and Sam's chest ached.

Chapter 15

AT FIRST LIGHT they were up and dressed. Sam and Gareth had agreed that they should ready the carriage, and then get the boys in it and wait. Tristan headed for the breakfast room with his heart pounding and his guts in turmoil. He still couldn't believe what was happening. He walked through the door and thankfully the room was empty except for Alfie, who stood by the window. He was clearly deep in thought.

"Penny for them?" Tristan said as he walked over to where Alfie stood.

"Not worth even that." He made an effort to smile. "Good night?"

Tristan shook his head and checked they were still alone. "Bloody awful."

"Same here. Are you ready to go?"

"Yes. I have left a note for Overdale claiming illness. Sam looked suitably wretched so I think that will be believed. No point in sending out alarms unnecessarily."

"Sensible idea," Alfie said.

Tristan just nodded. The idea of the company of likeminded men had seemed like a good idea, but he doubted he would ever do anything so foolish again.

They both made to leave, but the door opened and Wallingford strolled in.

"Gentlemen," he beamed. "I trust you had a pleasant night."

"Extremely pleasant. Thank you." Tristan bowed and smiled.

"You are up bright and early this morning."

"Indeed. Now, if you will excuse me..."

"I trust your tastes were well catered for?" Wallingford said, still standing in the doorway.

Ice slithered down Tristan's spine. "They were. Thank you." Alfie moved closer to him.

"Then I am pleased. Come, have you eaten? Overdale's cook is magnificent. I keep trying to tempt him away but to no avail." He headed for the sideboard where dishes were usually laid out for guests, but there did not appear to be any food there. Tristan glanced at Alfie and raised his brows in a question. Alfie looked grim.

"Good to know one's allies in this world, I always say," Wallingford said. "We need to know who we can trust these days, particularly men like us."

Tristan smiled again, and nodded politely wanting to yell that they were nothing like him. "Indeed. Now, if you would excuse us we simply must..." He broke off yet again as Sam appeared in the doorway.

"Aha!" Wallingford beamed. "Another of our allies."

Tristan sighed inwardly, and went to make introductions, but was surprised to find Sam staring fixedly at the man, a muscle ticking along his jaw and colour in his cheeks.

Tristan made the introductions, but Sam was standing stock still. Wallingford, however, was beaming. He pumped Sam's hand, but then seemed to retain it longer than was strictly speaking necessary. The colour had drained from Sam's cheeks leaving him looking deathly pale again, much as he had been after the knock to the head.

"I say, old chap," Wallingford said, peering at Sam, still retaining his hand. "Are you feeling quite the thing? If you don't mind me saying, you look as queer as Dick's hatband."

Sam seemed to unglue his tongue. "I am very well. Thank you."

Tristan's glance flicked between the two men and then it hit him like a blow to the chest. He remembered what Sam had said about knowing some of the men at the party from the brothel, and appearing in society together and someone possibly recognising him. Sam clearly recognised Wallingford, although Wallingford was putting a good face on it. The knowledge that Sam had entertained the man left him feeling cold and more than a little queasy. He was grappling with this new feeling of profound jealousy and distaste when Wallingford turned back to the sideboard saying something about a breakfast plate. Sam grabbed his hand and made a furious gesture to the door and mouthed, "*Get out. Now.*"

"Dammit," Sam said to Wallingford's back. "I left something in my room. Would you excuse me?" But before he could leave Gareth came sailing into the room wishing everyone a good morning in his flamboyant style but faltered when he saw Wallingford and then cursed roundly.

Sam grabbed Tristan by the hand and began pulling him towards the door but Wallingford got there before Sam and laughed.

"Good morning, my little flower," he said to Gareth, and Tristan knew for certain that Wallingford was one of their clients. He felt sick to his stomach. It had been convenient to imagine that he was the only person that Sam had serviced in the brothel, stupid and naive, but convenient. Having it waved in his face in this fashion made him feel sordid in the extreme.

Alfie had spots of angry colour on his cheeks as he watched the exchange between the men. "I do not have the faintest notion of what is going on between you good gentlemen, nor do I have any desire to find out," Alfie said, his voice dripping with disdain. "If you would excuse me?" he said, gesturing for Wallingford to move from the door.

Wallingford's response was to close the door, lock it, take the key from the lock, and drop it into his pocket.

"I am afraid I cannot do that as you have something that belongs to me. Something I intend to reclaim." With that he drew a pistol from his other pocket and held the muzzle point blank at Sam's chest.

They all froze.

Tristan swallowed and ran his tongue over his lips. "What are you doing?"

Wallingford moved closer to Sam and tucked the gun under Sam's chin.

Tristan's heart was hammering so hard he shook. He remained still for fear that a sudden movement might make the man pull the trigger. He waited.

Gareth was the one to speak, and the word he

said made the whole scene make appalling sense.

"Dante."

Wallingford smiled and pursed his lips into a mocking kiss in Gareth's direction. "Fear not, little one, there will be enough for you, too." Wallingford glanced at Alfie. "He always gets so terribly jealous when I share my affections."

The name was ringing in Tristan's ears. Dante. Dante. Dante. He forced himself to be outwardly calm. "What is it you want from us, Wallingford?"

The man smiled and pushed the gun tighter under Sam's chin, making his head move backwards. "Have a care, Chiltern. Do you know what will happen if I pull the trigger? The bullet will travel through his brain and explode out of the top of his skull, leaving a catastrophic hole." He spoke mildly as though making an innocuous observation rather than describing murder.

"I do know." Tristan said with as much calm as he could muster. "And I would like it very much if you didn't do that. I ask again, what is it you want from us?'

"From you? Nothing." Wallingford said with a smile. "Just Samuel."

Tristan had never considered himself an actor, but he found himself acting as though his life depended on it. Sam's certainly did. "Then take him. You will see no opposition from us." He raised his hands in an open gesture and looked at Alfie and Gareth.

Alfie laughed. "Take them both. They have served us well, but I have no desire to come between a man and his possessions." Alfie shook his head and walked over to where Gareth was standing looking stunned. "It has been a great pleasure, but I suspect your master would like you returned." He leaned in and kissed Gareth on the mouth, stroked his hair, and ran a hand beneath his coat to squeeze his arse with a lingering hand. Gareth jerked away and then slapped Alfie. Hard. Alfie's head jerked sideways under the blow and he shook his head.

Gareth stalked to where Dante stood. "Get us out of here. They are all perverted bastards." His dark eyes flashed.

Wallingford smiled and then looked at Sam. He handed the key to Gareth. "Unlock it."

Gareth took the key and slid it into the lock. It turned with a soft click. Dante held out a hand for the key and Gareth dropped it into his palm and stood beside them, eyes flashing, but Dante pushed him roughly back into the room.

"Samuel is all I need," he said and, without taking the gun from Sam's chin, led him through and locked it behind them leaving Tristan, Alfie, and Gareth staring at the closed door. When all was quiet from outside Tristan ran to the door and shook it violently. The lock was firm and it held.

"Dammit!" he shouted and hammered on the door with the flat of his hand. "Dammit, dammit *dammit!*" He felt as though his heart was trying to claw its way out through his throat. He hammered on the door again and then pressed his face against it, listening to see if he could hear where they were going. He felt useless. Impotent. Helpless.

"The window." Alfie walked to the glass and picked up a chair. He paused, and then threw it. It bounced off.

"We are two floors up," Gareth said, pacing up and down.

"I don't care. I need to get out of here," Tristan

said as he picked the chair up again and hurled it at the window. It bounced again. "For God's sake!" he shouted and picked up a brandy decanter. He hurled it with all his might and it cracked the glass. They all stopped, stared at each other, and then rushed to the window. Alfie pulled out his handkerchief. "Have a care," he said, and Tristan and Gareth followed suit. They managed to push and pull at the glass until the whole pane broke into shards and dropped the two stories to the ground. All three looked out. It was a long way down, and it would mean landing on grass that was now littered with broken glass.

"I'm going to jump," Tristan said.

"Roll as you land." Alfie said, brushing the glass from the window ledge with his handkerchief.

Gareth peered over the edge. "Why don't we lower him as far as we can? If we hold an arm each we can dangle him out and then he can drop."

"Excellent plan." Tristan stripped off his coat and rolled up the sleeves of his linen shirt to expose his forearms. "You'll get a better grip this way. You can throw my coat after me," he said as he hopped up onto the window sill.

Alfie and Gareth followed suit. "Double grip on the wrists," Alfie said, demonstrating. Gareth copied him, and between them the lowered Tristan over the edge. He shuffled with his feet, finding toe holds in the ancient brick and eventually he was stretched as far as he dared without dragging the others over.

"After three, release me," he shouted up. "One, two…three." And then he was falling. He hit the ground and rolled, jarring every last bone in his body but when he stood up everything seemed to work. He gave a swift thumb's up to Alfie and Gareth and then sprinted.

Trapped

❖

TRISTAN HEADED FOR the servant's entrance, hoping that he might be able to get back into the house undetected by Wallingford. He had no idea if Overdale would be looking for him, or if his servants had been alerted. He needed to find Sam, but he needed to go back for Ollie and Arthur, as well. He could only hope that Wallingford was pre-occupied with Sam and had left them in the bed chamber. His heart was thundering as he crept past the kitchens. The low hum of servant's voices filled his ears, but he managed to find the back stairs and run up them, boots ringing on the cold stone. He had no idea where they would lead to as the house was vast, but fortunately he recognised the corridor he ended up in and ran towards the breakfast room. He slowed as he spotted a couple of footmen, tugged at his sleeves to settle his cuffs and ran a hand over his hair.

He strolled up to them. "I say, could you do me an enormous favour?"

The footmen smiled and bowed.

"The breakfast room is locked. Could you be a dear?"

He bit his lip in frustration when neither had a key, but one of them trotted off to find one. It felt like hours before he returned, but return he did, and he unlocked the door. He didn't flinch at finding two men standing in there with one of the windows put out.

"Thank you," Tristan said, and when the footman disappeared, he breathed again and went into the room.

"Did you find him?"

"No. I just managed to get my way back here. He could have taken him anywhere. There must be miles of corridors in this damned place."

"Well, we will just have to search," Gareth said.

"I agree. We could split up?" Tristan said.

"Weapons!" murmured Gareth. "We need weapons."

"You have a knife. I slid it into your breeches whilst I was fondling your arse," Alfie said to Gareth.

Gareth's eyes widened. "You did?"

Alfie smiled.

Gareth stared and nodded, then nodded again.

"We need to see if the children are still there," Tristan said. "I will check the room."

"You look at the corridors by the bedchambers then," Gareth said. Tristan nodded and ran ahead. He reached the rooms, but as he feared, the boys were not there. He ran along the corridor trying the doors. Some opened, some did not. Those that did not he rattled the handles and called for Sam. Nothing. Not a sound, not another guest, nothing. Tristan plunged his hands through his hair as he got the end of the corridor and he hadn't located a soul. He ran back to where he began to go down the other wing, but as he did so he found Gareth racing along it.

"Tristan, Tristan," he called. "Alfie thinks they are leaving. Wallingford's coach has just raced down the drive at full tilt.

"Bastard," whispered Tristan. "We have to follow."

Tristan and Gareth ran to the stables, but they had to be about half a mile from the house. They arrived, out of breath and sweating, to find Alfie arguing with a groom, hands on hips.

"What is it?" Tristan said, mopping his head with his handkerchief as he approached the two.

"All the horses are gone."

"What do you mean, gone?" Tristan said, shoving the handkerchief back in his pocket. Gareth pushed past to go into the stalls.

"Sir, his lordship bade us exercise the remaining ones this morning. The grooms have them out on the hills. They won't be very long as they are back, maybe a couple of hours or so?"

"Remaining horses? Where are the other guests?"

"Mostly they have left, sir."

Tristan wanted to scream. They had been out-manoeuvred. Comprehensively.

"Thank you," Tristan managed and the man bowed and walked away.

"Well, we can either wait for the horses to return or leave on foot," Alfie said.

"What about our things?" Gareth said.

Tristan scratched his head and stared about him as though he might find an answer somewhere. "Ollie said that the children lived in a farmhouse nearby. We might be able to walk to that and find horses?"

"I doubt they would hand any over to us." Gareth said.

"I won't be asking them to," Tristan said. "I think we should go back to the house, pick up anything you want to take, and then if the horses have not returned we set off on foot."

"Where might this farmhouse be?" Alfie asked as they fell into step.

"I haven't the faintest idea."

"It might all be a trick?" Gareth said. "He might have set off down the road to make it look like he is taking Sam somewhere but has kept him back at the house."

Alfie nodded. "I thought about that, but I think that if that were the case, they would have left horses for us to follow."

They were silent for a moment. "I could stay behind and look?" Alfie said.

Tristan shuddered. "No. I think we need to stay together. I think Wallingford is capable of doing great harm. We just need to decide which direction to travel in and hope it leads us to the farmhouse."

Alfie nodded. "There is, of course, a much simpler way to work out how to get to the farmhouse."

Tristan looked at him expectantly, wondering what he had missed.

"We could ask the groom?" he said with an infuriating smile.

Chapter 16

AS IT TURNED out, the groom was enormously helpful. It took less than an hour to walk there. The groom had explained that the farm provided the house with produce, and Mr Mosely was the steward. He also mentioned that he would most likely be at home for the morning. Alfie had thanked him, and they set off.

When they arrived, they decided that, as Alfie was the only one that Mosely might not recognise, he should go and ask for assistance to see what he could find out. Alfie motioned for Tristan and Gareth to stay behind a wall, well out of sight. Gareth flopped onto the grass. Tristan peered over the top to watch what Alfie did.

He marched up to the door and hammered on it imperiously. He wiped his forehead with his handkerchief as he waited for a response.

"What?" a garrulous voice shouted from behind the closed door.

"I need assistance. Would you be so good as to open the door?"

The door inched open a crack to reveal a large, dark-haired man who peered out and stared at Alfie. It wasn't Mosely.

"What do you want?"

"I'm afraid my horse had a mishap and I need to get to London. If you could loan me a horse, or even better, a horse carriage, you would be doing me an enormous service," he said. "You would be very well paid," he added when the man looked unimpressed.

"Haven't got any," the man said, pushing the door shut. Frustration gripped Tristan hard.

Alfie hammered on the door again. "Would you be kind enough to open the door so I can speak to you properly?"

The door opened a fraction. "Nothing to say." The man slammed the door in his face.

"Let's head for the stables," Gareth said, struggling to his feet. "We can help ourselves and leave money if he won't listen. We can snoop about a bit to see if Ollie and Arthur are here."

Alfie came back to where they were hidden, and shook his head. "Miserable bastard."

"Make it look as though you are leaving and then double back. We will see what livestock he has and help ourselves. When he realises what we've done it will be too late," Gareth said.

"Good plan," muttered Alfie, and set off down the road from the main house and made a show of leaving.

TRISTAN AND GARETH hid a little way from the farm in an

old sheep shed whilst Alfie disappeared from sight.

"We still have no idea where he has taken Sam," Tristan said after a while, voicing the thing that had been hammering inside his head ever since they had set off from the house. He couldn't bear the overwhelming sense of helplessness, and the feeling that he had completely failed Sam that threatened to engulf him.

"He will end up back in Dante's, I would say," Gareth said. "I can only think that he means us to follow. Who knows what Dante is thinking?"

Alfie's footsteps quietened them. As he crunched his way over to the shed they stood up and brushed twigs away.

He looked out over the landscape. "There seems to be only one real road out from the house, so I think we must presume if we follow it we will eventually reach civilisation and be able to fathom the way back to London.

"They have a good hour on us, Alfie," Tristan said, heaving himself up. "Let's get a move on."

After some argument, they agreed that Alfie and Tristan would slip into the stables and see what was there, and Gareth would look for any sign of Ollie and Arthur.

Tristan edged along the low wall, feeling that at least he was doing something useful. He waited whilst a groom berated one of the stable lads for his lack of skill with the horses, and then, when they took the discussion outside, he and Alfie edged in cautiously checking that no-one was around. It was a very well stocked stable, probably ten or so horses, which surprised Tristan. The buildings beyond suggested that they did have carriages, but Tristan doubted he would have either the time or the opportunity to get to them. The horses whickered softly and stamped as he walked by them but he crooned softly, touching and stroking as he went. There was a door near the back of the stable that looked unused. Tristan motioned to Alfie, and they cleared some of the debris away. Tristan put his shoulder to the door. It moved. This would be a much better way out. If he could get three out, then they would be laughing.

"I will clear a path; you see if you can saddle the horses. If we can get them out this way, we stand a chance of not being seen."

He paused, listening, and then disappeared. Tristan looked at the three horses nearest the rear door. They looked like prime specimens. He paused by a bin and filled his pockets with carrots and slid into the first stall. He let out a breath of relief when he found tack hanging there. Swiftly, he bridled the horse, crooning as he went, and holding a carrot in his palm for the horse to find, he patted him gently on the neck, and then threw the saddle over as quickly as he could. Pleased, he moved to the second stable to begin again, and by the time he made his way to the third he was feeling flushed with success. All he needed to do now was lead them out...he paused as the main door to the stable slid open and a figure moved in and stood stock still. It wasn't Alfie.

Tristan's heart beat almost out of his chest as he cursed himself for his carelessness. Sun haloed the figure making it difficult to discern, but then the figure whirled and closed the door behind him and then ran into the stable.

Ollie. Tristan's knees almost buckled. "Ollie," he said. "Oh, Ollie, thank God you are safe. We were so worried." He took the boy by the shoulders.

Ollie stared at him a moment and then smiled. "What are you doing here?"

"They took Sam. Wallingford took Sam. You might know him as Dante?"

Ollie's eyes widened. "Dante?" he whispered. "Dante has Sam?"

"I am afraid so. I am here with Alfie and Gareth trying to get some horses so we can follow. Can you help me?"

Ollie regarded him for a moment. "Dante was here earlier. I hid."

Tristan stared. "Can you find out if he is still in the house? If Sam is with him?"

Ollie nodded. "I had better go back; they will wonder where I have gone. Where are you hiding?"

Tristan described the sheep shed where they had rested. Ollie just nodded. "Leave the horses. I will bring them to you. People won't take as much notice if I do it."

"Ollie?" Tristan stopped the boy as he made to leave. Ollie turned with raised eyebrows. "Don't do anything difficult, or anything that will put either you or Arthur in danger. Do you understand me?"

"Yes, my lord." He smiled, saluted, and trotted off.

BARELY HALF AN hour later, Ollie arrived at the sheep shed calling for Tristan. Alfie put a hand on Tristan's shoulder and motioned for silence. He slid away and then moments later when Ollie called again Alfie emerged from behind them and nodded.

"Over here," Tristan called, and the boy grinned

and ran over.

"I have found out things for you, but you have to promise something first." His too old eyes were serious.

"I will do my best."

Ollie took a deep breath and then stuck out his chin. "Sam isn't here anymore. Dante took him. Sam said he would take us with him to get us away from Mosely. If we help you find Sam will you take us to him and get us away from here?"

Tristan wanted to hug the boy, but he stuck out a hand. "It's a deal." Ollie shook.

Ollie was still staring. "And Arthur?"

"And Arthur."

Ollie swallowed and took a breath. "We have a friend. She's called Winifred. She only arrived yesterday, but if we don't get her out they will start taking her to the big house, too." Ollie frowned. "She's even smaller than Arthur."

Tristan opened his mouth and closed it again. "Winifred would be welcome to join us."

Ollie turned and yelled his brother's name and Arthur appeared clutching the hand of a small girl. They both came to stand by Ollie's side.

"This is Winifred. Winifred, this is Tristan. He's an earl. He's going to help us get away. He knows the king."

Winifred turned dark eyes to Tristan. She didn't speak so he just smiled.

"This way." Ollie grabbed Arthur's hand, pointed through the trees, and they duly followed.

They reached a clearing after about ten minutes of walking and Tristan gaped at what waited for them. A sturdy looking closed carriage with two horses, and two other horses stood loose, munching on grass.

"Ollie, old chap, you are an absolute marvel," Alfie said, pausing to ruffle the boy's hair.

"Sam was at the house," Ollie said softly to Tristan. "I didn't know, truly I didn't. I would have done something to help if I had, I swear it."

"I know you would. How long ago did they leave?" Tristan's heart was beating fast. Perhaps they were not too far away from them.

"Not very long ago. I asked about a little and found that they are heading for London and the club." Ollie paused, and then gave a small smile. "Apparently Dante has a black eye."

Tristan wanted to cheer on the one hand, but on the other felt a sense of deep unease about what Dante might do to Sam if angered more than he already was.'

"Good for Sam," Alfie said with cheer, and grinned at the boy. "Come, let us not waste a moment."

The small boys grinned back and clambered into the carriage, pulling Winifred after them, but Tristan saw the look on Gareth's face. "What?" he asked, not wanting the answer.

"Dante likes his boys to fight back."

There was nothing to say to that.

Tristan was frankly astonished when they made it back to London without incident. He had fully expected them to be caught, followed, challenged, but none of these things occurred. They had an uneventful journey, and got the children settled in his London town house without a problem.

His butler, Henderson, was eyeing them with some

misgiving as they stood in the calm of his study.

"How are your skills with young children, Henderson?"

"Non-existent, my lord," Henderson said, and offered a small bow.

"Could you procure clothing for them that would befit nephews and a niece of mine?"

Henderson blinked. Slowly. "Of course. Ah, nephews and a niece, my lord?"

"Indeed. Distant branch of the family, fallen on hard times and needed a rescuer, so I stepped into the breach."

"I see."

Tristan smiled at Henderson. Ever the impeccable servant he would never question his master's actions, but the questions flickered in his normally blank expression, none the less.

"They will need a nanny to care for them and a tutor to see to their education. I don't think they have had above much in the way of tutoring."

"Would you like me to arrange this for you?"

"Could you?"

"I have a cousin who is seeking work as a tutor, my lord. I wouldn't recommend him if I wasn't convinced that he could do a superlative job."

"Well then. Let me meet him."

"I shall arrange it, my lord." Henderson bowed.

Tristan hesitated, and then made a decision. "Henderson, the children were treated very badly."

Henderson's eyes widened a little. "I am sorry to hear that."

"I mean very badly. Very badly indeed. They look well, but they may take a little while to settle, and they are terribly afraid."

"You may be assured that I and the rest of the staff will make their stay as pleasant as possible."

Tristan took another decision. "I would like it to be known amongst the staff that, under no circumstances whatsoever, is the Marquess of Wallingford to be allowed entrance to the house. If he makes any such attempt, I am to be informed immediately."

Henderson's look was speculative. "As you wish it."

A knock at the door interrupted them. "Ah," said Tristan, smiling at Henderson. "This will be them now. I am sure that you will welcome them."

Henderson looked momentarily horrified, but then arranged his features suitably and went to open the door. It was indeed the children with his housekeeper, Mrs Crawley.

"Tristan!" Ollie said as he slid through the door. "We have a nursery for us all."

Arthur followed more cautiously, but there was the definite beginning of a smile on his face. "It is indeed all for you. Children, I would like you to meet my butler, Mr Henderson. If you need anything he will be able to help you. I expect you to treat him with the utmost respect though, he is a very, very valued member of my staff."

"Mr Henderson," Ollie said with wide eyes, and executed a small bow. Arthur followed suit and Winifred just stared. "I am very pleased to meet you."

Henderson's expression was inscrutable, but there was a kindness in his eyes that Tristan was sure that the boys saw, too. "Master Oliver, Master Arthur, Miss Winifred." He bowed to each in turn. "I am delighted to make your acquaintance."

The children were wide eyed.

"Between Mrs Crawley and Mr Henderson you

should be well catered for." He smiled at Mrs Crawley, who beamed back.

When the children left with the housekeeper, Henderson turned and gave him a speculative look. "May I speak freely, my lord?"

"Of course."

Henderson hesitated, bit his lip, and then appeared to take the plunge. "If Wallingford has any involvement with the children then it is little wonder they are subdued. You have my absolute word that I will keep them away from him and anyone connected with him."

Tristan gaped at the man. "What do you know of Wallingford?"

"Servants...talk."

Something very much like fear set up in the pit of Tristan's stomach. "Talk?"

"Lord Wallingford has a...reputation. Did you rescue the children from him? No. Don't answer that. It is better that we don't know. Perhaps if you could give some thought to the branch of the family from whence they came and then we have a clear explanation for their arrival in a bachelor household? I will make sure that it is well known."

"Henderson...I..." Tristan was stunned. "Thank you. I appreciate your honesty and your help."

Henderson hesitated again. "Might I be so bold as to enquire about your attire and your plans for the evening?"

Tristan glanced down at himself and grimaced. He was still dressed in his clothes from the previous day. "There is someone still in Wallingford's clutches that I need to find."

"Is it Mr Holloway?"

Tristan felt the flush hit his entire body and spill onto his face. Just how much of his life did Henderson and the staff actually know about?

"What do you know of Mr Holloway?"

Henderson hesitated. "Not a great deal. Just that you went away with Lord Alfred, and two others, and not all the gentlemen returned. You have also accumulated three children and Wallingford is involved."

"You are very observant."

"And very discreet. Of that you have my absolute word," Henderson said.

Tristan swallowed and nodded. "Thank you."

Chapter 17

SAM PACED THE room, heart pounding with a ferocious beat that echoed in his fist. His hand still hurt from punching Dante, but the elation that he had experienced when the man staggered and stared at him with wide eyed shock still coursed through him. In all his exchanges with Dante he had felt completely helpless. Alone. But now, he felt that that at least he had a fighting chance, and tolerating another round of his depravity was not something he was willing to take any more without a fight. He knew in his heart that the likelihood was that he would be forced, that Dante would return and restrain him in some way, but at least he had shown him that he was not the compliant, terrified boy that he had been. It wasn't much, but it was something.

Emotion was bubbling through him like the champagne they had drunk over the weekend. It felt as though everything was clear. He had in the past accepted what Dante and Mosely had imposed on him because it felt like they owned him. Well, no more. He needed to get out and get to Tristan. Get to those boys who needed saving before they too were ruined. He knew he needed to find work and purpose in his life, and he had no idea what that would be, but he was certain that he could not just live off Tristan's charity. He sat on the bed and pushed his hands into his hair and closed his eyes. He needed to get out and sort things. He stalked over to the window again and rattled it. It was shut tight, and even if he could force it, they were several storeys up so he would most likely kill himself trying to get down. He pulled open the chest that sat underneath the window and found all manner of implements designed to arouse. He found an alarmingly large glass dildo that would serve as a short club. He practiced a little with it, slapping it into the palm of his hand, and then paused. If he actually got out of this ridiculous predicament, he would use it on Tristan in the manner it was meant for. That made him smile for a moment. He grabbed chains and metal bars and put them at strategic points around the bed so that he could use them as weapons if needs be. He brandished the poker and lay it beneath the pillows on the bed. Some pairs of cuffs with mechanical closures were secreted on the off chance that he might be able to restrain Dante in some way. That would be a fine piece of poetic justice. He smiled again. Tristan would like that.

A rattle at the door made him shove the cuffs under a pillow and move to stand by the fireplace where the dildo was hidden behind the clock. He braced himself.

"Sam?" a soft, female voice whispered through the door.

"Iris?" he rattled the door handle. "Iris, is that you?"

"Are you alone?"

"Yes, can you get the door open?" He pressed an ear to the panel, then moved back as he heard the latch click. The door opened cautiously and there she was.

She pushed him back and came into the room, locking it behind her. "Are you hurt?" she said, touching his face.

"Sore knuckles. I hit him."

She picked up his hand and inspected the bruising. "He has a huge bruise on his eye. He is furious and I am terrified what he might do to you."

"I know. I need to get out, but he cannot find you helping me."

"I want to come with you." Iris stood rigid, mouth grim. "I want you to take me with you."

"Um…" Sam hesitated. He was fairly sure she knew were his inclinations lay, but…

She blushed. "Oh, for heaven's sake I am not interested in you that way," she said with such scorn that he flushed, too. "I want Clara to come with us. She is the only one for me."

He tried not to gawp, he really did. But it failed. "You and Clara?"

"Men are not the only ones with perverse desires, you know." She was snappish now.

Sam's eyebrows rose. "But you service the gentlemen so I think I can be forgiven for my assumption!"

Iris smiled a little and looked at him out of the corner of her eye. "Not all the gentlemen are gentlemen, if you get my meaning."

Sam's heart warmed and he grinned.

"So, will you take us?"

"Of course I will. Get everything that you need to take and keep it light."

"Already done. Waiting in the carriage by the door."

Sam laughed, took her pixie face in his hands, and kissed her. "I adore you."

She wiped her mouth and laughed. "Come on."

Sam followed her into the corridor outside the room and they sped along soundlessly. They almost made it. Almost.

"Planning another trip?" His voice stopped Sam dead. Dante stepped out in front of him, blocking their path, and Sam heard Iris swallow.

"I damned well am. I do not intend to spend another moment in this hell hole, so get out of my way." His bravado was meant mainly for Iris, but it helped to say the words, helped to feel that he was still in control.

"Then go," he said. "Go and leave Iris with me. She will take your place."

"Don't be ridiculous. Iris is coming with me."

Dante shook his head. The lust gathering about him was almost palpable. He enjoyed people's fear, he enjoyed shaming, humiliating and hurting, and he liked to take the unwilling. Sam made a move forward, but Dante stepped back, pulled his hand out of his pocket, and flashed a long blade, taking up a fighting stance with it.

Sam kept his eye on the blade, but spoke to Iris. "Get down the back stairs and get away."

"I'm not leaving you..."

"Fucking leave!" he yelled and threw himself at Dante, grabbing the arm with the blade and sending

them both crashing to the floor. He heard Iris cry out, but then do as he had bidden. He grappled with Dante, holding the arm with the knife, but Dante was older, more cunning, and in a trice he had a hand on Sam's balls squeezing enough to incapacitate. As Sam choked and slackened his hold he was flipped over, then Dante was on top. Blade to his throat, hand still on his aching balls.

"I am going to move very slowly, and you will get up. Another move like that and I will take great joy in cutting them off." He squeezed painfully and Sam was in no doubt that he would do exactly that. He got to his feet. At least Iris and Clara were out of the way. At least he had placed some instruments in the room that he might be able to use as weapons. At least he was still alive. He was mentally planning how to grab the dildo from behind the clock and then cuff Dante all the while keeping an eye on Dante's movements. He edged away, and was prepared when Dante rushed forward and launched a ferocious punch. He staggered back, holding up both arms and danced towards the fireplace, waiting for the next punch, but it never came. Dante feinted and as Sam moved, the man slammed his foot between his legs. Sam managed to move enough to lessen the blow, but it still felled him. He clutched his groin, and felt bile rise to his throat as nausea took him. He tried to breathe, tried to move, but Dante had him in cuffs so swiftly that by the time he could draw a breath he was manacled. Sam tried not to let the fight go out of him. He had no doubt that Tristan and Alfie would come and try and find him, but judging by the look on Dante's face, he was afraid of what they might find when they arrived.

When Dante looked over one shoulder and yelled, "Mosely, get in here!" Sam knew he was done for.

DANTE DRAGGED SAM towards the bed. Sam resisted. He lashed out with his feet, but Dante let him struggle for a moment before grabbing him by the throat and pressing hard on his windpipe. Sam's vision wavered and he tried to claw at his hand, but the cuffs made it impossible. Dante yanked his arms up and hooked the cuffs onto a chain that hung from the ceiling expressly for that purpose. Sam thought of all the times that he had used them for pleasure, but there was no pleasure here now. Nothing. This was not the kind of fear that arouses; it was the kind of fear that deadens.

"You disappoint me," Dante said as he paced up and down in front of Sam's strung out body, breathing heavily. "I thought you understood."

"Understood what?" he asked as he twisted to see if he could force the cuffs open by clenching his fists. The cuffs were not meant to really restrain if a person was determined, but they held fast.

"Understood that I do not allow my boys to leave."

"I am not your boy. I have never been your boy." Sam dangled from the hook uselessly. His feet touched the floor because he was so tall. His only hope was to get a good kick in.

"You think you belong to Chiltern?" Dante said with a laugh.

"Of course not," Sam snapped. He didn't want Tristan implicated in this sorry mess. "I tricked him into getting me out. That's all. He was an easy target."

Mosely appeared at the door and sauntered in. "Sam. How nice of you to drop in," he said, and laughed at his own cleverness. Sam tried to maintain his composure.

"How was Scarborough?" he asked and watched as Mosely flushed.

"Funny. Very funny."

"Right," Dante said, clapping his hands together and rubbing them. "By my reckoning the young earl and his coterie are about hour behind us. I think that gives us a little time to play." He glanced over at Mosely whose smile chilled Sam to the bone.

"In fact, if we time this well, the young earl should arrive in time to watch."

Mosely laughed as he walked towards Sam, unwinding his cravat as he did so. Sam waited. Waited, and tensed. He had one shot at this. He waited until Mosely's attention switched to removing his clothing, and then lashed out with his foot using everything that he had. It was a perfect shot. He slammed it into the side of Mosely's face sending him lurching. His hands were occupied with his cravat, so he fell heavily into the fireplace with a clatter, sending everything scattering. The fire was unlit, and Mosely lay sprawled on it, unmoving. Sam was breathing heavily as Dante moved. He opened a drawer, and pulled out a spreader with a smile. Sam's heart was near to exploding. If he got that thing on his legs he was completely immobile.

Dante edged towards him as though he were approaching a skittish horse. Sam watched his every move, waiting for a chance. Just one chance. Sweat trickled down his back as he positioned himself so that he could lash out again. Mosely was still unmoving, so it was just him and Dante.

Dante took a step forward and tensed.

TRISTAN RUSHED INTO the unlocked room in Dante's with Alfie and Gareth at his back. They all skidded to a halt at the sight that greeted them. Mosely was seemingly unconscious in the grate, and Sam was strung from the roof by a chain and cuffs. Wallingford appeared to be attempting to shackle his legs and Sam was fighting him with all he had.

Sam stared, eyes wide, and Dante took one look at them and laughed.

"How incredibly predictable you are, my dears." He dropped the bar and chains in his hands to the floor and dusted his hands together. "For someone you say you tricked into helping you escape, he seems dreadfully attached to you, my love," he said to Sam. "I think you need to tell him that it was all just a ruse before he gets hurt, and we can get back to our play." He looked at Tristan and smiled. "He loves being shackled and taken. Have you had him this way yet? No?" Dante made a sympathetic face and shook his head. "Such a shame you won't get the chance."

Tristan watched as the fight seemed to go out of Sam. His eyes closed.

"Of course it was a ruse. However, I paid for him and now he is mine. I keep what is mine," Tristan said.

Sam opened his eyes and swallowed. A single tear tracked down his cheek almost breaking Tristan, but he needed to get Wallingford, Dante, or whatever the hell his name was out of the way first.

"Well, I might be able to think of a way for you to

keep him, but he will come at a cost."

Tristan shook his head. "A cost?"

Dante's smile was unpleasant. "It is fortunate that you recently inherited the title. You are going to need the money that it brings with it."

"I don't understand."

Alfie came and stood beside Tristan. "I suspect he is talking about blackmail."

Tristan sucked in a breath and looked at Dante, who was smiling.

"Your cousin is an intelligent man, and also a wealthy man, so between the two of you, you will make me an even wealthier man."

Tristan's heart was pounding.

"We will agree on a sum from each of you that will guarantee my silence about your…nasty proclivities that would ruin you both and all your family were they known."

"What?"

"Well, not only do you find pleasure in unnatural activities with men, but with children, too." Dante shook his head in mock censure and sadness.

Alfie bestirred himself with an apparently languid sigh but Tristan could feel the tension rolling from him. "Very well. Once you let us know the sum we will confirm what we require from you to maintain our silence."

Dante laughed. "Touché. So you see, we are now equal. You can walk away."

"Let Sam go," Tristan said.

Dante looked him in the eye. "Not until I have the money."

Alfie put a warning hand on Tristan's elbow but he shook it off.

Sam wriggled in his bonds, the chain rattling in the silence. "Tristan, for God's sake will you get out of here? Don't you understand? It wasn't real. I don't love you. I am back where I belong so just go. Alfie, get him out of here. Neither of you belong here." Sam's words dropped chills down Tristan's spine but he didn't believe him for a moment.

He looked Dante in the eye. "Let him go." He pulled the pistol he carried secreted in his coat pocket and pointed it at him.

He heard Sam gasp, and felt Alfie move beside him. Dante's face was unreadable.

"You think that I would ever let him go to you?" he said, mildly, but then pulled a knife from his pocket and launched himself at Sam, aiming for his chest.

Sam yelled, Alfie leaped, but Tristan pulled the trigger.

Chapter 18

TRISTAN WAS STILL shaking several hours later when he sat with Alfie in the study of his town house. Gareth had taken Sam back to his rooms whilst they sorted out the mess.

"So what will happen now?" he asked.

Alfie passed him a glass of brandy and sat in the chair opposite. He stroked his chin and then tapped his thumb against his mouth before speaking. "I have spoken with the Prince Regent, and, with his permission, Wallingford's family."

Tristan started and stared. "The Prince Regent?"

"My dear boy, whatever Wallingford may or may not have been, he was a peer of the realm. A Marquess. Higher ranking than even you."

Tristan ran his hand down his face. "And I shot him," he said dully. "Do go on."

Alfie was quiet for a moment, but then continued. "I explained that there had been a very, very unfortunate incident in a brothel. A particular type of brothel, that Wallingford had been visiting." Alfie tapped his finger against his lip again before continuing. "I told them that there had been a violent incident and a man named Mosely had shot Wallingford dead in a row over a young man. In turn, someone punched Mosely, who sadly fell and hit his head causing him to also lose his life."

Tristan was staring at Alfie, dumfounded. He knew that his cousin had connections to the crown, knew that he was as secretive as he was inventive, but to take this story to the king and Wallingford's family…? Tristan was beyond speech.

Alfie continued. "The family now need a little time to come to terms with their loss, but also to decide how much of this they want made public. Given Wallingford's status, the king has granted them some influence over what is revealed publicly."

Tristan's heart thumped. "I am presuming they will not want any of this getting out?"

"I would concur. From the conversation I had with his grieving relatives there will be an announcement in the Times shortly announcing his sad, untimely demise. Heart failure, I suspect."

"And…"

"And they will be eternally grateful to our family for giving them the opportunity to hush up what might have been the scandal of the decade, and one that had the potential not only to ruin the family, but to touch the Prince Regent."

"Good God." Tristan was silent for a moment. "What about Overdale?"

"Apparently he has discovered he has urgent business in the Indies. Likely to be out of the country for the foreseeable future."

Tristan rubbed his face. So that was that. The fact that two of the country's most powerful men preyed on vulnerable children, and young men and women, would disappear along with Wallingford's funeral and Overdale's ship.

"This feels wrong," he said. "Dreadfully wrong. If we fail to expose what was really happening, if Overdale did have a part to play in the children being at the house, then shouldn't we do something about it?" Tristan's head was swimming.

"Am I condoning the silence about what really went on to protect myself?"

Alfie rubbed the back of his neck and pulled in a breath. "If you did tell the truth, and tried to expose them, what do you think would happen?"

Tristan shrugged.

"You would wind up dead and more than likely, so would I. No benefit in that. Better to stay alive and know that these things happen so that you can at least stop them where you can."

"So you know of such practices?"

Alfie hesitated and then just nodded.

"Sam said it was not uncommon." Tristan rubbed his face again trying to get his thoughts in order. He needed to see Sam. Needed to talk this through with him. Needed to hold him to reassure himself that all was well. Christ, what a mess. What kind of bloody world were they living in?

SAM SANK INTO the steaming hot water and let it close over his head. The muffled sound was soothing and he wanted to stay there. Stay where he did not have to think. His capacity to hold his breath gave way, and he emerged, sucking in a huge breath and stripping the water from his face as he did so.

He jumped when he opened his eyes to find Tristan staring down at him. "I didn't hear you," he said, and curled up his knees so he could wrap his arms around them. Tristan looked miserable. That beautiful, serious face was as miserable now as the day that he had appeared and Sam had begged him to help him escape. Sam had to look away.

"I know." He handed Sam a towel so he heaved himself out of the water. It seemed foolish to try and cover himself, but he did. He turned his back, roughly towelled his hair and shoulders, and then wrapped it around his middle before turning back. Tristan's head was bowed and he appeared to be staring at his feet.

"You can look now," Sam said, and smiled when Tristan raised his head. They were in the rooms that Tristan had procured for him.

"Did he hurt you?" Tristan's voice was low and he still avoided his eyes.

"Not much. You arrived before he could do any serious damage." He sagged into a chair and covered his eyes. He felt Tristan come and kneel beside him and rest his head on his knee. "I'm so sorry," he whispered.

Sam stroked his head. "Why are you sorry?"

"I failed you."

Sam sighed. "Exactly how did you fail me?" he asked as he stroked his head, loving the feel of the silky softness of his fair hair. "You rescued me from that place, you took me somewhere safe, you rescued me again from Dante, and this time shot the bastard. What more could a man ask for?"

Tristan looked up at him, his eyes were damp. "I should have understood you better, let you go to your cousin, but I just feel so protective of you. I don't mean to diminish you in any way but I don't seem to be able to stop being selfish where you are concerned. God, how does this work?"

Sam laughed softly and leaned down to drop a kiss on his head.

Tristan nodded. "There are no guidelines for us are there," he said with a sigh. "No role models, no social etiquette, no reference at all. It is as if men of our nature simply don't exist. Don't embark on relationships."

Sam's smile faded. He was right. "We don't exist. We can't."

Tristan stared up at him, fire in his blue eyes. "Well, I want to exist. I damn well will exist."

This was what he loved about Tristan. That huffy, buttoned up aristocrat who, beneath his starched shirt fronts, was as radical as you please. He stroked his head again and asked the question that had been burning him since they dragged Dante's lifeless body from the brothel. "What will happen to us?" he asked.

"With regard to Dante and Mosely?"

Sam nodded. When they had fished Mosely out of the grate they had found that he had struck his temple on the fender and was dead. Just like that. Both of them, dead. Sam couldn't quite believe it.

Tristan grimaced. "I wish I could regret it but I cannot. He was going to kill you."

Sam nodded.

"Alfie is sorting it out," he said after a brief pause. "Alfie has...connections. There will be an article in the Times before too long about Wallingford, and how he passed away unexpectedly. I imagine Mosely will just disappear. Alfie has seen Wallingford's family and told them that Wallingford was found shot dead in a brothel, and the man that shot him has been killed. Understandably, they don't want a scandal. Overdale has gone abroad."

"How on earth have you managed all that in an afternoon?" Sam was astounded. He had been terrified that the magistrates would carry him and Tristan away and somehow find out how Dante died, and what role Tristan had played.

"As I said, Alfie has connections."

"I'll say."

Tristan hesitated a moment. "There are people waiting to see you."

"Who?"

"Some rather lovely ladies from the brothel, the children, Gareth, Alfie...you are in demand."

Sam stared at him. "They are all here?"

"They were concerned."

Sam was moved. Moved that there were people in the world who cared about him. Moved that Tristan was here kneeling before him, caring about him, moved that Alfie had sought to ensure he didn't wind up in the gallows...He swallowed and nodded.

"I will dress and join you."

Tristan regarded him solemnly for a moment and then smiled awkwardly.

SAM WALKED INTO the room and took Tristan's heart all over again. He wondered if he was the only one who saw the uncertainty beneath the casual smile and the bright greeting. When Iris got up and threw herself into his arms he suspected he was not. He might have been jealous of the tight, hard hug he gave her with eyes screwed closed had he not already seen the love between Iris and Clara, Clara who had tears standing in her eyes and a wobbly smile on her face. He let her go, and she pecked him on the cheek and reclaimed her seat. Sam looked around and a huge smile lit his face.

"Ollie! Arthur!"

Ollie blushed from head to toe and stood, dragging his younger brother with him and they threw themselves at him. Sam hugged them tightly, then ruffled both dark heads. Tristan's heart squeezed yet again when Sam stooped and shook hands gently with Winifred, who stared at him wide eyed and then hid behind Ollie and sucked her thumb.

And then everyone was talking at once. Talking about what to do, about Dante and what would happen to the club and those who worked in it. What had happened to Mosely, all those things that mattered, but all Tristan wanted to do was beg Sam to come and live with him. Be with him. To love him.

A knock at the door quietened them, and Alfie went to answer it. He returned with a row of footmen bearing silver platters. They placed them on the table, along with crockery, cutlery, and glassware from a large hamper. They added several bottles of wine and then stood back and bowed. Tristan felt as open mouthed with surprise as Sam looked, but then joined in as they all fell on the food as though they had never eaten.

They had cleared the plates, and the staff had

disappeared with the empty dishes leaving them settled and replete, when another knock came.

Gareth grinned lazily. "Is this pudding?"

They all laughed. Sam made to get up and answer the door, but Alfie beat him to it. He disappeared into the small hallway, and Tristan heard an exchange of masculine voices. He glanced over at Sam; he appeared to be listening with a small frown.

Alfie appeared in the door. "Some gentlemen to see you, Sam. Captain Farrington and a Harry Valentine." He stood aside, and two tall gentlemen entered the room. Sam stared, open mouthed for a moment, but then shot to his feet.

"Harry! Bloody hell, Harry!" He strode across the room and grabbed one of them in a huge embrace that was returned with feeling. The man in his arms was startlingly handsome. Dark curls and dark, searching eyes that were dancing with laughter. His companion was a more subdued, fair haired man, clearly of military bearing, but definitely the more solemn of the two. Tristan had to surmise that this was the Harry that Sam talked of endlessly. He rubbed a hand across his mouth feeling a distinct sense of unease.

"Tristan, Tristan, let me introduce you," Sam was saying to him and holding out a hand, so he walked over and put a smile of welcome on his face. He stood beside Alfie as Sam made the introductions. Harry was eyeing him speculatively, and Farrington was unreadable. They shook hands in a very civilised fashion.

"How in God's name did you find me?" Sam said. Tristan waited for the answer with interest.

"I got your letter begging me to come. How could I

ignore that?" Harry said.

Stunned, Tristan held his breath.

Sam looked puzzled. "What letter? I wrote you a note saying that I'd left Dante's and that I was with..." He glanced over at Tristan. "That I was with someone, but I didn't ask you to come."

Harry frowned and pulled a letter out of his pocket and handed it to Sam. Sam scanned the contents.

"That is not my writing. It's far too neat."

Harry looked at Farrington. "I told you I wasn't sure."

Farrington nodded and turned to Tristan, concern in his eyes. "Is it possible that any post was intercepted by Dante? He has gone to inordinate lengths to get Harry back. If this is a trap we need to leave. Immediately."

"I would say that it was entirely possible that this whole thing was nothing more than an elaborate plan to get you all back," Tristan said, now firmly convinced that the invitation to Overdale, the children, Harry and his lover appearing...all Dante's doing.

"Then we should leave," Harry said. "Sam, you can leave with us if you need to, can't he, Charlie?"

Captain Farrington nodded.

"There is no need," Tristan said, moving closer to Sam. "Dante is dead. So is Mosely."

The words dropped into a little pool of silence, leaving Tristan feel quietly pleased that there was no need for Sam to disappear with his handsome friends.

"Dead? What the hell..." Harry was agape.

Tristan opened his mouth to reply, but Alfie stepped in. "There was an...unfortunate accident."

Harry looked staggered for a moment, but then turned to Farrington with a smile that was growing wider by the second, and something of Farrington's stern facade crumbled and he looked at Harry with such love and relief.

And then everyone was talking at once again. Tristan stood back and watched. Sam, Gareth, and Harry were with Iris and Clara and they were laughing, talking, and hugging each other. Farrington and Alfie were chatting to each other quite comfortably, probably having military things in common. Tristan could feel Sam slipping away as he found himself yet again on the periphery of the group. The children still sat in silence on the hearthrug so he went and knelt beside them.

"Have you had enough to eat?" he said.

They beamed up at him. "Thank you, my lord, it was lovely," Ollie said.

"I saved a cake," Winifred said, and held up a napkin. It was the first time that he had heard the child speak and something warm opened up in his chest.

"I think that was a very good idea. Is it for later?"

She regarded him with those solemn eyes for a moment. "No, it's for you," she said, and put the slightly squashed cake in his hand.

He had to blink several times and swallow before he spoke. "Thank you, Winifred. Thank you so much," he said. His voice was a little husky.

"What will happen to us now?" Ollie said. There was still a thread of concern in his voice.

"You will stay with us. I don't know exactly how this will work, but you won't be going back to Dante's or to Mosely's farm, that's for sure."

"Do you promise?"

Tristan swallowed. "I promise."

"Might I make a suggestion?" Alfie said. He had come to stand beside the children.

Tristan got to his feet, holding onto his cake. "Please do."

"I suggest that everyone repairs to your town house for the night. You and Sam might need to have a moment to yourselves?" he said with a meaningful look. "Then tomorrow decisions can be made."

Tristan nodded and within moments Alfie had everyone organised to leave.

Sam came to stand beside him so he took a deep breath. "Would you like me to stay here with you?" Tristan asked. "I understand if you would rather..."

"I would like it if you stayed."

Tristan nodded and tried to breathe evenly.

SAM WAVED AS the last of the mob disappeared through the door following Alfie, leaving him and Tristan in the rooms that Tristan had paid for. He waved at Harry. He couldn't believe Harry was here. His Charlie was a bit of alright, too. Fair haired, rather like Tristan, but a bit old and serious for his liking. He waved again, and then closed the door with a soft click and then turned back to the man that had come to mean so much to him.

Now they were alone he didn't know what to say. Didn't know where to start. How did a man say, *I love you, but I have to leave you?* He had no idea.

"You must be tired." Tristan squeezed his hand.

Sam nodded.

"We should retire."

Sam nodded again, and followed. They went through the rituals of preparing for bed until they were both dressed in nightshirts, clean, and ready to slide beneath the covers. Sam climbed in first and blew out the candle, then after a moment held up an arm, allowing Tristan to crawl in and settle his head on Sam's chest. He wrapped his arms about him and held tight, knowing how much they both loved to lie in bed and hold each other.

"I still can't believe Harry is here," he whispered into the dark.

"Seems like a good sort. Farrington, too."

"I'm glad for him. Charlie seems like a good man. Did you see the way that he looked at Harry? Like he was his whole world?"

Tristan kissed his chest gently and squeezed him.

"We need to talk." Sam's voice was soft; he didn't know where to begin.

"I don't want to talk."

"But..."

"Sam, we can talk later. We have plenty of time to talk. I almost lost you today and I am damned if I am going to lose what little time I have with you bloody well talking."

Sam opened his mouth to speak, but Tristan was climbing out of the bed and struggling with the tinder box to relight the candle at the bedside. Once it had taken, he stripped off his nightshirt and stood breathing fast in the candlelight. The golden glow lovingly caressed his body in exactly the way that Sam wanted to do. He sat up and pulled his own nightshirt off.

"Get back in here," he said, as he threw the garment to the floor.

"No. Tonight we do differently."

Sam was startled, but he smiled provocatively.

Tristan was trembling slightly, his chin lifted arrogantly. "Tonight, I shall take you."

Sam's stomach tightened and his cock shot hard as iron. The thought of Tristan...God.

He cleared his throat. "How do you want me?" His voice was hoarse.

Tristan held out a hand. "I want to kiss you first."

Sam slid out of the bed and took Tristan's hand, allowing himself to be pulled into his embrace. He closed his eyes and sighed. They held each other for the longest time, simply absorbing the incredible intimacy of naked skin against naked skin, hard male body against hard male body. Tristan was the first to move, he kissed Sam's neck, making him shiver, and then sought out his mouth again and kissed him. There was nothing in the world like kissing Tristan. He kissed exactly how Sam liked to kiss, and he fitted into his arms perfectly. The scent of his skin, his breath, his hair wrapped around him, held him and aroused him to an almost unbearable degree. Sam lost himself utterly in the sensation. The slip and slide, the pressure, the immense feeling of love that welled up inside him and threatened to overwhelm him, and the desperate, driving need for more. Tristan was completely in control as he tore his mouth away and kissed his way down Sam's throat, licked at his nipples and then sucked hard, making Sam groan and thrust against him. Sam grasped Tristan's arse and squeezed hard, loving the feel, the fullness, and the promise of what was to come.

"How do you want me?" he asked again.

"Lie over the bed," Tristan whispered against his mouth. "I want you over the bed."

Sam's heart thundered in his chest. He moved and hesitated, glancing at Tristan. They had never done anything like this before.

"This way," Tristan pushed him down gently, so he was laid face down on the quilt, but with his feet still on the floor and he understood exactly what he meant. Excitement made him shiver as he settled himself so that Tristan would be able to stand and fuck him hard.

He felt Tristan behind him, his thighs against the back of his legs, his balls soft against the curve of his backside. Then he stroked him. Ran his hands down his back from shoulder to the base of his spine, letting his fingernails scrape a little. Sam moaned into the bedcovers and pushed against him. Tristan did it again, this time a little harder and then let his fingers drift over the base of his spine again, but this time moved lower, tantalisingly lower until he took both cheeks of his buttocks in his hand, and Sam stopped breathing as he waited. Tristan ran his finger down Sam's crease, making his breath come in soft sobs of need as his whole body ached for more, needed more, but he didn't dare move. This was Tristan's moment, but it was killing him.

His felt him move and pour oil into his hands, and then his fingers returned and he parted his cheeks then sought, and pushed, until his fingers found his entrance. Sam sucked in a breath as he was breached, pushing back for more. Tristan prepared him with such care, but he needed more, so much more. Before he could speak, beg for it, Tristan lined himself up and surged into him. Sam shouted and pushed back hard. Being filled by Tristan was the most astoundingly intimate, satisfying moment of his entire life. He moaned as Tristan lay over him, covering him, holding him.

Tristan was shaking. He could feel it in the hands that gripped his hips and in the legs that lined up with his, but then he began to move and Sam's entire body lit up.

"Yes," he moaned, "yes, now…please, please."

Tristan held him between the shoulders with one hand and grasped his hip with the other and moved. His thrusts were short, tentative almost, and he bent and kissed him a few times, but as Sam cried out for more he let go and fucked him with long hard strokes into the mattress, leaving Sam moaning and writhing desperately. He felt Tristan's thrusts become shorter, harder, and then he connected with his gland and Sam yelled aloud at the sparks that lit up his already over-sensitive body. He managed to push his hand under himself to grab his desperate cock. All it took was a couple of tugs in time with Tristan and he was coming and howling, and as he did, Tristan cried into his back and emptied himself into him.

They lay together, panting, and Sam tried to pull his senses together but they were gone. He was gone. It was simply incredible. He felt Tristan pull out carefully and then brace himself with both hands on Sam's back. He was breathing as heavily.

"Did I hurt you?" he whispered, leaning down to kiss his shoulder.

Sam shook his head and licked his lips. "No."

He felt Tristan move away, and he came back with water and cloths. It took a gargantuan effort for Sam to move and clean himself, but when they were both done they slid back into bed, and Tristan resumed his position on Sam's chest.

"Are you…" he began.

Sam squeezed him. "Tris, it was the best fuck of

my life." It was the truth. He had never experienced anything like it.

Tristan's cheek that rested on his chest felt warm. "Oh. Well. There now. That's good. Better than talking?"

Sam laughed softly. "Much better than talking."

THEY SAT AT the table by the window sipping tea and eating toast. Sam dusted the crumbs from his fingers on his napkin, drained his cup, and sat resolute.

"I really do need to talk to you."

"By all means." The words were automatic. Polite, ingrained, but what Tristan really wanted to do was scream and say no and refuse to listen, take him back to bed and fuck him senseless again. He had hoped against hope that their activities through the night might have swayed him, might have made him want to stay.

"You have done so much for me; I could never repay you."

"I am not asking for repayment. I don't want repayment."

"I know." Sam rubbed at a spot on his breeches and kept his eyes down. "If I live here I will be as trapped as when I was in the brothel," he began.

Had he slapped him Tristan could not have been more shocked. He blinked and tried to process the pain that gripped him.

Sam looked up. "I…I can't live like this, Tristan. I adore you, but I cannot be a kept man. I cannot simply sit about all day and do nothing. And more to the point, I simply cannot countenance the possibility that you could ever be dragged into this...this cesspool that is my life again. I could ruin you, your entire family, I could get you hung. I cannot do that to you. I will not do it." Sam's eyes never left his and the pain in them was unmistakable.

Tristan swallowed, fiddled with his teaspoon for a moment, and then set it down. "I understand that this arrangement may make you uncomfortable," he said, feeling his way, "but there must be something that we can think of that doesn't mean you leaving me completely?" He glanced up.

Sam was frowning. "I want to feel like I am your equal. I want..." He sighed and pinched the bridge of his nose.

"My equal in what?"

"Everything. I want to be able to stand beside you." Sam threw his hands up in exasperation.

Tristan hurt. Every part of him hurt. "Well, unless you have found a way for you to become a...a wealthy, landowning member of the aristocracy I would say that is pretty much saying that what was between us is over."

Sam's silence said it all. Tristan couldn't look at him. He would not cry. He would not. "Where will you go?"

"I will look for work. I want to be able to support myself and a family."

That jerked Tristan's head up. "A family? Are you considering marriage?"

Sam's eyes were soft, pained. "No, I am taking the boys and the little girl with me."

Tristan didn't think he could hurt anymore but he was wrong. He had imagined keeping the children with him. Made plans for them. Thought he might have a place in their lives if not as a father, then as an uncle of sorts. He had allowed himself to imagine having a family, but Sam intended to not only leave him, but take the children, too. It was too much.

He stood, straightened his waistcoat and cleared his throat a couple of times, buying a little space in which to compose himself enough to speak. "I will leave you to get on. You clearly have a lot do."

Sam stood up, too, and watched as Tristan walked to the door. "Tristan?"

"Yes?" he paused, one hand on the open door. He stared at it. He couldn't look at Sam.

"It is for the best."

Tristan picked at a speck on the woodwork with his thumbnail. "I am sure it is. For you." He flicked a glance up at Sam and the words tumbled out unbidden. "Am I so fucking unlovable?"

Chapter 19

SAM STARED AT the closed door, mouth open. Unlovable? Unlovable? Christ, if he loved the man anymore he would die of it. He was leaving him *because* he loved him...

Sam rubbed awkwardly at the pain in his chest and tried to process what he had said, tried think about it from Tristan's point of view. Tristan who had no mother, felt rejected by his father, whose struggle with his needs set him apart from the rest of the world, from his peers and his family. Who, it seemed, clearly saw himself as not worthy of love. Sam had given him those words once but they had been a dreadful untruth. A ploy. He remembered the look of unspeakable vulnerability in Tristan's eyes when he had said it, and the look of pain when he had overheard Gareth say it was a lie. He sank back into the chair and covered his eyes.

❖

THE COMFORT AND familiarity of White's wrapped around Tristan and soothed him a little. His club was the one place where he could be alone with his thoughts in a place that did not hold memories of Sam in it. The low hum of conversation, the air, redolent of smoke, brandy, and polish; the clink of crystal and china were all calming and familiar. He shook out a copy of the Times and held it before him like a shield. A silent message about the need for solitude, a barrier against the encroaching world. He couldn't read a thing, mind; he just hid behind it whilst he thought. He was in a completely impossible situation. If he offered Sam work, paid work, Sam would still feel beholden to him. If he didn't then he would feel like a kept man and leave. If he offered Sam money to stay and Sam did stay, he would forever wonder if he had simply stayed for the money or because he loved him.

Brutal, really.

He sipped the brandy that had been brought to him. He was stuck in a mess of his own making. He had bought Sam from the beginning. Buying the affections of a man in a brothel, buying the sexual gratification he needed, buying Sam. He had never really thought of the man in the brothel, the man selling himself to others, selling his body, his self-respect, his...Tristan closed his eyes. He thought about those boys locked into the life of trading one's self for enough money to live, and the little girl that had been poised on the brink. When he had gone to Dante's it had been only to satisfy a deep and abiding need. He had not thought about Sam other than in terms of his own needs. He needed to be bedded by a man, he needed to have a man in his life, he needed...he needed...he needed. Sam had tried to explain today, but again he had only thought about how that impacted on his own life not that Sam might need, too. He folded the newspaper carefully. He remembered the way that Sam sank into his arms at night and loved to be held.

No wonder he wasn't loved. He really only considered himself. He thought about his abhorrence for what Dante and Mosely had done but in the end, he was complicit in that world as he had gone and bought into it by paying for Sam. He felt partly hypocritical and partly furious that men like him should be put in the position where they could not love freely. He took another drink and was forced to admit that had Sam been a woman he wouldn't be much better off because they could never have married because of the class difference. What was it Sam had said to him? That he was more trapped than most? Sitting in White's, surrounded by comfort and privilege, he had to admit he was trapped. His trappings offered immense wealth, comfort, and pleasure, but, when it denied him what he really needed, it was nothing more than a glorified prison.

Mind you, he thought as he took another sip, even if the world did allow for men to love men openly, he couldn't make Sam love him. He knew that Sam was fond of him, that he desired him, but when it came down to it there didn't seem to be much that Tristan could do to make him love him. As grand gestures of love went, killing a man had to stand up there, but it hadn't had a ha'porth of impact on Sam. He still didn't love him enough to stay; he still intended to go. He closed his eyes on a sigh.

The sound of someone clearing their throat dragged him from his reverie, and made him peer over the top of his newspaper. Captain Farrington stood there.

"Begging your pardon," the man said with a small bow. "Might I have a moment of your time, my lord?"

"Of course," Tristan replied. The words were ingrained politeness. He wanted nothing more than to be left alone, but found he was a little curious about this man who had managed to capture Sam's cousin's heart. He was good looking. Tall, fair haired, and serious.

Farrington sat opposite him. "I wondered how you were faring. Harry explained what happened."

"I am absolutely fine."

"Shooting a man is..." he looked off towards the window for a moment. "Never easy."

Tristan shuddered. In all the chaos that had ensued, the pain of possibly losing Sam forever, the fact that he had killed a man as yet stood unexamined in his heart. When he looked at it, it made him feel queasy.

Farrington went on. "I was trained to do it, but it never failed to make me feel ill. I can only imagine how you are feeling right now."

Tristan smiled sadly. "In fairness, I have been so caught up with trying to figure out how to persuade Sam not to leave I have given it little thought." He looked at the man opposite him. "Does that make me a dreadful person?"

Farrington smiled. He really was a very good looking man. "Not at all. When Mosely went for Harry I shot him, but only in the arm. I wished I had shot him dead. If I had, you and Sam might have been spared some of this."

Both men were silent for a moment, each locked in their own thoughts.

Tristan was the first to speak. "Funny, what a man will do for those he loves."

Farrington nodded. "Do you love him?"

Tristan balked a little at the personal nature of the question, but then capitulated swiftly. There were not many people he could talk to about the position he was in. He nodded and then pinched the bridge of his nose. "I do, but he is hell bent on leaving with you and Harry. Not only that, he intends to take the children with him." Tristan swallowed.

"We rescued a boy from Dante," Farrington said. "Julian. Probably the same age as Ollie. He lives with us and Harry acts as his tutor."

"How did you persuade Harry to stay with you?" Tristan asked. Was there something that he hadn't thought of, something he could offer that might make a difference?

Farrington looked at his hands for a moment, and then looked up. "I asked him."

Tristan nodded and smiled. "And he said yes?"

Farrington just smiled.

"So it was that easy?"

"I wasn't sure he would. I had only known him a day." Farrington's eyes took on a faraway look as he remembered. "But it was enough for me to know that I loved him. To know there would never be another for me. Fortunately for me, he loved me, too."

"You are a lucky man."

"I know."

Tristan wanted to be happy for Farrington, but

Trapped

inside he was a seething mass of misery. Why couldn't Sam just love him back?

"How long will you be staying?" he asked.

"Probably a week or so."

Tristan wasn't sure if that was a good thing or not. Could he spend a week with Sam and then let him go? Could he spend a week with Sam knowing he didn't love him?

"Might I make a suggestion?"

Tristan looked up at Farrington.

"Stop thinking too much."

Tristan opened his mouth to speak, but then laughed and shook his head.

SAM STOOD OUTSIDE Alfie's townhouse for long moments trying to compose himself. He was still struggling to come to terms with the fact that in his attempts to protect Tristan, and find some kind of self-respect for himself, all he had managed to do was make Tristan feel unlovable. Unlovable. Just the word made his chest ache. He had spent some time talking with Harry, and between them they had come up with some ideas. All he needed was some help from Alfie to try and find a way forward that would suit them all. That would allow him to lead some kind of productive life, love Tristan, and look after the children they had rescued.

He shook himself, straightened his coat, and ran lightly up the stairs to the door and rapped on it. He stretched his neck a little and cleared his throat. The door opened, and he was admitted.

He found Alfie in the drawing room with Gareth,

Charlie, and Harry. He smiled at Harry. He had promised to make sure that he and Charlie would be in attendance.

Sam cleared his throat. "I need to speak to you all," he said, head held high. "I am looking for work."

Alfie's eyes glinted. "Really?" he drawled. "What makes you think that we would be interested?"

Sam restrained himself. "Not that kind of work," he snapped. "Real work."

"And I repeat, what makes you think that we would be interested?"

Outrageous arse.

Gareth shushed him and Sam felt slightly mollified when Charlie and Harry bade him continue and pay Alfie no heed.

"I want to build some sort of a life with your cousin, but, at the moment, I have nothing to offer him." He pulled in a breath and stuck out his chin. "I love him."

Alfie was standing by the fireplace watching him, unblinking.

"You both have estates. You must have estate managers?" he said to Alfie.

Alfie actually laughed and Sam clenched his fists. "Indeed I do, but, my love, you are a whore, what do you know about estate management?"

It all happened very quickly, and then, Sam was nursing bruised knuckles, and Alfie was wagging his jaw and blinking rapidly. The others were talking loudly. Sam shook his hand and wondered if he had broken something, the pain was so intense. "Sorry," he mumbled, "shouldn't have done that but..." He shook his head and turned to leave, but Harry and Charlie stood with him and stopped him.

"I think that the boy deserves to be heard," Charlie said. Sam smiled at him. Charlie was a good man.

Alfie sighed and straightened his coat. "Sam, you have my most heartfelt apology. Sometimes I simply cannot help myself, and you do make it so damnably easy...oof!" Gareth's elbow connected nicely with his ribs, winding him a little.

Sam bristled, but restrained himself.

Alfie coughed and pouted a little at Gareth, but then turned back to him, and this time is usually taunting eyes were serious, and his customary bored drawl was missing.

"If you would hear me out, I do actually have had something of an idea that might be of interest to you."

"You have a guest, my lord." Tristan frowned as he handed over his hat and coat to the footman, who had waited for his late return. Who on earth would be calling at this hour? He headed for the library and opened the door to find Sam standing by the fireplace. Tall, manly, and handsome. His heart stopped for a moment and then flung itself against his ribs like a crazed bird. He wondered if he would ever be able to look at him without that happening. Somehow he doubted it.

"Sam." It was all he could say. He turned and closed the door behind him and tried to breathe.

"Two things," Sam said, and paced a little. Tristan could tell he was anxious so he just nodded.

"First. I...I have a proposition for you. I cannot claim credit for it, I had some help, but I think if you will listen you will see that, as an idea, it has merit."

Tristan swallowed and stared. "I am listening."

"You have an estate. Not your principal seat, but a small estate not far out of the city. Alfie told me that it is in need of repair and that you were considering selling it."

Tristan thought for a moment. "Havering? The old abbey?"

"The very one. Alfie tells me that it is in a state of disrepair and in sore need of attention. That the tenant farmers need more from you than they are getting, and...well...and it might need a young, strong steward to manage it, and a team of people to restore it to its former glory." Sam cleared his throat. "It would also be an excellent home for your newly discovered wards."

Tristan's breath caught. "Wards?"

Sam nodded. "Wards. Ollie, Arthur, and Winifred need a home and a family and you did manage to find a branch of the family that was vague enough that we could claim the children sprang from it. You would be their guardian, and we would need a nanny and a housekeeper along with a tutor...."

His heart was thumping. Sheer genius. "Iris, Clara, and Gareth?"

"Yes. And maybe some others from Dante's. They will need work, and some of them want good, decent work. And the children. There will be more children."

Tristan was warming to the idea. "Why would I remove them to Havering and not take them to the Park?" Tristan thought of the Earl of Chiltern's vast principal seat in Surrey with a shudder. He had hated being there as a child.

"Because they need a home of their own, somewhere quiet and not so publicly associated with you.

Somewhere that you might eventually bequeath to them? Alfie said it was free of entail?"

"And...I would need to spend a lot of time there?"

"Naturally." Sam smiled. "Alfie said you used to love it as a boy."

He nodded it was true. As a boy he had spent many happy times there, but since he had grown to manhood it had fallen into disrepair, but not so much so that it wasn't recoverable. He had looked into it when his man of business had suggested selling it.

Sam swallowed, and continued. "Charlie and Harry suggested that it may be that there is a need for homes for children who fall foul of types like Dante, or Wallingford, whatever you want to call him. Charlie has a big house in Yorkshire if the children needed to take the sea air, or to get away from the city, and they think that they might even purchase a property by the sea for that purpose."

Sam stumbled to a halt and drew breath. "What do you think?" he whispered, his eyes wide and anxious.

Tristan was unable to speak. He just nodded. Several times, and he blinked a lot. It was a splendid plan. So splendid, he didn't trust himself to speak. Sam ran on. "Alfie is looking into Overdale's business with the orphanages. He said he has a horrible feeling that there is definitely something going on there, with Overdale supplying young children to brothels and houses from the orphanages."

Tristan choked. He still couldn't even begin to fathom that, but at least he might be given the chance to work with Alfie in exposing whatever was going on and put an end to it. "Then I shall work with him. Help him in any way that I can."

"So, between us, Alfie, Charlie, and Harry and

the rest of them, we will be able to give them somewhere safe. Charlie reckons we could even teach them their letters and prepare them to find good jobs so that they can make a good living. Have a good, respectable life."

Tristan was struggling to process the whole thing. "Why didn't you speak to me about any of this?" he asked. "It is a remarkable idea." He shook his head. He didn't want to jump to conclusions, but it sounded very much like Sam was saying that he wasn't going to run away, that there might be a way for them to spend time together.

Sam closed his eyes and then opened them. "Well, this is the second point." He coughed and rubbed his hands together.

"I hurt you," he said. "When I talked of leaving, I thought that I was doing what was best, even though it broke my heart, but I hurt you."

Tristan had to look away. "Don't worry about that. I am perfectly fine. I apologise if I was overly dramatic. Again," he added.

Sam continued as if he had not interrupted. "I needed to be sure that I had something to offer you before I spoke to you again."

Something to offer me? Tristan waited, barely breathing.

"Secondly, and most importantly, you are the *most* lovable man that I know."

Colour exploded in Tristan's face. "Don't be ridiculous," he began, but then Sam was taking him by the arms and holding him tight. Looking directly into his eyes and making him look back at him. His eyes. His beautiful, crystalline grey green eyes shone.

"You *are* loveable. Incredibly lovable." Tristan

stared as Sam took a deep breath and closed his eyes as he continued. "*I* love you. I love you so damned much. I don't blame you if you don't believe me after what I did, but it is the truth. The absolute truth. I love you."

Tristan blinked hard.

"Then why did you insist on leaving me? No, don't answer that," Tristan said, holding up a hand. For once in his life he just needed to listen, but somehow words kept tumbling forth that he knew would more than likely precipitate an argument.

"Because I thought I had to," Sam said, capturing his hand. "Because I needed you to respect me. How could you respect me if I lived off you and sat about doing nothing? When all I have managed to do with my life is to fall into debt, sell my body, and almost get your family ruined and you killed?"

"Respect," Tristan repeated, and turned the idea over in his mind before replying. "Actually, I have enormous respect for you." It was true. It had taken Sam's words for him to realise it, but he really did.

Sam scoffed, but Tristan held up a hand and continued. "I respect the fact that you fought hard to survive when you lost your home, you fought hard to get out of Dante's." He slanted a glance at Sam. "I respect the fact that you have tried to do what you see as the right thing, even though I didn't like it above much."

A small smile curved Sam's mouth and he looked a little incredulous. "Really?"

"Really." Tristan ran his thumb over Sam's knuckles. "There is so much to respect about you, but me? Why on earth would you respect me?"

Sam looked a little perplexed. "Well, all this?" he

said, gesturing to the house. "The small matter of you being a peer of the realm?"

"I didn't earn it; it was given to me. An accident of birth. I haven't done a single thing in my life to deserve any respect that is shown to me, other than be born in the right place into the right family." It was true. He'd never thought of it that way before, but there was little to remark on in his life.

Sam's eyes sparkled. "I always thought you were a bit of a radical under all that fancy clothing."

Tristan ducked his head and laughed.

"I respect the fact that you helped me when you had no need to, you cared for me when you had every right to throw me in the gutter and, well...you shot Dante and made sure I won't hang for killing Mosely."

Tristan closed his eyes and rested his forehead against Sam's shoulder, loving how he was pulled close. He hated himself for asking, but couldn't help it. "Do you really love me?"

Sam's arms tightened around him. "Yes. I don't blame you for not believing me but, yes. I do."

"I do believe you, I just...like to hear it."

Tristan pulled back so that he could look at Sam. He touched his lips with his fingers and then kissed him. Just a fleeting touch.

"I love you, too."

Sam let out a sigh and touched their foreheads together. "Thank God. I thought you did, hoped you did, but I was afraid that I'd ruined it all."

"I loved you from the first. I never stopped." He looked up and smiled. "I might have hated you for a bit in the middle, but..."

Sam looked shocked for a moment, but then laughed and they laughed together.

"So, what do we do now?" Tristan said.

Sam shrugged. "If you agree we set things in motion to remove to Havering."

Tristan nodded. "Tell me again."

"Well, we can move into…"

"No, not that bit. The other."

Sam's grey green eyes glinted. He smiled slowly, tilted his head to one side, and let his gaze roam all over Tristan's face, warming him. All that he felt was clear to see, and Tristan's breath caught again as he spoke.

"I love you."

The Wrong Kind of Angel

Chapter 1

CHARLES FARRINGTON HAD long ago resigned himself to the fact that his deviant nature meant he was destined to be alone. He found himself unable to return the affections of a lady, and was unwilling to set up a pretence, so he embraced his solitude and satisfied himself with the very occasional foray into London for business and places where he could seek out likeminded company. After Napoleon's eventual defeat he had resigned his commission and set up home in small, but pleasant house on the outskirts of a small village on the edge of the North Yorkshire moors, not too far from the coast. There was a distinct lack of local young ladies who might wish to pursue a bookish ex-officer, which pleased Charles, but this also meant that there was a complete lack of likeminded company which in many ways was a relief. To counteract the lack of company, Charles surrounded himself with things that gave him pleasure. Things like his growing collection of snuff boxes, his garden, and lately his writing of, what he considered to be, rather daring novels involving dashing young men flinging themselves into battle. So life, for the most part, was pleasant. Or so he told himself.

Over the past year or so he had spent rather more time with his writing, and to his everlasting surprise he had published some of his stories, making a small sum of money from it. This supplemented his military pension nicely, and supported his rather expensive snuff box collection. So, as winter approached, he was happy to while away the dark hours hunched over his manuscript, fortunate in the fact that he could afford a good number of candles. As Christmas drew near, and the weather worsened, he tucked himself away with only his cat, housekeeper, and groom for company. Mr. and Mrs. Darnley lived in the village and came in daily to wash, clean, and feed both him and his horses. Horatio, an enormous ginger tom, kept the mice at bay. It was a good arrangement.

They had established a routine for the Christmas period that suited all of them; Mrs. Darnley left the house laden with food for both him and the cat, her husband organised the livestock for him, and then they returned to their family on Christmas Eve, not returning until after Boxing Day. He couldn't quite countenance the idea that they would forsake their large, jolly family during the Christmas period to hang around to see if he needed anything. When the weather turned particularly nasty, he begged that they leave early on Christmas Eve.

"But it isn't even lunchtime," Mrs. Darnley said, shaking flour from her apron.

"Have you seen the weather?" Charles said, pointing to the window. "If you and Darnley don't go now you may not make the village. I would not wish to be answerable to your entire family if they missed out on your dinner."

She looked out and sighed just as her husband came into the kitchen, stomping snow from his boots making Horatio flick his tail in disgust.

"Darnley, my dear fellow, will you have words with your good wife?" Charles said. "You need to leave. I have enough food to feed an army. Several armies. I will not starve if you leave now."

Darnley stuffed his cap in his coat pocket. "He's right, m'love. Temperature is dropping and there's a north wind coming in. I reckon snow's set in for a day or two."

All three stared at the whitening landscape and listened to the howling wind for a moment and then Mrs. Darnley sighed. "I don't like leaving you here alone."

"My dear Mrs. Darnley. No harm shall befall me. I will enjoy the solitude and no doubt laze the days away in front of the fire."

"You should consider getting someone to live in, you know," she said for the hundredth time as she bustled about. "Not right, a lovely gentleman like you on his own. Not right."

Charles smiled at her. "I give you my word I shall consider it," he said, laying a hand on his heart. What she really meant was that he should find a wife.

With a little more huffing and puffing the Darnleys finally left, but not before she had made him a pot of tea. After he closed the door on the dreadful weather he took the tea and the plate of cake into his study, piled the fire high with logs, and settled himself in with a sigh as the well-banked fire blazed and drove away the worst of the cold. Listening to the howling wind and watching the falling snow blanket the landscape from the safety of his study made him feel exceedingly cosy. He picked up the paper, sipped his tea, and propped his feet on the stool. Horatio promptly settled himself on his lap and he was tempted to kick off his shoes and toast his feet by the fireside Mrs. Darnley had adorned with holly, making the room feel almost festive.

By early evening the snow had covered the land as far as he could see and the wind was causing spectacular drifting. Charles banked the fires in the study, the kitchen, and his chamber. There was no point heating anything more. He had catalogued more of his snuff boxes, written a couple of chapters of his book, and tidied his papers again, so he picked up a book on the history of York and helped himself to a glass of brandy.

After a while his eyes began to tire. He tipped his head back and closed them for a moment and indulged himself. He pretended he was not alone. Pretended that there was someone with him; someone special. Someone who would come into the room and take the chair opposite him, but first would lean over, run a hand over his hair, and kiss him. Someone with whom he could exchange a Christmas gift, kiss under the mistletoe, and retire to bed with. Wake up with. So vivid was the image, so clear the warm promise of the kiss, that when there was a noise at the front door he wondered if he had conjured it from his imagination. He jerked upright and listened. There it went again. Charles hastened from the room into the freezing hallway, pulling the study door closed behind him to preserve the warmth. He dragged the bolt from the ancient door and heaved it open, wincing at the blast of icy air and wet, swirling snow that hit his face.

Standing propped in the door was the most handsome young man he had ever seen in his life. Charles' jaw actually dropped. He was tall, with sodden, inky black curls plastered to his hatless head and eyes so dark they appeared black in a sharp angular face. He had the sort of direct, piercing gaze that made whomever was subject to it faintly uncomfortable. The eyes fluttered shut.

"Thank God," the man muttered and staggered over the threshold. Charles grabbed him awkwardly and shoved the heavy door back, shutting out the freezing snow and wind. The man was dead on his feet. He swayed badly and Charles caught him under the arms, staggering a little as he did so. He was soaked to the bone and the icy chill of his body soaked into Charles. The man's head lolled and Charles braced himself to hold him up, but he regained his balance a little and stood, swaying precariously. Charles maintained his grip on him just in case.

Before he could speak, the man's eyelids fluttered open and Charles found himself eye to eye with that searching gaze.

"Oh..." he said. Dark brows narrowed into a quizzical frown, and those equally dark eyes ran over every inch of Charles' face. "Oh..." he said again, and Charles held his breath, barely daring to move when the man ran his hand over his hair, actually touched him, and then trailed a thumb across his cheek. Charles' mouth went dry and his heart thundered in his chest.

"Are you an angel?" the man said and brought

his other hand up so he was cupping Charles' face. Charles couldn't have spoken or moved if his life had depended on it. "You must be," he continued, his voice dropping to a whisper, and his eyes continued to search Charles'. "You are all golden. A beautiful, beautiful golden angel," he said in an odd singsong voice, and tilted his head to one side.

Charles' knees were about to buckle so he held on to the stranger and presumed he was talking about his fair hair. "Thank you for saving me, beautiful angel," he whispered, his eyes appeared to lock onto Charles' mouth. "Thank you, thank you...thank you..." the stranger whispered as his mouth came closer, closer to Charles' until it hovered so close over his that he could feel the warmth from the stranger's skin, his breath, his very being.

Charles was not sure who closed the fraction of an inch until their lips met, touched, and held, but he knew that the strangled sound of naked, shocked pleasure and need came from his own throat. It had been an age since he had been kissed; he pressed his lips to the other man's and squeezed his eyes shut. The stranger sighed and his lips moved over his with increasing, rhythmic pressure that Charles, after a faltering start, echoed. The man held his face, and he held it still whilst he dragged his lips away to touch them to Charles' eyes, his forehead, and then came back to his mouth.

They kissed until the man pulled back again and Charles let go of him. His hands were shaking, so he balled them into fists and tried to breathe, tried to speak, but he couldn't. The man smiled. Smiled right into his eyes. "Beautiful, beautiful angel, thank you," he said, and crumpled to the ground.

Chapter 2

CHARLES WAS SHAKING from head to foot with a soul deep ache coursing through every fibre of his being. It was unlike anything he had ever experienced before in his life. The young man was sprawled on the floor, unmoving.

"Sir?" Charles said as he sank to his knees to shake the man. "Sir, can you hear me?" There was no reply, but the man was clearly freezing, his lips having taken on an alarming bluish tinge. Charles took one large hand in his and chafed it, but to no avail. He continued his ministrations as he looked around the entrance hall frantically for inspiration. He needed to get the man dry, warm; get some food or drink inside him, and hope that he regained his senses. He doubted he would be able to get to the village to summon assistance, and by the time he got back it might be too late. What in God's name was he to do?

Fear and anxiety bloomed in an almost overwhelming wave. What if he was unable to revive him? What if he...Charles squeezed his eyes shut.

Stop it. Just stop it, Farrington.

Forcing away the encroaching panic, he settled on a plan. He would bring bedding from upstairs, fashion it into a temporary billet before the fire in the study, and carry, or more likely drag, the stranger to it. The unconscious man was similar in height to Charles, perhaps a little taller, and was slender in build, but moving a dead weight was never easy.

He ran a hand over the wet curls. "I will be right back," he said, and then paused. He couldn't resist stroking his thumb across the man's temple. Then he ran upstairs.

Within minutes Charles had created a neat bed on the floor in front of the fire in the study. A quilt lay on the rug with a selection of soft pillows, blankets, and yet another quilt raided from the guest rooms.

He hurried back into the hallway to find his guest in exactly the same position as he had left him. Charles hesitated and rubbed a hand over his mouth, considering how best to move him. In the end he tugged and pulled until the man was flat on his back, and then managed to get behind him and lift his shoulders to get a grip around his chest, but he didn't move. Frustrated, Charles looked around the ancient hallway and then hit upon an idea. He removed all the rugs from the floor between the door and the study revealing the old, polished wooden floor, braced himself behind the man again, and managed to get his arms firmly around his chest so that he could drag him. The old polished wood assisted this enterprise admirably. He stumbled and fell a few times when the water in the man's clothing clung stubbornly to the floor, whacking his knee quite painfully as he did so, but eventually he got the man parallel with the bed before the fire. The cat trotted over and sniffed tentatively at the stranger, but recoiled immediately and leaped into the chair.

Panting, he laid the man down and considered how he might get him onto it. He scratched his head and then pulled off his coat and rolled up his sleeves.

"Come along old chap," he said to the man. "We are going to have to roll you onto the bed. Can you lend a hand?" The man remained motionless. Charles made a mental note to increase his physical activity, as his strength had clearly dwindled since his departure from the army, but as he stooped to move him, he bethought himself. His guest was sodden. His clothes were saturated and if he wrapped him in the blankets like that he would never get warm.

Charles hesitated, ran a hand over his mouth, took a deep breath, and then started with the shoes and stockings. The long, slender feet were ghostly pale and wet; the skin wrinkled and puckered.

"You poor thing," Charlies muttered as he took each foot and dried it. Once done, he took a deep breath and then unbuttoned the man's breeches and stripped them down his legs in a brisk, businesslike fashion, but his heart stopped for a moment when he realised that beneath them the man was naked. He blinked, looked away, then returned to towelling him dry. Getting rid of the coat, waistcoat, and shirt turned out to considerably harder as the wet fabric clung stubbornly, and the man was incredibly heavy, but eventually Charles had him laid before him naked.

His heart skipped along at an alarming rate. The man was young. Probably much younger than his own thirty some years and in his unconscious state he looked terribly vulnerable. Charles covered him with the blanket and quilt and tucked a pillow beneath his head. His heart was thundering in his chest as he tried to banish images of sleek muscles that ran down a tailored torso from surprisingly wide shoulders to narrow hips. Through school, university, and the army Charles had encountered many naked men, but this one was unspeakably beautiful.

Charles pulled the door to, hurried to the kitchen, and prepared a pot of tea, needing to be away from the man for a moment or two. He loaded a tray with milk and sugar along with a pile of bread, Twelfth Night cake, and cheese and then was forced to grip the edge of the table and take several deep breaths. He had never been kissed like that before in his life and it seemed to have triggered something in him that was like a live thing coursing through his entire body, but gathering into his heart and his groin. His chest was so full it hurt, and his cock simply throbbed. Beside the intense physical reaction remained a very real fear deep within him that he would not be able to revive him, or would not know how best to help him to heal, and if he took with a fever, he was not sure he had the right things to hand.

He mentally reviewed the books in the library and could recall some treatise on medicine and healing. A physician was at least an hour's drive away in good weather. Goodness only knew how long it might take in the snow and wind. He eyed the plate of food that he had prepared. Wasn't one supposed to starve a fever?

Shaking his head and sucking in several long breaths, he attempted to compose himself and shake off the feeling of complete inadequacy before he headed back.

Holding onto the tray he put his shoulder to the door and then leaned on it to shut it, intending to put the food and drink on the table, but jumped when he realised the man was awake. Awake and staring at him with his mouth open. Charles stared back.

"You're real," the man whispered as he struggled to sit up. "Oh, Christ, you're real."

Chapter 3

CHARLES SET THE tray down, carefully avoiding his gaze. "I am indeed." Firelight flickered over naked shoulders; a log cracked and hissed and they both jumped. "How do you feel?" Charles asked.

The man ran his tongue over his lips and scrubbed one eye with the heel of his hand. "Dreadful. Are you going to shoot me?"

"Shoot you...?"

"Beat me?"

Charles stared and then realisation dawned. The kiss. He cleared his throat and felt his face heat.

"Ah...no. No." He wanted to say more, but the words stuck so he shook his head.

The man managed to sit up, only swaying a little, and as the coverlet fell to his lap, he looked down at his naked chest. He said nothing about his state of undress but shot Charles a questioning look.

"You were soaking and freezing," Charles felt

compelled to explain. "I...ah...um...undressed you and dried you." He cleared his throat again and then gestured to the tray awkwardly. "I brought something to eat and drink. You should eat. Unless you have a fever?"

The man's eyes were riveted on the food. "I'm not feverish."

Charles put the tray on the floor and after a moment's hesitation, folded himself to sit cross legged in front of the stranger. It was as if they were engaged in some bizarre picnic in front of the roaring fire. He poured the tea and passed a plate of bread and cheese. The man fell on it and devoured every scrap, in the way that young men do, then polished off the cake with two cups of tea. He wiped the back of his hand over his mouth.

"Thank you," he whispered. "Where are my clothes?" he said, eyes darting around the room.

"Drying in the kitchen. You don't have to leave," he said and immediately looked away. He got to his feet and lifted the tray. "I have plenty of rooms if you would like to stay the night. The weather is atrocious."

"That is very kind of you."

No, it's not. Charles ran a hand around the back of his neck and searched for something to say. "It's Christmas. The season of goodwill." He sighed inwardly.

"Christmas day?" the man asked with a frown.

Charles glanced over at him. "Not quite. Christmas Eve. Happy Christmas." Dear lord. He had definitely been alone too long. He risked a glance at his guest and saw a shadow of a smile on the man's face as he pushed the covers away and moved to stand. Charles whirled around to give him some privacy, but not before he caught a glance of that long, sleek body and what he would have sworn was the beginning of an erection. He closed his eyes and tried to breathe normally, but his heart was almost beating him to death.

"I could loan you some clothes while yours dry?" he offered.

"Might you have a robe or something for now?"

"Yes. Of course. A robe." With that, Charles fled to the safety of his bedchamber.

HE SAT ON the edge of the bed for a moment, breathing heavily and blinking at the fire. After a moment, he threw more logs on to keep the blaze going. It was the only other room in the house that was warm apart from the study and the kitchen. He didn't bother keeping any other areas heated and aired as there was usually no point. He couldn't offer a guest room that was horribly damp and unaired. The man would have to sleep in his chamber. Charles let out a faintly hysterical laugh at the thought and sank his fingers into his hair. It took a moment, but he pulled himself together and found the warmest robe he possessed. It was a heavy blue brocade that his aunt had bought him a few years before. She said the colour reminded her of his eyes. He smiled at the memory and tucked it over his arm.

"This one is quite warm." Charles handed the gown to the man who was standing hunched over by the fire, draped in a blanket, warming his hands.

He straightened and smiled. "You are indeed an angel."

And there it stood between them again. The kiss.

"My Christmas angel," the man said, moving closer to take the robe. His hand brushed Charles' as he took it and he felt the contact ripple through him. He averted his eyes as the man shook off the blanket and shrugged into the robe and again caught sight of that lengthening cock. His own was as hard as marble and, without the protection of a coat, in all likelihood, frighteningly obvious.

"Would you like something else to eat?" Charles said, hoping the edge of desperation in his voice was not too evident.

"If it would be no bother?"

"Of course not," Charles said, and yet again, fled.

Chapter 4

HENRY WILSON, WHO more often than not went by the name of Harry, wrapped the loaned robe around him and watched his host almost run from the room. He sank into the chair by the fireside before his legs gave way.

"Fuck," he said to the room. He felt like death. Exhausted from running, hiding, and then from trudging through the damned snow, but he was not completely dead he realised as he adjusted himself.

He was damned lucky. Lucky to have found shelter, lucky that the chap who had taken him in didn't shoot him, or throw him back out into the snow after that kiss. Fancy being so stupid. He shook his head in disbelief. He had learned the hard way to keep his peculiar preferences to himself when in public. What were the chances of falling into the home and the arms of a fellow sodomite? He was bloody grateful though. He looked at the door that his host had closed behind him. He couldn't linger. Daren't linger no matter how delightful his rescuer might be. His angel. His Christmas angel. Christ, the man was gorgeous. Harry ran his hands over his face. This was a complication that he didn't need and certainly couldn't indulge, but the look in those dark blue eyes almost undid him. Longing, curiosity, loneliness; shame. He ached to take him in his arms and show him that there was no shame in the desire that he felt. But, where some men would be happy for a quick tumble, instinct told him that this man would want more. If his angel handed over his body, his heart would likely be attached, too, and that would never do.

Harry willed the fog that clouded his brain away and tried to focus. He had to reach the coast which was probably still at least half a day's drive away, maybe more in this weather, and that would be if he could find a horse, work out the way to go, and if it stopped damn well snowing. He rubbed his face. Could he persuade his angel to loan him a horse and some money? He groaned and pinched the bridge of his nose. He probably knew the answer to that. It was what he was good at.

The door opened and his host returned pushing a trolley laden with food. Harry's mouth watered.

"My housekeeper left me well stocked so I warmed some stew. I hope this is acceptable?" His angel looked up with a shy smile, dark blue eyes framed by fair hair. The man was a fair bit older than him and as neat as wax. When he looked around, he realised that the room was also frighteningly neat.

"That would be wonderful; you should have let me help," he said, trying to get to his feet.

"I think you need to recover first," his host said as he placed a bowl of stew and a plate of bread on the table at the side of Harry's chair and gestured for him to remain seated. He took a bowl himself and sat opposite. "I hope you don't mind the informality; the dining room is freezing."

"I don't mind at all."

His angel put the bowl down and looked a little sheepish. "Forgive me, I haven't introduced myself. Charles Farrington." He stood and held out his hand. Harry ignored the lure of the food, stood up, too, and took the proffered hand. "Harry Valentine." Only a small white lie. "Please, call me Harry."

"Harry," Farrington smiled and shook, lingering over the handshake a little, so Harry squeezed the hand nestled in his.

"You should call me Charles." Those blue eyes burned now and Harry felt his resistance slip as he stared back and felt heat burn through him at the contact. He felt Farrington's breath catch.

Harry swallowed and pulled his hand back. "Does anyone call you Charlie?" he asked with a cocky grin, breaking the spell.

"No."

"I think I might do. This looks delicious."

Charles, decent chap that he was, followed his lead and returned to his seat and picked up his bowl. Harry picked up his own and watched covertly. Long, fine boned fingers held the spoon as he ate, movements neat and economical. There was also a stubborn thrust to his chin that Harry would have wagered got him into difficulty at times.

"So," Charles said, dabbing his mouth with his napkin. "How did you end up at my door, Harry?"

Harry finished chewing, and put his own bowl down. It bought him a little time. "I'm afraid I got myself hopelessly lost." Not a complete lie. His grandfather had always told him that if you must lie, stick as closely to the truth as you can.

"Easily done around here," Charles said with a smile, but his eyes were watchful.

"My horse threw me and ran so I tried to make it on foot. I was headed for the village of Hackness." Again, not a complete lie.

"If the snow lifts in the morning I can guide you to the village. It is not far." He passed Harry more of the of rich fruit cake.

"If it would not be too much trouble...?"

"Not at all."

Harry ate the cake, pondering a little. "Do you have my coat? I'd like to check that everything is still there."

Charlie arched an eyebrow and Harry felt himself flush with the sheer stupidity of the statement. He held up his hand as he chewed to swallow the mouthful of cake quickly.

"That sounded dreadful. I am so sorry, I never meant to infer that you..." He coughed a little and held his hand up to his mouth. "I collapsed on the road here and I am sure I felt someone..." He gestured vaguely.

Charlie smiled a little. "I see. I will fetch the coat."

"You don't have to do it immediately, please finish your food." Harry's heart was thumping. He needed to get his thoughts together. He was usually much better than this with people.

"It's no problem." Charlie said and left the room but the soft smile made Harry's heart thump even harder.

"Christ." He closed his eyes and used the moment to get try and get a lie straight in his head. How much could he share? Should he share anything at all? Would Charlie be quite so attentive if he knew the truth? He doubted it.

Charlie came back into the room and laid the coat gently across Harry's lap. Harry smiled his thanks and began rifling through the pockets which of course were empty. He let the searching become increasingly frantic and then he laid it down and put his head in his hands.

"What's wrong?" he heard Charlie ask.

"It's all gone," he whispered. "My money, papers, everything." He screwed up his eyes and to his surprise the tears that sprung there were genuine. He was sick and tired of running, sick and tired of looking over his shoulder. Sick and tired of having less than nothing, being less than nothing. He covered his eyes with his hand.

He felt Charlie kneel by his chair and take the coat gently from his hands. Harry lifted his head and stared at the man by his side. His eyes were really quite beautiful. Blue, clear and honest. And, at the moment, looking at him with such tenderness Harry wanted to weep again.

"Don't distress yourself. Whatever you need I can help you with."

"That's too much to ask." Harry whispered, hating himself.

Charlie reached out and brushed a finger over the corner of Harry's eye collecting a tear with a frown. "Please don't." He took Harry's hand in his. "Let me help you."

Harry wanted to die. Wanted to roll over and die. Either that or throw himself into Charlie's arms and tell him the whole sickening, sordid truth. Instead he nodded. He couldn't speak, so he just nodded and watched relief spread over Charlie's face materialising in a lovely, lopsided smile.

Chapter 5

CHARLES HELD HARRY'S slender hand in his and watched as he agonised. There was definitely something that he wasn't telling him, Charles was certain of that, but then Harry capitulated and agreed to accept his help. The relief that flooded him was enormous and the extent of it surprised him. There was something about Harry that called to him so strongly it frightened him.

"Would you like some brandy?" he said, extricating his hand from Harry's. He needed to break the contact.

"Thank you."

Charles poured two glasses and returned to his chair, handing one to Harry as he went.

"If you don't mind me asking, how old are you?" Charles settled himself in his chair and took a sip of the brandy before settling the glass neatly on the coaster and adjusting it so it was nicely central.

Harry smiled weakly. "I'm two and twenty. How

about you?"

"Ah, a mere youngster. Two and thirty."

Harry took a long drink of the brandy and closed his eyes as it slid down his throat. "Positively ancient," he said as he opened them again and they both laughed, restoring a lighter atmosphere.

"Do you live locally?" Charles asked. He was certain that the boy did not, he would have remembered him.

"No, I was travelling through to the coast."

"To Scarborough?"

Harry nodded and took another drink.

"Once the snow has lifted it should be quite easy to get you to Scarborough, it's only a couple of hours' drive. Have you relatives there?"

Harry hesitated a moment and then nodded. "Yes. I'm hoping for work."

"Then we shall have you restored to your family in no time." Charles raised his glass in salute. Scarborough. Not so far that he couldn't visit on occasion. He swallowed. What on earth was he playing at? Planning visits to a man he barely knew, who although he shared a similar nature wasn't necessarily attracted to him. Why would he be? Harry was young, stunningly handsome, and he was…well. He swirled his brandy in his glass. Women seemed to find him attractive but he wasn't terribly sure about men. Attempts at forming any sort of attachment had been awkward, and in all honesty, he had concluded that he was not very good with people and certainly not good at involving them in his life in any way. He certainly would not encourage anyone to rely on him. But if the boy did find him attractive…"

"Penny for them?" Harry said, jerking him from his

reverie and making colour rush to his cheeks. Harry smiled, then grinned knowingly, making Charles blush even more. Dear God, who was the boy here?

Charles cleared his throat, suppressing his own smile. "Did you say you were heading for Hackness?"

Harry's eyes sparkled in the firelight and a smile lingered on his lips. "Yes. I was hoping to hire a horse."

"Didn't you say your horse threw you?"

"It did. It was hired. I don't know what happened to it. I was trying to find somewhere to stay for the night but couldn't."

Charles looked at him and laughed a little. "No room at the inn?"

Harry stared for a moment and then broke into infectious laugher. "Indeed. My very own nativity. I presume that Hackness has an inn?"

Charles nodded, the smile lingering about his lips. "The Cock and Bottle," he said, reasonably straight faced.

Harry's eyes widened and a delighted smile lit his face. "Really?" He laughed. "I'd love to see the sign outside,"

"Cockerel. There is a picture of a cockerel on the front," Charles said with mock censure.

Harry let out a snort of laughter. "Not a…"

"No!"

They stared at each other and then dissolved into a bout of juvenile laughter. The more they laughed, the funnier it became. Charles scrubbed at his eyes and wondered when he had last laughed so much. He had a good ten years on Harry but he was shocked at just how much he liked sitting by the fire, making boyish jokes and listening to his laughter. Harry was still sniggering when Charles moved

The Wrong Kind of Angel 261

to refill their glasses and stoke up the fire. When Charles passed Harry his glass Harry's fingers managed to drift across his, and Charles felt the touch all the way to his bones. He couldn't remember the last time he had been touched, let alone held, and now his entire body ached. He wanted so much for Harry to stand up, take him in his arms, and hold him tightly, it was a physical pain. He rubbed his chest as he sat down.

"So, do you do anything, Charlie?"

Charlie. He let his eyes close for a moment. No-one called him Charlie except his sister. He pulled in a breath and smiled. "I collect snuff boxes and I write books."

Harry's face lit up. "What sort of books?"

"Adventures. I write stories about travelling the world and finding adventure. Do you read?"

"I do. My mother taught me. You must lend me one of your books. I'll tell you if it's any good."

Charles laughed. "Too kind."

The laughter subsided between them and drifted into a comfortable silence. Charles stared into the fire and sipped his brandy. After a while he looked over at Harry to find his head lolled to one side and his brandy glass tilted precariously. He was fast asleep. Charles moved soundlessly over to his chair and pulled the glass from his fingers. He never moved.

"Harry?" Charles said in a low voice, but he was sound asleep. "Oh, Harry," he said, touching a finger to his hair that had now dried into a mass of endearingly untidy dark curls.

❖

CHARLES LEFT HIM sleeping and went to bank the fire in the kitchen so it would burn through the night. He then went to his chamber and did the same and made a decision. He was going to invite Harry to share his bed. He closed his eyes at the thought. He had never spent the night with a man in his bed. Ever. He was going to do it. Fate had conspired to throw them together during the only short period of time in the year where he was completely alone, and if life had taught him anything it was to accept what was thrown at him. Good and bad. He took two hot bricks from the fire with the tongs and placed them in bed warmers. He slid one into each side of the bed and took a deep breath.

Chapter 6

HARRY WOKE WITH a start and for a moment wondered where he was. Shaking his head, he looked around but Charlie was nowhere to be seen. A large ginger cat sat on the rug by the fire, watching him with unblinking eyes. He got up and padded in his bare feet to the window. The snow was falling steadily in huge white flakes with the wind piling it up everywhere. There was nothing he could do tonight. He squeezed his eyes closed and tried to force back the panic that threatened to seize him. He could only pray for a thaw overnight. If Charlie was true to his word he could be on his way first thing and in Scarborough before luncheon. He'd have been there now if it were not for the miserable bastard who threw him off the stage when he realised he hadn't purchased a ticket. He'd thought he'd done a good job of shamming him, but clearly there had been something that aroused suspicion. At least he had got most of the way, and at least Julian should have made it to Scarborough by now. He just hoped to Christ that he was safe somewhere and had left word where to find him.

The door opened and Charlie came back. He was now dressed in a robe like the one that Harry wore, but Harry could see that he wore little beneath it. His breath caught at the sight of his naked throat and bare feet thrust into slippers. Oh God. Oh God oh God. Harry ached at the sight of him, and his cock was so hard it hurt. Beautiful Charlie. So good, so honest so…vulnerable. He had taken advantage of his good nature, lied to him…

"It's time we retired," Charlie said, not quite looking at him. Harry didn't speak.

"You can have my bed," he said, and then took a deep breath. "We could share it if you wish." He hesitated, still not looking at him. "But please don't feel obliged. You may not necessarily find me attractive…"

Harry almost broke in half. If he found him attractive? He was the most attractive man he had ever seen. Did Charlie not know this? He looked at him, looked at the muscle ticking along his jaw, his averted eyes, and he got his answer. Groaning, Harry marched over to him and pulled him into his arms. Charlie's arms came around him and held tight as he pushed his face into Harry's throat.

"Christ, Charlie, you are the most attractive man I've ever met."

"But?"

The words were muffled and Harry's heart heaved. "But there is so much you don't know about me. I am not a good person. I am…Charlie," Harry closed his eyes. "Charlie, I want nothing more than to spend the night in your bed but I must leave. I must leave in the morning." The words tumbled out of his mouth.

Charlie just held him tighter. "So you want me?"

Harry pressed his mouth to Charlie's neck for a moment. The man was ten years older than him but he felt like the older one. He pushed him away leaving him standing bewildered, arms slightly outstretched as though reaching for him. Harry stuck his chin in the air and tugged at the belt on his robe and let it fall open, revealing his painfully erect, leaking cock. He took hold of Charlie's unresisting hand and placed it on himself.

"Does that answer your question?"

Charlie's long slim fingers curled around him and Harry couldn't breathe properly. All the air had gone from the room. He took hold of the tie binding Charlie's robe and pulled. As he did so, Charlie let go of his cock and stood stock still, breath shallow. His hands were by his side, and his head down in an unconscious pose of trust and submission. Harry's mouth went dry. He took Charlie's face in both hands and kissed him hard, then, pulling back, slid the robe from Charlie's shoulders. It fell to the ground, leaving him naked. His body was pale, muscled, and peppered with an assortment of odd scars. Harry touched his finger to a particularly large one on his shoulder.

"How did you get these?"

Charlie swallowed. "Army."

Harry nodded and carried on cataloguing them with his fingers as he moved lower. His chest was hairless, but there was soft golden hair below his navel leading to his cock. Harry swallowed and sank gracefully to his knees. In one move he took him in his mouth.

Charlie shouted and gripped his shoulders probably to keep upright, and then the shout turned into a loud, agonised moan as he thrust gently into Harry's mouth. Harry was filled with him, overwhelmed by him. He breathed in the unique musky scent of him and squeezed his balls as he sucked him hard. He wanted to be gentle, to tease, and to arouse, but he couldn't. Part of him was angry with Charlie for making him feel, for making him regret the fact that he couldn't ever stay, but mostly was just so damned aroused he couldn't bear it. Seeing this handsome, aristocratic man so desperate for him, but asking not taking, begging not demanding, filled something inside him he hadn't really realised was empty.

He pulled his mouth off. "Do you have oil?"

Charlie was panting and shaking. He cleared his throat. "Robe. Pocket." Harry rifled through the pockets and came up with a glass bottle. Charlie sank to his knees, his legs apparently giving way. Harry unscrewed the glass and then hesitated. "How do you want this?"

Charlie just looked blank.

"Do you like to give or receive?"

A dark flush stained those angelic cheeks but Charlie held his gaze from his position on his knees. "Receive. Please," he whispered and Harry's heart felt too big for his chest.

"On all fours in front of the fire," he said and Charlie moved into position without a murmur. Harry looked at him. Kneeling in front of the roaring fire, light cascading over his pale skin, head down braced on his hands. He wondered how long it had been since he had given this to anyone.

He put the oil down carefully on the hearth and made himself go slow. He wanted this to be good. If this was the only chance he had to be with this man he wanted to make the most of it. He ran his hands down Charlie's back, shoulders to buttocks, and explored the texture of his skin, the shape of his muscles. Like his front his back was peppered with scars. Some large, some small. There was a wicked, long scar down his left thigh. He dropped a kiss on the base of his spine, making Charlie squirm. Harry took his hips in both hands and kissed a little lower and felt the shiver that ran through him. He parted his cheeks with his thumbs and Charlie went still. Absolutely still. Perhaps he wasn't ready for that.

"Breathe, sweetheart," he whispered when he realised the reason for Charlie's stillness. The man had stopped breathing.

Charlie's breath hitched and he trembled. "Please..." he whispered.

Harry poured oil into his hands and coated his cock, then ran his fingers down Charlie's crease. He rubbed gently, teasing his entrance until Charlie made a soft, desperate sound. He hesitated and toyed a little more and then inserted one finger; teasing, opening. Charlie made a sobbing sound, so he added another finger and stretched him before pushing both inside to rub against his spot. He found it and Charlie yelled aloud and pushed against his hand. "Now, now...please..." he panted.

Harry poured more oil on himself, determined not to hurt Charlie, and then pushed inside, bit by bit until he was fully seated and Charlie was moaning low and soft. He curled himself over Charlie's back, kissed his neck, and wrapped an arm around his chest.

"Are you ready?" he whispered in his ear.

Charlie nodded. Harry knelt up, held onto Charlie's shoulder and hip, and pulled out a little. This was not going to last long. Charlie's long, muscled body was vibrating with need and Harry was so lost, so gone that just...Oh God. He surged into Charlie and set up a punishing rhythm. Charlie's arms gave way and he sunk to his elbows and Harry followed, curving over him and pounding hard. His vision blurred and he knew he was close so he wrapped a hand around Charlie's cock and pumped it in time with his thrusting and then Charlie was shouting aloud and spending. Harry fucked him through it and then collapsed as his body emptied itself into Charlie in the longest, hardest orgasm of his entire life.

They collapsed onto the floor, Harry managing to roll off, wincing as he pulled free. Charlie lay on his stomach so he tugged him a little until his head lay on Harry's chest, his leg twined with Charlie's, and he held on for dear life. How in the name of all that was holy had he gone from thinking that the man was attractive, but that there was not possibility of anything between them, because he was sure that Charlie would want more than he could give, to rolling on the floor in the front of the fire with him. What the fuck was he to do now? As his arms curved protectively around Charlie he felt panicked as he wondered just whose heart might be in danger.

Chapter 7

CHARLES LAY SPRAWLED on Harry's chest. On the rug in front of the fire in his study. He couldn't move. Didn't want to move. Ever. The younger man had his arms around him tightly, possessively, and for the first time in his life he felt complete. Full; whole. It felt as though this was who he was, this was what he was meant to do. He was meant to love another man and there was nothing that would change that. He knew he couldn't keep Harry, he had made that plain, but that didn't stop the welling of feeling inside him. But they had the night, possibly the day tomorrow and he intended to make the very best of it before he too left him.

"Did I hurt you?" Harry whispered a little while later as he sifted gentle fingers through Charles' hair.

"No. It was wonderful. Thank you."

"So polite," Harry said with a soft laugh. "It was wonderful for me, too."

Charles ran a finger down Harry's naked chest and kissed his nipple, making him squirm.

"You are remarkable," Charles said softly. When Harry didn't reply, Charles squeezed him tighter. "Don't worry, I remember everything you said. I know you have to leave." He wriggled a little so he could lift his head and look up at him. Harry's eyes held wariness, tenderness…so many things. "I know it is just for tonight, so let's enjoy what we have."

"Truly?" Harry said with a small smile.

"Truly."

Harry's smile broadened. "Is there any more of that cake left?"

Charles stared at him a moment and then laughed, dropping his head onto Harry's beautiful chest and rubbed his face in the soft hair that dusted the space between his nipples.

"What?"

"Nothing. We shall eat cake by the fire. Naked."

"Best way if you ask my opinion," Harry said, shuffling around.

Charles got up and headed to the kitchen to seek out something to clean themselves with and brought the rest of the rich fruit cake with him and a platter of cheese.

"Here you go," he said, offering the bowl and towel to Harry, having cleaned himself.

Harry took it and tended to himself whilst Charles folded both robes and put them neatly on a chair, then cut more cake and poured more brandy. They pulled up armchairs in front of the fire by Harry's makeshift bed and sat themselves on the floor, leaning against them, and each other, wrapping the other blanket around their shoulders.

"This is the most wonderful Christmas," Charles said around a mouthful of cake. He held his hand to his mouth as he chewed and then smiled. "Snowed in with a magnificent cake and a beautiful man."

Harry laughed and leaned against him. "Snowed in with a magnificent cake and a beautiful angel." He settled his head against Charles shoulder and put his hand on his chest. Charles covered the hand with his own and lay his cheek against Harry's soft hair. They stayed like that for a while, just staring into the firelight, each lost in their own thoughts until Harry shivered.

"You're cold," Charles murmured, lifting Harry's hand to his lips.

"No, just someone walking over my grave."

"You can tell me, you know."

Harry fidgeted. "Tell you what?"

Charles looked down at him, laid so trustingly against him, naked and vulnerable. He smiled and kissed the top of his head. "You can tell me what troubles you, what had you running in the snow, what brought you to me."

Harry scrunched up. He drew his legs up tight and burrowed tighter against him. "There's nothing wrong."

In that moment the ten years between them felt like a hundred. Charles kissed his head again. "If you say so, but you can always talk to me. I would never judge you." He could feel the tension in Harry's body as they sat silent, but then he uncurled in a sinuously beautiful movement and rolled over to straddle Charles' lap. Charles caught him by the waist, a smile curving his lips as he watched Harry's erection grow.

"Oh, to be twenty again," he laughed. "Insatiable boy."

Harry's answering grin was wicked. He leaned

forward and put his hands on Charles' shoulder, his hair a wild mass of curls, his eyes endless, unreadable pools of darkness. He leaned forward and let his mouth hover over Charles', nipping at his lips. Charles moaned and reached up but Harry held himself just out of reach. He touched his lips to Charles' chin, his nose and Charles followed, trying to latch onto his mouth until he growled with frustration, grabbed Harry around the waist, and tumbled him onto his back. Harry went down laughing and let Charles grab his hands and pin them up over his head. He lay there, smiling, arms spread, and Charles' breath stuck in his chest. His heart squeezed so tight it hurt. He straddled Harry and put a finger in the centre of each of his palms, and then ran them gently down the tender skin of the underside of each arm, watching each finger in turn, touching, feeling; absorbing him. He touched the backs of his fingers to the hair under his arms and then ran his hands over his chest. Harry's breathing was uneven. Charles brought his gaze up to Harry's face. His eyes were wide, watchful; filled with an aching desire that was echoed in every part of Charles' body. He leaned down slowly and pressed his lips to Harry's, swallowing the soft moan. He kissed his eyes, his forehead, wanting to imprint every part of that beautiful face in his memory. Harry remained still and allowed his exploration for a little while, but then surprised Charles by grabbing them and flipping them over. Charles found himself on his back, a little winded, with Harry grinning down at him.

"Let's go to bed." He dropped a hard kiss on Charles' lips. "It's Christmas and I want my angel."

Charles ran his hands down Harry's sides and took his arse in both hands, massaging his taut cheeks. "Insatiable boy," he said again.

Harry growled. "I. Am. Not. A. Boy." Every word was punctuated with a kiss until they were both laughing. Harry languished against him for a moment and then jumped up and offered a hand. Charles let him pull him up and tow him out of the room. Charles glanced at the mess before the fireside and opened his mouth to speak, but took one look at Harry and abandoned it.

Chapter 8

THEY RAN THROUGH the house to the bedroom because it was bloody freezing. Harry kept hold of Charlie's hand as he ran behind him. It was a lovely house. Soft, thick carpet, shiny polished wood. It felt like a home. Something inside Harry ached. Charlie stopped outside what looked like a bedchamber door and turned. His face was soft in the candlelight, his hair pale.

"This is my chamber." He touched the door.

"Well, let's get in there. I'm freezing my cock off out here." He huddled against the warmth of Charlie's body and smiled when he was held tight.

"What?" he asked when Charlie didn't move.

Charlie kissed his temple. "I've never had a man in my house before, in my chamber, so I am savouring the moment."

Something akin to panic shivered down Harry's spine at the feeling of being...cherished. Of feeling cared for. He wrapped his arms around Charlie and, shaking the feeling away, held tight. Charlie kissed him gently again and then opened the door.

A blanket of warmth hit Harry as they slid into the room and closed the door quickly behind them. Along with the warmth came the scent of sandalwood and polish that he knew instantly he would always associate with Charlie. The sandalwood was Charlie, the polish; his house. The fire crackled and spat as he looked around. The room, like the rest of the house, was immaculate with everything lined up with military precision.

He spotted the large bed with two bed warmer handles sticking out. One each side. "Did you plan this?" he said, incredulous.

Even in the firelight Harry could tell that Charlie blushed furiously. He swallowed and gestured awkwardly. "I hoped." He nodded. "I just hoped you might..."

Harry moved closer. Firelight danced over Charlie's nakedness. "Hoped what?" he said and reached out to take hold of Charlie's hand, but he moved away rubbing the back of his neck.

"Nothing. I don't know, just...perhaps there might be...you might...want me." He headed towards the bed and began fiddling with the sheets.

Harry immediately went and stood behind him, wrapping his arms around him and holding him tight. He kissed the side of his neck and rubbed his nose against his ear.

"I do want you," he whispered. He closed his eyes and buried his face in the warmth that was Charlie. His heart beat was heavy. He sucked in a breath and turned Charlie so they could hold each other properly.

"I still have to go," he said, more for his own sake.

He felt Charlie smile. "I know. Probably for the best. I'm not very good with people. Best not to rely on me."

What the hell was that supposed to mean? Before Harry could ask he was swept up in Charlie's arms being kissed in a way that disconnected his brain. He gave up thinking and threw himself into a kiss that made his legs weak.

He pulled away panting. "We didn't bring the oil," he said.

"I have more oil there," Charlie said nodding to a bottle sat on the table beside the bed.

Harry grinned. Charlie flushed again and let go of him to remove the warming pans, then then they tumbled into the bed laughing and shivering until they found the warm parts.

"My feet are freezing," Harry said, trying to tuck them between Charlie's warmer ones. Charlie yelped and a skirmish ensued that left them both sweating and laughing. They huddled under the blankets and explored soft skin, hard muscle, and aching cocks. When Harry was happy that Charlie was close to the edge, he reached out for the oil. When Charlie started to roll over he stopped him.

"I want to do it facing you," he whispered. "I want to see you."

Charlie hesitated.

"Like this," Harry said, pulling a pillow down so he could stuff it beneath Charlie's backside and settle himself in the space between his thighs.

Charlie looked serious as he reached up and took Harry's face between his hands. He sighed.

"My beautiful boy."

"My beautiful angel," Harry replied and they kissed for a moment.

Harry applied the oil to his hands and found Charlie's entrance, making him moan. He stretched and rubbed until Charlie was writhing beneath him.

"Pull your legs right up," he murmured as he oiled his cock. He daren't touch it too much he was so close. He wasn't sure how long he could last.

"Right up," he said, positioning Charlie's hands to hold up his thighs. "That way it won't hurt."

"Hurry," Charlie whispered, "please hurry."

Harry lined himself up and eased in, suddenly conscious that he might be sore from before. He rocked himself gently, watching his face.

"Tell me if it hurts. Are you sore?"

"It's perfect," Charlie whispered.

CHARLES HELD TIGHT. Held tight to the man, the moment, and the pleasure that rippled through every fibre of his being. There was nothing in the world that would ever compare to being filled by Harry Valentine. Harry's face was pressed against his neck and he could feel the tremors that rippled through him. Cocooned in the warmth of the bed, confined by the blankets and firelight, it felt as though they were in their own, private place where no-one or nothing could intrude. He let his hands roam down Harry's back, his buttocks, his shoulders until Harry started to move. Gently at first, slowly, making each thrust long and deep as though he was memorising every second in exactly the way that Charles was. Harry's lips found his and they kissed. Harry's tongue delved into his mouth just as his cock delved into his body and Charles took him in. All of him—and felt claimed.

Someone wanted him, someone needed him. As Harry's thrusts grew harder, faster, shorter, Charles waited for him to find that spot inside that lit up the world and when he did he cried out long and loud, moaning and writhing, thrusting to meet Harry until he spent so hard, the darkness closed in on him for a moment. He felt Harry go rigid and heard him shout as he emptied himself, body and soul, into Charles. Sweating and panting they clung to each other as though the other were the only other person in the world, the only other person that mattered.

CHARLES CLEANED HIMSELF and then tended to his lover. His lover. He liked that. He climbed back into the bed and settled his head on Harry's chest. Those hard arms came about him and he closed his eyes.

"That was the most amazing...Christ, Charlie, I'm almost dead," Harry said.

Charles just held him tighter.

"Did I hurt you? You must have been sore from last time; I should have thought..."

"Harry, I am fine. Truly." It was the truth. He was. His body was perfectly fine but his emotions felt stripped raw and flayed.

"Oh, Charlie," he murmured nuzzling his head. "Do you mind me calling you Charlie?"

Charles thought about it for a moment, trying to push back the feelings that the name evoked.

"Charlie is fine. It's just..." he hesitated. "My sister used to call me Charlie."

He felt Harry shift so that he could look down at him. "Used to?"

Charles stared at his chest, tracing a pattern with his finger. "Yes. She died."

Harry was quiet for a moment. "I'm so sorry," he whispered. "Was it recent?" His hands stroked Charles' back.

Charles shook his head. "Carriage accident. I was ten, she was eight." He forcibly beat back the terror that threatened to consume him. "Mother and Father died, too."

"Were you with them?"

Charles felt like he was drowning. "Yes. Lucky to survive." It was hard to breathe. He couldn't quite believe he had told Harry. That he had allowed the memory to surface. He couldn't move. He felt Harry's arms tighten about him, felt his lips in his hair.

"I couldn't save them. It took them a while to find us." Charles was back in the carriage, listening to the terrified horses screaming, listening to his father...

"Oh, love," Harry whispered into his hair.

The darkness, the sounds, the fear all bubbled up out of nowhere and swamped him. He tried to push it back, but before he could the tears started leaking from his eyes. He tried to stop them, shamed by them, but Harry kissed them and that opened the floodgates and Charles, for the first time in his life, wept for his lost family, and for himself.

When the storm subsided, he lay quiet in Harry's arms. Harry was still gently stroking him and every now and then would kiss the top of his head.

"Sorry," he murmured, and tried to move away.

Harry held tight. "Stay there."

They lay in silence for a while. Charles was drained. Completely drained. Emotion was not something that he dealt with on a regular basis, in fact, his life was ordered specifically to avoid it, but laying in Harry's arms he found he could think about his sister and parents without feeling like he was going to fall into some unnamable, inescapable void.

Charles moved a little and looked up at Harry in the firelight. "I think you should call me Charlie."

Chapter 9

HARRY HELD CHARLIE as he slept and wiped the tears from his own face. He trailed a finger down Charlie's back, wondering at the network of scars and his life as a soldier. He didn't look like a soldier, but that didn't mean anything. He kissed Charlie's head and closed his eyes. He couldn't even begin to imagine how young Charlie had felt losing his whole family like that, but having held the man in his arms as he wept, he felt connected to him in a way he couldn't explain and felt ill-equipped to deal with. Every moment that he spent with Charlie made him feel torn. He needed to get back on the road to Scarborough, but he couldn't shake the feeling that his angel needed him.

He dozed a little, keeping one eye on the huge clock on the mantel that was just about visible in the firelight. He needed to watch the weather and be out of the house and on the road as soon as the snow let up. He needed to keep ahead and could only pray that the snow had held up his pursuers in the same way.

He needed to get to Scarborough and get to Julian. The only chance that he had of doing that was in a carriage and with money. There were two ways that he could accomplish that. He could steal from Charlie. He could take his horse and carriage, steal some money...the thought of doing that was so abhorrent it made him shudder. A few hours ago he would have done it without a backward glance. The other way was to tell all. Tell him everything. The whole sordid story of his life and beg him to help. He was fairly sure that Charlie was goodhearted enough to make sure he got to Scarborough, but once he knew the truth? Well, that would most certainly put paid to anything that there might have been between them. He squeezed his eyes shut. Who was he fooling? There could never be anything between them. For a start, Charlie was a toff and he was from the gutter. Moreover, and more importantly, they were men. Men were not allowed to love men. He would never be able to have a family with another man. His kind were not even deemed fit to live amongst decent people; not fit to live. He was not the kind of man who had Christmas miracles. He was the wrong kind of man.

Charlie stirred and then seemed to go quite still. Harry swallowed. He hoped that he didn't regret it. Men got funny when they regretted sexual congress with another man and seldom wanted to be faced with their transgression. Charlie's head came up. He blinked a couple of times and then his face dissolved into that beautiful, shy, lopsided smile and Harry relaxed.

"Did I lean on you the whole night?" Charlie whispered.

"You did."

"That must have been damnably uncomfortable," he said, not moving.

"Not a bit." They smiled at each other. Soft morning smiles that held the reflection of the night before, flushed cheeks that recalled the pleasure and rekindled the delight.

Charlie moved off him. Harry followed and rolled him onto his back. He pulled the blankets around them as he did so because the fire had dwindled to almost nothing and there was a distinct chill. Charlie went willingly and opened his legs so that Harry could lay between them and then wrapped his arms around him.

"Your turn to lean on me," Charlie whispered, his eyes serious, inviting and filled with something that looked frighteningly like tenderness.

Harry groaned and ignored the double meaning. He leaned down to kiss him and they stayed like that for an age. Kissing. Just kissing. It was so damned intimate. More intimate than the scorching pleasure they had engaged in the previous night, more satisfying that any fucking that Harry had ever engaged in. Just a man, holding him tight, kissing him, and offering himself without wanting anything in return.

Charlie's hands were in his hair, holding his head. Harry moved a little so he could bring his own hand between their bodies. He lined up their cocks and took them both in one hand and as the kissed, he stroked. Their rhythms became intertwined and softly, gently, intimately they held together and as Harry's crisis neared, he pulled his mouth away.

"Open your eyes and look at me."

Charlie's eyes opened. Serious and intent. Harry

kept on stroking hard until Charlie's eyes started to flutter and his body tensed and then Harry kissed him again before he spent. Harry followed moments later.

They lay in the cold and the mess and Harry knew he could not put it off any longer.

"There is something I want to tell you, but we should dress first. You'll get cold." Harry glanced down at Charlie who lay beneath him, eyes wide and unblinking. Harry felt ill.

"Why don't you tell me here? We can clean up and..."

"No. Let's get up." Harry knew that when he told Charlie the truth he would not want to be naked in bed with him covered in his spend. As much as he wanted to hide under the blankets, for Charlie's sake he needed to be up and dressed.

Charlie swallowed, leaned up, and pressed a kiss to his jaw. "Very well." He threw back the covers and strode naked across the room. He threw more wood on the fire and then stood shivering by washing stand as he cleaned himself up as the fire crackled and smoked a little. When Charlie had done, Harry got up and cleaned himself, too.

Charlie went through a door in the corner of the room and came back holding an assortment of clothes. "Here you go. They should fit. Yours were in a bit of a mess."

Harry took them. The clothes were simple but handsomely made, unlike his own. Charlie disappeared back into the small room so Harry dressed quickly. They were a little loose, apparently Charlie had more muscle than he did. He was messing with the cravat in the mirror and making a hash of it when Charlie came back looking terribly tidy and handsome. He smiled and took hold of the ends, then stood behind him to tie it.

"We look like a couple of tulips," Harry said to Charlie's reflection in the mirror with a smile.

"We do. You do realise that it is only five o'clock, don't you?"

Harry nodded. He took Charlie's hand and kissed it, then walked to the window. He took a breath and pushed back the curtain. He prayed that they were so snowed in no-one would be able to get to him for months. Well. That was one Christmas wish that wasn't going to be answered. There was still a significant amount of snow drifted about the house and the countryside, but it was starting to rain rather than snow. Harry felt guilty as he thought of Julian stranded in Scarborough and waiting for him. Charlie came up beside him.

"Should be gone soon," he said.

Harry squeezed his eyes shut but opened them before he turned around. "Let's eat. I'm starving."

Charlie lifted his hand and cupped Harry's cheek. "You can tell me anything. Just take your time."

Time. He didn't have time. He had no time at all. He trooped after Charlie miserably as they headed for the kitchen.

Charlie made a pot of tea and put some bread to toast and then dropped some eggs into a pan. He mixed the eggs and moved the bread like an expert.

"You've cooked before," Harry said as he watched.
"Army."
Harry huffed a laugh. "You can tell."
"How so?"
"Scars all over you, neat and fussy."
Charlies scowled. "I am not fussy."
"If you say so." Harry had to laugh. He was the

fussiest person he knew. Nothing was left out of place. "I'll wager you thought I hadn't noticed you tidying up all the time."

Charlie shot him an amused glance and scooped the eggs out of the pan and divided it onto two plates. He plastered the toast with butter and then disappeared into what looked like a pantry and returned with a platter of roast ham. He put generous helpings onto each plate and then put one down in front of Harry. It looked divine.

Charlie sat opposite. He lifted his cup of tea in salute so Harry followed suit. "Merry Christmas."

Harry smiled and clinked his cup with Charlie's. "Merry Christmas."

They ate in silence and Harry appreciated Charlie not putting pressure on him to speak. He was trying to work out a way to explain that wouldn't end up with Charlie hating him, but concluded that there wasn't one. He put the toast down.

"I stole money." He looked at his hands on the table as he said it.

"How much?"

"Two hundred and fifty pounds. Well, I didn't exactly steal it, I owe it, but I ran away."

Charlie was watching him but his eyes were unreadable. He had no idea what he was thinking. "Men are chasing me for the money. I managed to get on the stagecoach from London to Scarborough, but they realised I hadn't paid and threw me off a few miles back."

Charlie nodded. "You didn't have enough money with the two hundred and fifty?"

Harry's head drooped a little lower. "No. I stole some more for the stagecoach fare and..." Harry felt sick.

Charlie reached over the table and took his hand. "Do you want to borrow it?"

Harry looked up, Charlie's instant kindness almost breaking him. "Oh, Charlie that's just the start of it…" He squeezed Charlie's hand. "When I tell you the rest you won't…"

Before he could say more a banging on the kitchen window made them both leap apart guiltily. Charlie was on his feet immediately, but Harry was frozen to the spot at the maniacally grinning face in the kitchen window.

"Don't let him in!" Harry leaped up, knocking over his chair with a clatter and grabbed Charlie's arm. "Don't let him in…"

Chapter 10

CHARLES STARED AT the faces at the window for a second and then turned to Harry.

"Calm yourself. Who are they?"

Harry was shaking, his eyes wide and terrified. "I can't believe they found me here. How did they find me here?"

"I have no idea. Tell me who they are."

Harry flinched as the man banged on the window again and shouted. "They've been sent by the man I owe money to. Dante sent them."

"Dante is the man that you owe money to?"

Harry nodded.

Charles looked at the men in the window. He had no idea how the bastards had found him, but there were not getting Harry.

He pulled his shoulders back and stared at them. "You must go to the front of the house," he shouted through the window.

The response was abusive but Charles ignored it. After some shouting and gesturing they set off grudgingly, so Charles ran for the study with Harry on his heels. He grabbed a key from the drawer of his desk and opened his cabinet. Inside was his brace of pistols. He checked them. Both were primed and ready and in perfect condition. He lifted his coattails and shoved one down the back of his breeches.

"Can you fire a pistol?"

Harry looked horrified. "No."

"Fair enough." He shoved the other beside it and grabbed his knives. "Put this inside your coat where you can get to it." He secreted his own throwing knife and then gestured for Harry to follow. He spoke over his shoulder as he opened his safe. "You came to me to get the money you owe. Right?"

Harry stared. "Harry. Listen to me. You came to me to get the money. This is what I will tell them and then I will give them the money." He held up a pile of notes and then shut the door and closed the cupboard.

"Charlie, they are dangerous—I mean really dangerous," Harry said, apparently coming to life. He grabbed his arm, genuine fear in those dark eyes. "Let me deal with them. You don't have to do this. All they want is me. I will hand myself over to them and they will go. Charlie, you can't get involved. I can't let you get involved in this. I can't let them hurt you. We are outnumbered."

Charlie took his hand and kissed the back of it. "This is my home." He didn't feel the need to say anything else.

HARRY COULD ONLY stare at the man who stood before

him, arming himself and preparing to take on Dante's men for him. His gentle, charming angel had transformed into the soldier that he apparently was. Charlie stalked into the hall, flung open the door, and stood looking at the men. Harry's heart sank. Bill Mosely. Bill Mosely hated him with a passion and would gladly take any opportunity to disembowel him. With him were two men that he had seen at Dante's but didn't really know. All of them were big, ugly, and hard. They didn't stand a chance.

Charlie looked them up and down. "You must be the three wise men?"

Absurdly, Harry wanted to laugh. He put his hand to his mouth.

"Funny man," snarled Mosely as he barged his way in with the other two following. Mosely was big but it was all fat. He was probably ten years older than Charlie, but he was a nasty bastard through and through.

"Hold it there," Charlie said, holding up a hand. Something in his voice registered with them because they stopped. Harry wondered if Charlie had been a general or something. "I presume you have come for the money?" he said.

The men looked at each other and then Mosely grinned. "Nice work, Harry lad."

Charlie ignored the comment, but Harry went cold. Clammy sweat coated his skin. "From what Harry tells me three hundred should cover what is owed."

"Selling yourself short, Harry lad?" Mosely said and then turned to Charlie. "Three hundred what he owes and then another three for the service he done you." Mosely sneered.

"Fucking molly," he spat, looking Charlie up and down. "A round thousand will keep us quiet. We saw you."

Chapter 11

CHARLES' HEAD WAS racing but he remained absolutely calm. Service? He watched the men carefully. They were hard men, of that there was no doubt and there was only one way to deal with that in his book. They were outnumbered, but Charles had the advantage of surprise.

"Are you threatening me?" Charles asked with a smile.

The big man grinned and glanced back at the other two. "You could say that. I don't believe you've spent the night with Harry without fucking him, he's one of our best whores, so I want the money for the service because that belongs to Dante as surely as if you'd fucked him in the brothel, and some to keep my mouth shut."

Charles looked at Harry. He was frozen. His face was a mask of horror. Charles didn't want to think about how much truth might be in the man's words, but he wasn't prepared to be blackmailed in his own home.

"Well, now," he said rubbing his chin. "That's a shame."

"What's a shame, molly boy?" The man grinned.

"I was quite willing to give you the three hundred." He took the notes out of his pocket, waved them at the man but then put them back. "But now I'm going to have to kill you."

He said it in a very matter of fact way, but at the same time pulled one of the pistols from his waist, pointed it at the man, and fired.

The sound in the confines of the hall was deafening, and the smoke almost choked them. The man screamed and went down. It was only a flesh wound to the arm, but it would take him a moment or two to realise that. The other two men shouted as he pulled out the second pistol and his throwing knife. One swift, hard throw and it was embedded in the thigh of one, and he pointed the pistol at the heart of the other.

"Get out of my house." He didn't raise his voice.

The uninjured one dragged his comrades as they scrambled and staggered out and Charles slammed the door behind them and threw the bolt.

HARRY'S LEGS ALMOST gave way. He had never seen anything like it in his life. Bill Mosely, Dante's brutal muscle, reduced to a quivering mass of tears and snot by the quiet, unassuming man standing before him. Charlie looked at him for a moment. It was a searching look, but then he took him by the arm and led him back to the study.

"I think you had best tell me all. They will no

doubt be back."

Harry crumpled into the chair by the fireside and ran a hand over his face, closing his eyes for a moment as he steeled himself.

"From the beginning? We may not have a lot of time," Charlie prompted.

Harry sucked in a breath, straightened his spine, and stared into the fire. His head and ears were still ringing with the spectacle that he had just witnessed. He looked up at Charlie, seeing him in a new light, but he needed to pull himself together. It was time for the truth no matter what it cost. The words came out in a tumble.

"My father died in the war and my mother took up with another man. I hated him and he hated me. I kept out of his way and worked on a farm in the summer and in inns where I could find work in the winter. I gave as much to my mother as I could, and kept myself to myself." He paused and steadied his breathing and clenched his hands into fists to stop them shaking. "For as long as I…I always…" he coughed. "I like men. Always have. My stepfather caught me with another man." He nodded. "Caught me." The memory of it robbed him of words. He couldn't look at Charlie. "He wasn't big enough to take me on, I was almost twenty by then, so he waited and got friends. They set on me and…yes…well…I nearly died." He sucked in another breath. "Anyway, he told the whole village and I was run out with no money. Everyone I'd ever known, friends…they…" He cleared his throat.

"I went to London and looked for work and a place to stay but the city was full of men looking for work after the war and, after I almost starved, I worked out that men will pay me to fuck them, or to let them fuck me. So that's what I did."

"I see," Charlie said softly and Harry couldn't even begin to work out what he meant by that.

"Then I met a man. He was handsome and kind, and he said he would look after me. He took me off the street to his club. It was a club where rich men went and paid for a night with another man in safety and comfort, not down the back of an alley. At first, they gave me rich, young, handsome men to entertain which was no real hardship at all. They gave me a beautiful room, food and clothes, champagne, and they gave me money to gamble with." Harry rubbed the back of his neck. "And I gambled. Hell, did I gamble."

He fell silent for a moment, and risked a glance at Charlie, who had sat himself on the other chair facing the fire. He was watching him carefully, but his expression was blank so Harry couldn't tell what he was thinking. He carried on. "So then, when I was completely sucked into the life they gave me, he told me how much I owed him. Said I had a gambling debt, but that it would all be right as ninepence because I could work for him and pay him back. He took back all the money that I had earned, moved me into a tiny room in the attic and I shared with a couple of other chaps that were in the same position. It was damp and cold, and then all I got was dirty, stinking old men. He gave me pennies and I had to feed myself from that although they gave me decent clothes."

"So he lured you in and then turned the screw?" Charlie said.

"Exactly. I was stuck owing a sum of money that I could never hope to pay back. I ran away a few times but they always found me because everyone knows Dante and is terrified of him. The last time I ran they…if I thought the beating my mother's husband gave me was bad…" He shuddered at the memory. "They gave me to Bill Mosely, the man you shot just now…" Harry couldn't speak any more.

"I wish I had known. I would have shot him in the heart," Charlie said in a conversational tone that made Harry blink.

"Anyway, it didn't take me long to realise that was what they did because I saw it happen time and time again. They lured in young men who had nothing, and then trapped them. I tried to warn a couple but they didn't believe me." He rubbed a finger over the leather of the chair arm and watched its progress. "Anyway," he said after taking a couple of deep breaths. "I worked out that I could get out and get out of London. I thought about going to Leeds but decided that would probably be even worse. I friend of mine went to work on the fishing boats in Scarborough so I decided to head for there. I'd always wanted to see the sea." He glanced up at Charlie but looked back down. "The stagecoach runs from London; takes a day or two, so I managed to steal enough money for a ticket, a few shillings in my pocket, and I had it all planned. I was on the verge of leaving when…" He swallowed. "When they brought in Julian."

Harry wasn't sure, but Charlie seemed to tense. Harry looked over at him, remembered fury burning his stomach as he sought the words to explain to Charlie just how sordid, how dreadful his life was. In the end, he could only state the truth.

"Julian is twelve. His balls haven't even dropped." Harry said and looked at his lap. I hadn't realised that they made boys—" he gestured, "—but they did." Harry covered his eyes for a moment and then looked up at Charlie. "They had done pretty much the same to him, and he was horribly battered about." Harry shook his head. "Anyway, they brought him back in the day I ran, so I took him with me. I grabbed him and ran."

"What happened?"

"Well, I patched him up as best I could so he didn't look too bad, but I only had one stagecoach ticket, and not enough money for another, but with a bit of flummery we managed to make it look like we had two and off we went. Thought I'd done a good job, but then the driver realised he had more passengers than had paid and it was either me or Julian. So I left him on the coach; told him to get to Scarborough and wait for me. Told him to leave a message at the inn at the end of the route and I set off on foot. I was going to see if I could steal a horse or beg a ride, but then it started to snow so badly I could hardly see and it was so cold." He shuddered, remembering the fear that had gripped him when the thought he was going to freeze to death. I thought I'd had it until I saw the light in your window."

Charles looked a little pale. "How did they track you to here?" he asked.

"I have no idea, but if they found me they may well have worked out where Julian was going." Realisation only sank in as he said it and it made his heart lurch. "I have to go…" He stood and hesitated. "Charlie, you have given me so much already, but if you could loan me a horse…?"

Charlie stood up and came to stand in front of him. He looked into his eyes for a moment, making Harry anxious, and then seemed to come to a decision. "I will take you. I have a carriage that is heavy enough to get through the snow. We had better get ready."

Harry was almost open mouthed. "I can't ask that of you," he said, reaching out to touch his arm.

"You didn't. I offered." Charlie looked him square in the eye and gave a small smile. "We need to get a move on."

"But..."

"But what?"

Harry didn't know what to say. Charlie had listened to the whole sordid story and was standing there as if he had said nothing. He wondered if he had misunderstood.

"Charlie, don't you understand? I'm a prostitute, a whore," he said gently.

Charlie frowned. "Did you fuck me for money and to persuade me to help?"

Harry thought for a moment and pursed his lips. "No. The thought crossed my mind that I probably could, but I decided that you were too decent. I decided not to, decided that I wouldn't, but then..." Harry's breath hitched a little at the memory. "When you wanted me...I couldn't..." He covered his eyes with his hand. "Christ, Charlie, it has never been like that with anyone. No-one ever wanted me, needed me like you did."

Charlie's frown lifted. "Well then. Let us head for Scarborough and hope we find Julian before Mosely does. And let's hope for his sake he never crosses my path again." The last was said with utter determination.

Chapter 11

CHARLES PILED BLANKETS into the back of the carriage along with his reloaded pistols, his rifle, and shotgun. He added a basket of food for them just in case, and left a plate of meat for the cat. Shivering, he checked the horses and decided that all was in order and they needed to leave. He was doing a good job of not thinking too closely about what Harry had said. He couldn't deny that the thought of Harry in that situation shook him badly. The thought of Harry with other men made his gut hurt almost unbearably and he couldn't put a name to the feeling that this new knowledge flooded him with, but he had been an innocent boy lured into something beyond his understanding and entrapped. He had heard of Dante's; it was an extremely exclusive club in London but he hadn't realised that it catered to his kind as he had never been there. The thought of paying for someone to...well, that had always left him feeling a little cold.

He also found that he was deeply moved by Harry's actions to remove the child from the brothel. Sometimes he seemed terribly young, but at other moments more of a man that most would ever be. What saddened him was the exuberance and affection that had been so evident over the last day was were completely gone. He was despondent and low. Charles patted the horse one last time and then headed back into the house.

"Chin up," he said as Harry cleared away the last of the breakfast dishes neatly. He even understood Charles' need for order.

"It's up," he said with a weak smile.

Charles felt awkward. That easy affection had been blown away by the intervention of Mosely and his henchmen, and Harry's tale. Where they had been warm, comfortable, and affectionate they were now awkward and he didn't quite know how to regain that closeness and companionship. He had no idea how Harry would react if he tried to kiss him. He moved closer and Harry looked ready to weep. His eyes were glassy. Charles lifted an arm and awkwardly touched his cheek with the back of his fingers and watched Harry's eyes flutter closed. He reached in and kissed him on the mouth. It was a clumsy, closed mouthed kiss but it seemed to galvanise something in Harry who moaned softly and wrapped his arms around him and held him tightly. Charles pressed his face into Harry's neck. This was what he needed. To be held so tightly it hurt by those hard, wiry arms.

"Oh Charlie," Harry choked. They stayed like that for a moment and then parted awkwardly. Charles patted his arm and they headed for the stable.

❖

HARRY SAT HUDDLED in his borrowed clothes next to Charlie who drove at a fair clip. He pulled his hat lower to keep the icy wind off his eyes. It was the most stunningly beautiful morning. They had eventually left the house at around half past six, and Charlie said it would take around two hours to get to Scarborough. The snow and rain had stopped and the sky was clear. So clear that the stars seemed to go on endlessly. Everywhere was eerily quiet, the sound dampened by the covering of snow. As Charlie moved the horses steadily on Harry could do nothing more than sit beside him and lean on him to try and share some of the warmth from his body, and listen to the crunch of the wheels as they drove.

Charlie's coat was a huge, many-caped affair and he had loaned him a similar one. He had wrapped a scarf around his throat, covering his mouth and nose. Harry had done the same, so they no doubt looked a peculiar sight as they trotted through the snowy lanes. They covered the first hour of the journey pretty much in silence, but it wasn't an uncomfortable one. Harry felt that Charlie needed a little quiet, and he felt that he had probably said quite enough.

"Would you like to get out of the cold for a short while? We could have something to eat?" Charlie asked after a few more miles. It was still dark, but the sky had the beginning of a pinkish glow as though sunrise was struggling to push its way through the darkness. Pretty as it was, the cold wind was biting and becoming unbearable, so Harry was glad of the suggestion.

"Only if you do."

Charlie found a spot on the road that was wide enough for them to pull over without causing any kind of obstruction, not that they had seen another coach or traveller at all, and jumped down and tethered the horses to a handy tree.

"If you look in the back there is a basket of food. We can shelter for a little while, warm up, and get something to eat. If we get back on the road quickly we could be in Scarborough not long after sunrise, probably around half past eight or so."

Harry jumped down and clambered into the back. The interior of the carriage was dark, but sheltered. It felt marginally less freezing and it was certainly a huge relief to get out of the wind. Charlie heaved himself in and the whole thing rocked, but they got settled side by side and Charlie delved into the basket and pulled out bread and the last of the ham from breakfast. They ate in silence.

When they had finished, Charlie packed the wrappings neatly and placed them in the basket. Harry put a hand on his arm.

"I have no notion of how I will ever repay all you have done for me, but I will. You have my word on that. I will find a way." He meant it. Meant every word.

"There is really no need," Charlie said.

Frustration ate at Harry. They were bundled up so much he couldn't get near to him. He wanted to hold him, kiss him…he was so quiet. Harry was desperate to know what he was thinking. He pulled his hands free of the gloves that he wore and managed to slide one hand around Charlie's jaw. He felt him jump.

"Charlie," he whispered and leaned as close as the carriage would allow. He brushed his lips against the corner of this mouth and after a moment Charlie turned, caught his face in his gloved hand, and brought their mouths together. They kissed gently. Charlie was the first to pull away, but he leaned his forehead against Harry's.

"Do you hate me?" Harry said. Their breath formed little clouds between them in the cold.

Charlie shook his head. "No." The word came out on a puff of air and something inside Harry uncurled a little. He breathed heavily and closed his eyes.

"We must go," Charlie said, but didn't move. Harry leaned on him for a moment and then pulled away. They got out of the carriage and settled themselves on the seat. Harry pulled his gloves back on and pulled his hat down.

Chapter 12

THE SUN WAS rising as they neared Scarborough. The town lay in the east, so they watched the sky fill with winter fire on what was the most peculiar Christmas morning Charles had ever experienced. Harry leaned on him and he was grateful for the warmth and company. His face was freezing and he was cold to the bone and he had no doubt Harry was, too. He glanced at his companion who sat upright as the fields gave way to the town. The air was filled with the smells of salt and seaweed and as they came into the town and drove to the cliff where the stage would alight they had the most magnificent view. They could see the sea crashing against the beach far below them, filling the air with noise and spray, and the ruins of the ancient castle that sat high on a headland guarding the town that curved around the bay. Harry's face was a delight.

"Have you ever been to the coast?" Charles asked.

"No. Never seen the sea." Harry wasn't looking at him.

"Good view?"

Harry turned and grinned. "Very."

They pulled into the Bell Inn on Bland's Cliff, the hooves clattering over the cobbles as they slowed into the yard. Charles was pleased to navigate the tight bend without scraping the carriage.

"We are probably best starting here as this is where the stage usually lands. The mail coach, too." Charles jumped down and handed the reins over. Harry landed beside him and as the horse and carriage were led away they made for the inn.

"They do the most delicious breakfast here," Charles said.

Harry nodded. "Do you think they will today? It is Christmas, after all."

"Let's see?"

They were headed for the entrance when Harry caught his arm. "Listen," he said, tilting his head. Charlie listened to the crashing of the waves below them. The air tasted of salt and the shriek of the seagulls above them became deafening. Harry turned delighted eyes to him. Charles wanted to take him in his arms and listen with him and share his joy, but they were in public so he gave him a pat on the arm and walked on.

The door was open so they both walked in, removing their hats and pulling off gloves as they got inside. The inn was warm and welcoming, and there were a few people sitting around. Charles walked up to the bar and a man appeared with a huge smile.

"Sirs, season's greetings. What can I do for you?" He wiped his hands on a white apron. Charlie arranged breakfast and coffee for them whilst Harry found a seat by the window near the fire and where he could watch people walk past, and no doubt see the sea.

"Happy Christmas," Charlie said as he sat himself opposite.

"Happy Christmas," Harry said and his face softened into a beautiful smile. His eyes were warm and his smile tender.

Charlie glanced around. "You probably shouldn't smile at me like that," he said. He hated to say it, but Harry's face was so expressive at times.

Harry ducked his head. "Sorry."

"Don't apologise."

When breakfast was served, they were called to a huge table where they had the company of several other travellers. A large dog positioned itself hopefully by Harry's leg, and the proprietor brought out platters of food. Charles watched Harry eat freshly baked rolls and local shrimps. His own stomach seemed to be tied firmly into a knot and was lodged firmly under his breastbone. He toyed with a piece of ham and drank some coffee. Where they hell did they go from here? He was surprised how strong the need to make things right for Harry was. He needed to find the boy, restore that smile to Harry, and be sure that he was safe from the brutality that he had endured. Equally as strong was the notion that he did not want to lose Harry, but for the life of him couldn't think of a single thing to offer to induce him to stay. He turned when he realised that Harry was speaking.

"I'm going to speak to the landlord and see if Julian left me a message."

Charles nodded. Harry folded his napkin and put it on his plate and headed off towards the bar.

Charles took a drink of his coffee and waited. The room was pleasant and everyone in high spirits. They had exchanged season's greetings with their breakfast companions and branches of holly decorated the table. Charles was amused to see a sprig of mistletoe tied to the candelabra. He took another sip of his coffee and imagined that he could kiss Harry under it.

At the far end of the table was a young couple. A young man, probably not much older than Harry, with his pretty young wife. Every now and then they would steal loving glances at each other, and share shy smiles. Charles was fairly sure that they held hands under the table, playing with each other's fingers. They tilted their heads together as they spoke and she smiled shyly up at him, eyes filled with affection and warmth, much as Harry's had been earlier. The intimacy between them plain for all to see. How wonderful it must be to show the affection that was held in one's heart without fear. Harry's one tender look in his direction had been enough to have them thrown out, or much, much worse. He stared into the depths of his cup.

"They have no word," Harry said as he sat back down. "Nothing. The stage coach came in, but he does not recall a young man and certainly no message has been left." Worry was etched into his face and Charlie was at a loss to know what to suggest.

"What did you tell Julian to do?" he asked.

"I said to leave word as to his whereabouts. I gave him all the money that I had, but..." He ran his hands through his hair.

"Come. Try not to worry. Let's see if we can take rooms here and then we can start looking for him."

❖

CHARLES SHOOK OUT his clothes, hung them neatly, and placed his shaving equipment by the washstand in a neat line. He paused by the window. The view out over the sea was beautiful. He hoped Harry and an equally good vista. The room was warm thanks to a fire roaring in the grate, and clean. The whole place had that soft, underlying smell of hops and polish that alehouses did, but all in all the facilities were acceptable. A soft knock at the door interrupted his thoughts.

"Can I come in?" Harry said with a smile as Charles opened the door. He stood back to allow him through.

"My room is wonderful. I can see the sea," he said.

"Mine, too."

Charles was startled to realise how much he wanted to share a room with Harry. Share his joy at the sea as well as his fear about Julian.

"We should get our coats on and go and look for Julian," he said.

Harry nodded, and brushed his dark curls back with his hand. Charles moved to get his coat, but Harry caught his hand. Charles halted, the tension between them palpable. His heart thumped hard against his chest.

"Charlie..." Harry's voice was roughened. He pulled Charles closer and slid a hand over his jaw. Charles pushed his cheek into Harry's palm, closed his eyes, and let himself be pulled into him. Harry brought their lips together in a chaste kiss, and then gathered Charles into his arms and held him tight.

"Tell me we will find him," he whispered. "Tell me all will be well."

Charles clung to Harry and squeezed his eyes shut. "We will find him."

"My angel," Harry whispered into Charles' hair.

"What will you do when you find him?" Charles asked the question that had been burning inside him since they had begun the journey in the dark Christmas morning.

"I don't know. Find work, find lodgings…"

Charles nodded, still holding tight. "I will help."

"I know. I know I can rely on my angel to save me."

The words jarred. Charles pulled out of his embrace and scrubbed his face. "Best not to rely on me."

Harry snorted softly. "You are exactly the kind of angel a man can rely on," he said, reaching for him again.

"I'm the wrong kind of angel for that," Charles said feeling the familiar weight of guilt and sadness crush his chest. "My record of reliability is not good."

"Rubbish," Harry retorted.

"Ask my family."

Harry stared at him, clearly shocked. "Charlie, you were a boy. You couldn't have done anything," Harry said, his voice sounding appalled. He came up behind him and slid his arms around his waist.

Charles closed his eyes, unable to move. "Ask the men under my command." He waited for the crushing pain and waves of sickening guilt. There was pain, and there was guilt, but not as strongly. It didn't threaten to suck him under as it usually did. He waited for Harry to ask him to explain. He didn't know if he could.

"You lost men?"

Charles nodded.

"Men that you were close to?"

Charles screwed his eyes shut and nodded again.

Harry's cheek was next to his own. "It was a war, sweetheart."

Charles crumbled a little at the endearment. He leaned into the embrace and allowed himself to be held. Allowed himself to be comforted for the first time. Harry kissed his temple, and Charles straightened before he ended up weeping again.

"Come. Let's find the boy." His voice was rough.

Harry let him go, and Charles swiped at his eyes with his fingers and sniffed. God, he was turning into a watering pot.

Chapter 13

THEY STEPPED OUT of the inn wrapped up against the chill, and after admiring the sea again, they headed up into the town. The place was quiet, with few people around.

"Do you have any idea where to start?" Charlie said.

Harry shook his head.

"Well, let us walk about the streets a little and work our way down to the harbour. He may well have gone to look at the boats and the lighthouse."

Harry nodded. That was Charlie. Neat and methodical. Harry just wanted to run about like a madman until he found Julian. He made himself follow Charlie's plan. At least Charlie seemed to know his way about.

A thought occurred to Harry. "Do you visit Scarborough often?"

"Not really," Charlie said. "I've been a few times. I quite like walking on the cliffs, and visiting the bookshop."

Harry glanced at him. "Is there much...society?"

Charlie stared forward. "No. I go to London for that."

"Oh." Harry wondered if he had offended him so he shut up. He'd certainly never seen him in Dante's club. He wondered if he had someone in London that he visited. The thought was sobering.

They walked and walked and Charlie took them past another couple of inns where travellers might be. They popped into the Talbot and asked the landlord if any messages had been left, but there was nothing. It was as though Julian had simply disappeared. Charlie led them through more small streets until they were heading down the road towards the harbour that nestled beneath the massive cliff on which the ruin of a castle stood. It was quite dramatic, and Harry could see that either the boats or the castle might appeal to a small boy.

"Can you get up there?" Harry asked nodding towards the castle.

"Yes. The militia are stationed there."

"He might have wanted to look at the castle?"

Charlie frowned. "If he has any sense he will be hiding and not exploring."

Harry nodded. "The carriage would have arrived last night. He had some money for food, but I can't imagine where he would have stayed." The thought of him spending the night out in the freezing cold worried him. "He's small," Harry added.

"I'm just worried that Mosely got here before us," Charlie said as he stepped around a huge pile of rope and fishing pots. The sound of seagulls was deafening as they screeched about the bay, adding to the cacophony of sound that the waves made crashing on the beach. By the boats and pots the smell of fish almost overwhelming. Charlie stood with his hands on his hips, staring around as though willing Julian to jump out at them. He sighed.

"Perhaps he went to look at the dippers."

"What are dippers?"

Charlie smiled a little. "In the better weather people come to the Spa House and bathe in the sea. The men just dive in naked and swim, but the women go the strangest lengths to get ready, using little huts."

Harry raised an eyebrow. "Naked men?"

"Indeed," Charlie laughed.

"Surely not at this time of year?" Harry grimaced and cupped his hands over his groin.

Charlie actually laughed at that and it was good to hear. "No doubt."

"I like it here," Harry said and was surprised to realise that he did. "Do you think I will find work?"

"Not the best time of year," Charlie said as they set off walking along the seafront in the direction of the Spa House. "During the summer the place gets busy with people coming to take the water and bathe in the sea so there might be work then. At the moment, probably not as much."

Harry refused to be daunted. "I'll find something. I've worked at most things so I can turn my hand to pretty much anything. I'm pretty versatile." He slid a sideways glance at Charlie and grinned. "You should take a house here. You could come and see me. Save you going to London."

Charlie stopped walking, making Harry stop and turn to face him. Charlie was looking horrified.

"What?"

"I don't...you expect..."

Despite the cold Harry went hot all over and he

felt the colour explode in his cheeks. Charlie didn't need to say more.

"Well, I know I haven't done anything to make you think highly of me but, Christ, Charlie, if you think that I would do that, your opinion of me is lower than I thought." He put a gloved hand to his chest where his heart physically hurt.

Charlie stared at him for a moment and then went to take his arm, but then let it go quickly but he stood close.

"Harry…I'm sorry…I…" He shut his mouth and closed his eyes, brows drawn down. He took a breath and opened his eyes. "I am so sorry. I didn't mean…It was a stupid, horrible thing to think."

"I'll say." Harry tucked his hands into his pockets and carried on walking. Charlie followed in silence for a while.

"Let's try up here," he said pointing.

Harry looked at him and nodded. He couldn't help feeling stupid for thinking that Charlie might want anything to do with him after they had found Julian. Stupid for thinking that he might be able to see past what he had done. Once a whore always a whore, apparently. They walked up a narrow path that brought them onto a lane that ran parallel with the coast.

"See that inn?" Charlie said. Harry nodded. "It's hundreds of years old and rumour has it that it has hidden pathways to the sea that smugglers use."

Harry felt himself smile. "Really?"

"So I'm told."

They walked a little farther, but the path was littered and filthy, so they took a turn down by some fishing boats and climbed over the ropes and jumped down. As he did so, an oilcloth at his feet moved and a small, battered face appeared.

Harry's breath caught in his throat. "Julian?" he whispered.

The boy tried to sit up but fell back. His eyes were wide and immediately they filled with tears. "Harry!" he whispered. "Oh, Harry, you came."

Harry sank to his knees and pulled the old oilcloth off him.

"He's here," Julian whispered, clutching at Harry's arm, eyes wide and terrified. "Mosely, he's here."

Chapter 14

CHARLES' SKIN TIGHTENED with horror as Harry lifted the boy who was now sobbing weakly. When Charles moved closer, the child cringed against Harry.

"Hush now," Harry whispered to him. "Hush now, this is Charlie. He's been helping me to find you."

The child peeped out and Charles tried to give him a reassuring smile.

Harry kissed the top of the boy's head. "Charlie shot Bill Mosely in the arm."

The child looked up at Harry and then at Charlie and scrubbed at his nose with his sleeve. "He had a sling. Did you do that?"

Charles nodded with a smile. He wasn't sure he could speak.

"Come on, let's get you cleaned up and fed." Harry set off walking with the boy in his arms. "Why didn't you leave a message at the inn?"

"Mosely was waiting for the carriage. It got held

up because of the awful weather. We were supposed to get here yesterday, but it only arrived a little while ago." Julian rubbed his eyes. "When they threw you off the driver decided to stop overnight because the snow was so bad. As we drew in this morning, I spotted him. Honestly, Harry I couldn't believe it. I jumped off the back and ran as fast as I could. I didn't dare go in anywhere, and then…" his voice wobbled. "I was robbed. They took all the money you gave me, Harry. I'm so sorry, so sorry, we don't have anything now."

"Don't worry about the money," Harry said. "Is that all they took?"

Julian nodded, much to Harry's relief.

"But it was all you had. You gave it to me, trusted me with it and I lost it." The boy was weeping again.

"Shh, don't cry. Charlie helped me. He paid my debt to Dante and helped me get here. We have rooms at the inn, it's warm and there is food…"

"Really?" The boy peered around to look at Charlie.

"Really," Harry said. "We only have yours to pay off now and when that is done, we are free. Completely free. We can live here; I will find work soon."

"I can work, too," the child interrupted. "I can work with the fishermen."

CHARLES FELT A curious sense of isolation. As though he had been discounted now, and as the two of them planned their future, he was amazed to realise that the feeling was jealousy. He was *jealous* of the bond that the two of them had, of the plans they made together, of the life that they might have. Horrified, he shoved the feeling aside.

"Might I interject?" he said walking alongside.

"Of course," Harry said with a smile. "Interject away."

Charles rolled his eyes. "We may need to clean young Julian up a little before taking him to the inn, he looks like a ragamuffin. When we get there, I will arrange for him to have a bed in your room."

Harry peered down his chest at the boy and laughed. "He's right. Come on."

They found a wall and sat Julian on it whilst Charles fished out a handkerchief and a comb from his pocket. He dipped the handkerchief in some water that had collected in an upturned bucket and applied it to Julian's hands and face. They dusted off his clothes as best they could and combed his hair. Nothing could disguise the bruising on his face though, or removed the pinched, hungry look. He also found it quite hard to stand without his legs buckling. A combination of hunger, fear, and exhaustion coupled with a severe beating had debilitated the child.

"We need a story," Charles said. Harry nodded. "Julian, do you have family?"

Julian's gaze dropped to his lap. "No."

"Very well." Charles thought for a moment. "I am your guardian and you ran away?" he suggested, looking at Harry.

"Why did I run away?" the child asked. Charles frowned.

"You didn't want to go to school?" Harry chipped in.

Charles shook his head. "The schools are on holiday."

All three stared at one another. Harry grinned. "Come on, Charlie, you're the book writer. Think of a story."

Julian's eyes widened. "You write books?"

Harry clapped Julian on the back and laughed. "He does. Adventures, too."

Julian smiled. For the first time since they had picked him up the boy smiled. Charlie smiled back. "Very well." He put his hands on his hips and thought for a moment. "Julian's parents died in a tragic accident and he came to live with me as his guardian. His father was a close friend of mine in the army, but Julian has never met me before and didn't want to come and live with me. Stricken with grief, he escaped my house and managed to get as far as Scarborough, but fell into the hands of footpads and was robbed and left for dead. I am filled with remorse for not caring for him better, so I followed him, calling on my...secretary, Harry, to find him and persuade him to come home and to promise to be a better guardian to him."

Harry doubled over laughing and Julian clapped his hands in delight.

Charles couldn't help the smile that spread across his face. "If we tell the people at the inn, they will be overcome with sympathy at our plight. I shall be the villain, but I will be dreadfully remorseful."

The merriment lasted a moment or two until Harry's face fell.

"What is it?" Charles asked.

Harry tried to regain his smile, but failed. "It's a brilliant tale, but...it wouldn't really work."

"Why ever not?"

Harry looked away. "How would we explain that you were going home and leaving us here?"

Silence ticked between them for several moments and Charlie's heart pounded in his chest. "I..." he began but they were interrupted by a chillingly familiar voice.

HARRY JUMPED AT the sound and whirled around. Charlie moved to stand in front of him and Julian in such a protective movement that Harry's heart swelled despite the fear that gripped him.

"Well, well, well. If it isn't all three dirty little shitten pricks," Mosely said. Harry's skin crawled and fury bloomed in his gut.

"No idea why you are calling names, Mosely," he said, stepping out from behind Charlie. "You never complained when you bent over and took it."

"I've never been touched a man in my fucking life!" Mosely spat.

Harry's mouth ran away with him. "No, you like children."

"Bastard!" Mosely sprang forward, but with one arm in a sling he was seriously hampered. Charlie stepped forward, intercepted him, and felled him with an incredibly effective smack to the jaw. The other two stood back, wary of what Charlie might do next, no doubt. Mosely, however, had no such sense. He staggered to his feet and rushed towards Harry, dragging a knife from his pocket as he did so, but Charlie kicked his hand, sending the knife spinning, and then launched at him with another savage blow to his jaw that sent him back to the ground. This time, though, Charlie followed him down and, sitting on his chest, pinned him, and hit him again and again until Harry clamped his arms around him and dragged him off.

"Enough, enough..." he crooned in Charlie's ear. Charlie struggled until Harry let go, but he got to his feet, glaring at the man with the bloody face grovelling on the ground.

Charlie's nostrils flared. "Bastard. He doesn't deserve to live."

"I know," Harry said holding out a hand towards him. Mosely's cronies were long gone, leaving just him, Charlie, and a stunned Julian. The sound of running footsteps broke them apart as two fishermen ran towards them.

"Are you hurt?" One of them bent to look at Mosely, whilst the other laid a hand on Charlie's arm.

Charlie shook his head as he shook out his hand and then stuck it under his armpit. "Thank you, but no, I am unharmed. This man robbed my ward and attempted to do the same with us." He gestured at Harry and Julian.

"He's out for a bit. I'll get the magistrate," the man kneeling on the ground beside the now unconscious Mosely said.

"Don't think he's going to thank us for that. He'll be eating goose with the family."

"True. Might be best if we just throw him in the gaol and make him wait a bit."

"Can you do that?" Harry said.

"Most certainly," the older of the two men said.

"It's where he belongs," Charlie said and held out his hand. "Farrington. Captain Farrington. Pleased to meet you. This is my ward, Julian, and my cousin, Harry Valentine." He gestured to Harry and Julian and Harry's mouth hung open. They had agreed that this wouldn't work. They all shook hands. It was decided that gaol was definitely the best place for Mosely, and one of the men disappeared and then came back with a cart. They loaded Mosely onto it and waved as the two men towed him away.

Harry looked at Charlie who was sucking his knuckles. "Sore?"

"Bloody hard-headed bastard," Charlie said, and then grimaced when Julian laughed.

"What now?" Harry said.

"Well, I think Mosely may find himself incarcerated long enough for us to be away. The magistrate will not welcome an interruption to his Christmas, so we might have a little time. What about the other two?"

Harry shook his head. "I don't really know them. Do you?" he said to Julian. Julian shook his head. "I suspect that without Mosely leading them they won't tackle us." Harry grinned. "Or more specifically, they won't tackle you."

Charlie nodded. "In that case, we should go back to the inn and have something to eat. We can then decide what would be best."

They walked together, the silence only broken by the sound of the seagulls crying overhead. The sun had come out and the church bells were ringing.

"Charlie?" Harry began.

"Not now."

Harry subsided. Julian was looking decidedly wobbly and Charlie had set a brisk pace.

"Here, hop up," Harry said, gesturing for Julian to climb on his back. He settled the boy's arms around his neck and hitched an arm under each of his legs and carried him. Charlie slowed a little.

❖

IN THE END the innkeeper required very little explanation about Julian. He had a bed made up for him in Harry's room, and pocketed the extra money without comment. Harry helped him to wash and bathe his wounds.

"What are we going to do, Harry?" the boy asked as Harry rubbed him vigorously with a towel.

"I don't know. I need to speak to Charlie."

Julian slid into the nightshirt that Harry had given him. "Are you two lovers?"

Harry sighed. "You shouldn't know about things like that. You're too young."

"Maybe, but I do and he looks at you like you're his whole world."

Harry paused and then handed Julian a comb. "Really?"

"Yes." Julian dragged his hair neat. "Same way you look at him."

Harry sank onto the bed. "He's…I've never met anyone like him in my life. He is…" Harry shook his head. "I don't want to leave him." He looked down at his hands, the truth of the statement made his chest hurt.

"Then you'd better tell him that," Julian said. "Can we eat now?"

CHARLES KNOCKED ON the door of Harry's room as the waitress stood beside him, holding a huge tray of food. Harry opened it and let them in. Julian was seated on the bed in an enormous nightshirt looking much better than he had earlier. They all waited until the girl had put down the three plates of mutton pie and a huge plate of twelfth night cake and cheese. The door closed and Charlie let go of a breath he hadn't realised he was holding.

"How are you feeling?" he said to Julian.

"Much better. Thank you, Captain Farrington," he said.

"Call me..." He hesitated a moment and then smiled. "Call me Charlie."

All three of them fell on the food as though they hadn't eaten for months and drained the mugs of ale that came with it.

"You must be getting tired of fruit cake and cheese," Charles said with a smile. He'd fed Harry endless amounts of the stuff.

"Never," Harry said on a groan. "Love it"

Charles smiled scooped up some remaining crumbs. Julian sat watching them both.

"I didn't know you were a captain," Harry said.

"Didn't I mention it?"

"No. I did wonder if you were a general or something though when you shot Mosely and knifed the other."

Charles laughed. "Not a general, but I did do a lot of unarmed fighting. I learned to look out for myself and because I am quiet people tend to make the mistake of underestimating me." He gave Harry a small smile.

"Well, I shan't be making that mistake," Harry said with a laugh.

Charles gathered up the crockery and cutlery and put it on the tray to move everything out of the way.

"Charlie likes order," Harry said to Julian as Charlie put the tray outside the door and closed it.

Charles turned to face them both. He didn't know what to say. They both looked well fed and happy, despite Julian's bruises. They boy's eyes shone as he looked at Harry and in the warmth of the fire with a belly full of food Charlie was sure that they would survive. The fact of the matter was; they didn't need him anymore.

"I will pay for the rooms to be held for you for as long as you think you need them. For as long as it takes you to find work." The words tumbled out. He vaguely registered Harry's shocked face and he was fairly sure that Julian kicked Harry on the leg.

"I should leave you now," he said and nodded. He turned, but as he got to the door Harry was beside him.

"Julian, I need to speak to Charlie," he said and pulled the door open. "Your room."

Charles walked the short distance to his door and let Harry follow him in.

"You can't leave now," Harry said, pacing the room and dragging his hands through his hair. "You can't."

"I...why?"

"Didn't it mean anything to you?" Harry demanded. His eyes were a little wild.

"Didn't what..."

"Us." Harry pulled him close and kissed him. Kissed him hard and Charles sank into him with a groan and when those hard, wiry arms imprisoned him, Charles let go and kissed him back. He sank his fingers into his dark curls and ground himself against Harry. He moaned when Harry lifted him off his feet and pushed him against the door. And then they were rutting against each other frantically. Charles wrapped one leg around Harry, kissing him all the while, but within moments he had to drag his mouth away as he spent so hard it robbed him of breath and thought. Harry made a strangled sound, buried his face in Charles' neck, and followed.

They clung to each other as the waves subsided and then Charles moved to adjust himself in the rapidly cooling puddle of mess in his breeches.

Harry stepped away an inch, but pressed their mouths together in a soft kiss. "I don't want you to go," Harry said against his mouth. "I don't want you to leave." He kissed him again.

"I can't stay forever," Charles said.

"I know, but you don't have to return today. You could stay tonight. It's Christmas. An angel shouldn't be alone at Christmas." Harry nuzzled his ear and Charles eyes drifted closed. "What if we need you to protect us again," he said and kissed his neck.

"I told you, I'm not that kind of angel."

"Well, you did a damned good job of protecting us today. We'd both be bound and gagged and headed for London were it not for you." Harry's voice had gone from cajoling to serious. Charles pulled back to look at him.

"Charlie, I...I don't want to lose you yet. Stay tonight? Please?" Those dark eyes locked with his and were filled with longing.

"Very well. I'll stay," Charlie whispered.

Harry leaned his forehead against his and, closing his eyes, sighed. "Thank you."

Charlie put his arms around him and held on tight. What were they to do? Were Harry a woman he would be begging for his hand. Rushing him back to his home to make him his forever. But Harry was a man.

He was shocked to feel tears prick his eyes. It was so unfair. So damned unfair.

Chapter 15

CHARLIE STAYED. Harry held him in his arms all night long. They didn't make love because they decided that Julian should be in the room with them to keep him safe, so the three of them talked until the small hours, and then, when Julian fell asleep, Harry held Charlie tight. He seemed to like that. They held each other with an edge of desperation that went beyond passion, and when sunrise edged the darkness away Harry lay and watched it paint the room in pinks and oranges as Charlie lay sleeping. He didn't want to move; didn't want the moment to go. Didn't want the day to begin because he knew it would take Charlie from him. Christmas was over.

EVENTUALLY, CHARLIE stirred, his fair hair tickling Harry's chest and his hand stroked his stomach, edging downwards. Harry smiled and caught it before it went any further and Charlie dragged his head up, blinking at him sleepily. Harry nodded to the truckle bed where Julian was snoring softly. Charlie smiled. Harry watched him yawn and stretch, then rub the sleep from his eyes. He wanted to absorb every moment. Charlie rolled onto his back and stared at the ceiling, flinging one arm above his head. Neither spoke. Harry put his hand on Charlie's thigh, and Charlie put his hand over Harry's. They simply lay together.

When Julian awoke and asked if it was breakfast time, Harry jumped up and threw logs on the fire to warm the room. They had managed to keep it going through the night, but the remaining embers did nothing to ward off the morning chill. They huddled under blankets until the fire roared and the chill subsided and then Charlie went back to his own room, leaving Harry and Julian sitting side by side on the bed.

"Is he really going?"

"So it would seem."

"Did you tell him how you feel?"

Harry thought for a moment and then pulled a face. "Well, I didn't say it but I think I showed him."

"Did he say anything to you or did he just 'show' you, too?"

Harry frowned. Was that what they had done? Shown each other rather than say the words? If that was the case...

Before he could wrap his head around the notion any further the door burst open and Charlie came in. His hair was awry and his cravat undone. He slammed the door behind him and both Harry and

Julian jumped.

"Charlie…"

"Hush." He held up a hand. "Just listen."

Harry and Julian exchanged a glance.

He opened his mouth and then closed it, planting his hands on his hips. He closed his eyes momentarily, sucked in a breath, and then let it go.

"I looked into the matter and I would be able to rent you a house for six months. A year. However long it took you to find work and get on your feet."

Harry was taken aback. "Ah, thank you." Charlie looked a little wild and most unlike himself.

"I will see to your bills and make sure that you are safe."

"Charlie, I…"

He cleared his throat and held up a hand. Clearly he had more to say. "I thought that it was important that you have a choice. A genuine choice."

"That's…very kind." Harry frowned. "A choice in what?"

Charlie closed his eyes. "What to do. You can make a life for you and Julian here, in Scarborough or…or you can…"

Harry's heart was hammering. He didn't dare hope. "Or what, Charlie?" he whispered.

"I don't want to leave you. I want you to consider coming back with me." He said it as though he didn't imagine for a moment that Harry would say yes.

"My housekeeper has been trying to persuade me to employ someone, a secretary or something, to live in with me because she is firmly convinced I am incapable of looking after myself, so it would not be a surprise to her or her husband." He spoke fast; without pause, and then stopped to draw breath. "At all."

He cleared his throat. "You wouldn't really be my

secretary but it would serve as a reason for your presence in my home and if we take Julian and say he is my ward then you can also be his tutor. Or something. Anything. You could be my cousin if you prefer." He seemed to run out of breath completely because he slumped a little, leaving Harry and Julian staring at him.

Harry's chest constricted as what Charlie had just said in that mad rush started to sink in, but Charlie took another breath and carried on.

"Just think about it, please." He cleared his throat. "I know you have only known me a day, and I am not an easy man to live with, I know I am…fussy and…"

"Yes."

Charlie stopped and stared. "What?"

Harry was grinning now from ear to ear and Julian had his hands over his mouth. "I said, yes. Yes. What do you think, Julian?"

Julian held tight to his mouth and nodded but tears dripped from his eyelashes.

Charlie was staring. "Yes to which part?" he whispered.

"I want to come with you."

Harry watched the words register with Charlie; watched the surprise and then joy fill his face and then he threw his arms around him and held him tight. They clung together a moment and then pulled apart to draw Julian in and then they were all laughing, crying, and talking at once.

Epilogue

THE CLOCK STRUCK twelve and Charles touched his champagne glass to Harry's with a clink. "Happy New Year," he said.

Harry grinned and snuggled closer, his naked body warm and sated. "Happy New Year, my angel."

Charles shook his head, but Harry reached over and put a finger over his lips. "Don't say it. You are exactly the right kind of angel. My angel."

Charles smiled and nipped at the finger on his lips. The odd thing was he didn't feel like an imposter now. He still grieved and mourned the loss of his family; his men, and the pain was still there, but it didn't crush him anymore and make him feel like he should have died, too. If he had died, he wouldn't have been there to save Harry and Julian. His family.

The Darnleys had taken both Harry and Julian to their hearts, and Julian was recovering nicely with the mothering that he got from Mrs. Darnley, to say nothing of the food and fussing. Even his cat had taken to them both and could often be found curled in Harry's lap. They had decided that the best tale would be that Harry and Julian's parents had been killed, leaving them in difficult circumstances, and Charles, as a distant cousin, had given them a home. The Darnleys seemed quite happy with the explanation that Julian and Harry were family and Charles could see no reason for anyone else to doubt it.

The only cloud on the horizon was Moseley and the possibility of him, or the man Harry referred to as Dante, returning for them, but Charles was ready for that.

He turned his head so he could look at Harry. "I love you," he said and watched Harry's face flush and those beautiful dark eyes shine.

He blinked a couple of times and cleared his throat. "I love you, too."

Charles nodded and smiled. That was the first time they had said it aloud to each other. It seemed the right thing to say in the first moments of a new day, of a new year.

"I have one last confession," Harry said leaning over to kiss him on the lips.

"What?"

"Harry Valentine isn't my name."

Charles stared at him and laughed. "Well, what the hell is it? I can't start calling you anything else, you are my Harry. Always will be."

Harry grimaced and kissed him again. "It's Henry Wilson."

"Henry Wilson." Charles tried the name but then shook his head.

"I would be happy to keep Harry Valentine," Harry said.

"Then we will keep him."

Charles drained his glass and then reached over and took Harry's out of his hand and placed them both carefully on the bedside.

"Any more revelations?"

Harry shook his head, his eyes darkening.

"Come here then. I intend to start this year as I mean to go on."

Harry Valentine laughed and, rolling over, wrapped his angel tightly in those hard, wiry arms.

About the Author

Ruby lives in Lancashire in the northwest of England. All through school she was told that she would never get anywhere if she didn't stop daydreaming. Eventually it occurred to her to write down the daydreams, and *voilà*! The beautiful men in her head came to life.

Ruby writes historical and contemporary gay romance but has a definite weakness for handsome men in billowing white shirts, breeches, and cravats. Oh, and she loves tea. Lots of tea.

For more information, visit rubymoone.com.

CPSIA information can be obtained
at www.ICGtesting.com
Printed in the USA
LVHW011629191119
637872LV00011B/739/P